Richmond upon Thames Libraries

Renew online at www.richmond.gov.uk/libraries

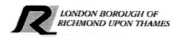

LONDON BOROUGH OF
RICHMOND UPON THAMES

Published in the UK by Scholastic, 2023
1 London Bridge, London, SE1 9BG
Scholastic Ireland, 89E Lagan Road, Dublin Industrial Estate,
Glasnevin, Dublin, D11 HP5F

SCHOLASTIC and associated logos are trademarks and/or
registered trademarks of Scholastic Inc.

Text © Brianna Bourne, 2023
Cover photo © Shutterstock.com

The right of Brianna Bourne to be identified as the
author of this work has been asserted by her under
the Copyright, Designs and Patents Act 1988

ISBN 978 0702 31418 6

A CIP catalogue record for this book is available from the British Library.

Printed by CPI Group (UK) Ltd, Croydon, CR0 4YY
Paper made from wood grown in sustainable forests and other controlled sources.

1 3 5 7 9 10 8 6 4 2

This is a work of fiction. Names, characters, places, incidents and dialogues are
products of the author's imagination or are used fictitiously. Any resemblance to
actual people, living or dead, events or locales is entirely coincidental.

FOR MY GRANDMOTHER, MARY JOSEPHINE MCDONALD.
AS A CHILD, BEING WITH YOU WAS MY
CALMEST, SAFEST PLACE.
SOMEHOW, SO MANY YEARS LATER,
THAT'S STILL TRUE.
THANK YOU.

flint

THIS IS WHERE I'm going to die.

From my spot in the back seat of our Jeep, wedged in between overstuffed suitcases, I stare sullenly at the ultramodern "cabin" in front of us.

It's all sharp angles and gleaming wood. And glass—so much glass. The low-slung October sun glints off huge floor-to-ceiling windows with a glare so hot it stings my eyes.

It's the only house in view, tucked neatly into the Pennsylvania forest. All around it, bright orange leaves flame on branches. The whole scene could be on the cover of some glossy architecture magazine.

Not exactly what I pictured when I thought about where I'd spend my last forty-one days.

Forty-one days. I can't believe that's all that's left for me.

I blink hard. Swallow down the tightness in my throat that's been permanently lodged there for exactly half my life. Well, almost exactly half.

Outside the car, birds chirp in the autumn sunshine. Inside, the three of us—my mom, my dad, and me—are silent. Nobody even makes a move for their door handle. This is a threshold, and no one wants to take the next step.

"Well, we made it," Mom finally says with forced brightness. Her words ping off the tension like a needle thrown at plate armor. Weariness smudges her at the edges, and I know it's from more than just the long drive.

The me-about-to-die thing isn't all that's making this awkward. I haven't seen my parents in the same room since their divorce, and now Mom's riding shotgun in the Jeep like old times, sharing a bag of M&M'S with Dad. Acting like we're a normal family again.

When Mom came up with this plan, she said it'd be like a vacation. Pretty dismal vacation, in my opinion, but I was a good son and kept that observation to myself. I know this trip is really so I don't have to spend my last few weeks alone while they're at work.

She asked where I wanted to go, listing a string of beach towns and bustling cities, but we've been down that road before. When we first found out about my expiration date, she dragged us to a million places, determined to give me as much *life* as she could in the time I had left. But weekends in New York City and boring drives to national parks didn't make us feel any better—and it nearly bankrupted them. I'm already an emotional burden. I won't let myself be a financial burden too.

So instead of letting Mom plan a postcard-worthy last hurrah, I told her I wanted to go to the one place I knew wouldn't leave my parents in debt. The town where I grew up: Carbon Junction.

My dad grumbles something, then yanks the keys out of the ignition. "Can't sit here all day," he says. I can always count on his grumpy ass to bail us out of moments like this.

We get out of the car, stretching our stiff legs in the autumn chill.

I'm wearing my standard black T-shirt and black jeans, and goose bumps break out on my bare arms, spreading in a rush from my shoulders to my wrists.

Mom comes over and side-squeezes me, looking up with an encouraging smile. She's not super short or anything—I'm just abnormally tall.

Of course, she notices the goose bumps. "Oh, Flint, you must be—"

"I'm not cold," I interrupt. We've been over this. It's my standard response every time I refuse to wear a jacket.

The thing is, I'm lying. I am cold—I just like that it hurts. If I stay cold and hungry and miserable, when the end comes, it won't hurt. It'll be a relief.

We trudge up the driveway to the front porch, our shoes thumping hollowly on the deck. This cabin wasn't here when we lived in Carbon Junction. A lifetime ago, the three of us in our cozy house on the other side of town.

Dad checks the Airbnb instructions on his phone and pushes the code into the keypad on the door. The dead bolt retreats with a mechanical whir, and he plunges unceremoniously into the house. Mom and I hesitate for one heavy second, then we follow him in.

The cavernous space is painfully modern, with hard floors and even harder-looking furniture.

"I'm sorry it's not more . . . homey," Mom says as we look around. "I can get some pillows for the couch. A few area rugs. Make it a bit warmer in here."

Mom's an interior designer, the Leslie Larsen of the tiny,

struggling Philadelphia-based Leslie Larsen Interiors, and if I so much as nod in agreement, she'll spring into action and completely overhaul this place.

"It's fine, Mom," I say, plopping down on the couch. "Don't get anything."

My divorced parents exchange a look, further cementing the fact that this is going to be weird.

I rub my knees. In the Jeep, my legs were crunched up, and my kneecaps were pressed against the front seats. But other than my sore knees, I feel . . . fine.

That's the worst part, I think. That I'm healthy. There's not a single thing wrong with me. No chronic disease eating away at me, no defective organs. My body should be able to keep on trucking for years, decades even. But it's October 23, and sometime on December 4, it's going to stop like a watch that's run out of batteries.

That date has become more important to me than my own birthday. I've written it on every form I've ever had to fill in. Pre- or post-half-life? they all ask. In school, I'd watch as my classmates circled *pre* with carefree swishes of their pens. I'd draw a tight box around *post*, nearly ripping the paper. Everyone around me would get to skip the next question, but I'd have to answer it.

Deathday: December 4.

Birthdays and deathdays. All lives are bracketed by them. Everyone half-lifes; I'm just one of the unlucky people who had it happen when they were a little kid.

I shake off the memory of the day I twinged. Of the sudden,

4

splitting headache that I remember and the seizure afterward that I don't. That day was the demarcating line that was drawn down my life, separating it into before I knew when I was going to die and . . . after.

Dad scratches at his stubble. "Flint, why don't you go get our stuff out of the car?"

Mom's chin snaps up. "Don't make him do that, Mack."

"Why not? He's perfectly capable."

"It's fine, Mom," I cut in, before this devolves into one of the "differences in opinion" they used to have.

I don't mind getting suitcases out of the car. At least Dad still makes me do normal shit. That's why I chose to live with him after the divorce. Well, that and because Mom's efforts to stay positive and cheerful around me were wearing her down. She pretended she was fine, but she was getting thinner and more washed out right in front of my eyes. I couldn't watch that. Be the reason for it.

While I'm busy bringing our stuff in, Mom messes around in the kitchen trying to get the fancy coffee machine to work, and Dad sticks his head into the cabinet under the sink, probably improving the water pressure or something. Since my dad's name is Mack, we joke that he's a "Mack of all trades" because he's had so many weird jobs over the years. Before I was born, he was one of those guys who put out fires on offshore oil rigs, then he was a guide for a whitewater rafting company. Now he manages a team of industrial welders in Philadelphia, and he can fix just about anything.

I should be happy my parents are here with me, but I wish they'd leave me here and go back to the city. Back to their jobs and their friends and their separate, Flint-free lives. I don't need them here. I can die just fine on my own, thanks.

Finally the Jeep's empty. It locks with a *beep-beep*, and I head toward the house—but something stops me when I get to the door.

I can see Mom and Dad through the glass. They aren't bustling around the kitchen anymore—they're frozen, perfectly still. Mom's at the coffee maker with one hand pressed over her face, the other propped on the counter, like she doesn't have the energy to stand up straight. Dad's on the other side of the kitchen, staring at her back with a helpless expression I've never seen on him before.

I make a big deal out of opening the door and shutting it behind me.

When I turn around, Mom's upright, smoothing her sweater, blinking hard. But there's the same hush over everything that you'd find at a funeral. A thickness in the air. A dead body in a box at one end and everyone tiptoeing around, saying careful things. Only in this case, the dead body isn't in a box yet—I'm still up and walking around.

This whole idea is stupid. We can't pretend we're the family we were eight years ago.

I go to the back window and stare out over the forest so they can't see my clenched jaw. I force myself to breathe, to focus on the leaves rustling on the trees.

Through the half-bare branches, I can make out the backs of a few houses on the other side of Maynard's Creek, which burbles in a dark ribbon at the bottom of our sloping backyard. I know the street on the other side—it's called Harker's Run. Weird how the name comes back after all these years.

My old life in Carbon Junction is almost more real to me than my eight years in the city.

But at least one thing has changed—one of the houses has been painted bright purple. It looks out of place in all the burning, dying colors of autumn. I narrow my eyes. I don't remember there being a purple house on that street. But as garish as it is, it's not the part of the view I hate the most.

Above the tree line, two buildings sit on top of the biggest hill in town, proud and exposed. The Castle and the Crown.

The Castle is the old coal power plant—apparently the three giant smokestacks look like turrets. It shut down years ago. It's rusting and rotting now, cordoned off with a mean chain-link fence, but from far away it's still massive and imposing. Back in the day, virtually everyone in town worked there. When it closed, the town would have been sucked under by poverty and weeds if it hadn't been for the other building on the hill—the Crown. Because that's where everyone in Carbon Junction works now. Or nearly everyone, anyway.

The Crown is a brutally modern tower of white concrete rising thirty stories over the town, topped with a circle of curved spikes that look like some evil, alien crown.

How painfully ironic that my hometown—the place where I was born and the place where I'm going to die—is home to the Half-Life Institute, the world's premier research facility into the phenomenon humans have been living with since the dawn of time.

If I had the energy, I'd give it the finger.

I think my mom is secretly pleased that I wanted to come back to

Carbon Junction. The Institute exists primarily to figure out what's causing the half-life (which I doubt they'll ever make any progress on), but they offer all sorts of supplemental "support" programs too. If she thinks she can wrangle me into talking to one of the Institute's therapists, she's dead wrong.

The sun shifts behind a cloud, and for a second, I can see my own reflection in the glass. God, I look rough. I'm just so *tired*.

Something thwacks into the glass right in front of my face. I jolt back, startled.

On the deck, lying on its side, is a small gray bird. As I stare, the bird twitches once, then exhales, its tiny chest deflating. It doesn't move again.

For a second, I'm in shock. I've never seen anything *die* in front of me before.

The ever-present lump in my throat swells. "Mom? There's a dead bird on the deck."

"What?" She comes over right away. "Oh god, honey, don't look. I'll get Dad to put it in the trash can on the driveway."

"Wait." I feel connected to this bird now. After all, I'm going to die here too. "Do we have a box or something?" I ask.

Mom softens. "Of course."

While she's looking for one, I rifle through the kitchen drawers. I didn't think to pack a shovel for this cheerful little vacation, so a serving spoon will have to do.

Mom hands me an empty coffee pod box. "Will it fit in here?" she asks.

I nod and head for the back porch.

"Flint, wait—take a coat."

I turn around and she's already holding it out to me.

"Please?" she adds.

I take it, but I have no intention of wearing it once I'm out of her sight.

She snags my elbow. "Is there anything you want to do this afternoon?" she asks. "I was thinking maybe we could order some Thai food, and Dad can set up the TV?"

"I'm pretty tired, Mom. I might just crash in my room."

That's not going to go over well. I know what she expects from these final weeks. Neither of them could take an entire month and a half off work, but there's still plenty of room for Quality Family Time. And Mom will want me to talk about my feelings.

"Flint . . ." She reaches up to push my hair back from my face. "I know this is hard, but we can do some fun things, even though you're—"

She can't say it, even after eight years of living with it.

She holds her hands out helplessly. "You can't just do nothing here. You deserve to live a little."

"*Little* being the operative word," I mutter.

Hurt flashes on her face.

I want to say sorry, to hug her and hold on like I used to when I was a kid. But I can't. I have to make sure she doesn't miss me when I'm gone.

I sigh. "Thai is fine, Mom."

She gives me a stretched-thin smile, but at least it's a smile. "I'll order it now. Love you."

"Yeah," I mumble.

Outside on the porch, I crouch and nudge the bird's limp body into the box. Then I set off through the trees. I stop next to a towering hemlock and peel off my coat. As I push the serving spoon deep into the cold soil, all I can think is *Forty-one days.*

A wave of something bleak and endlessly shitty grips me.

I thought I was used to the countdown. But now that there are six weeks left, I keep getting these waves of hot, clammy panic. Some days it's worse than others. Sometimes I can almost make it go away, but now that we're here, the tightness in my throat is impossible to swallow down.

I've been through a lot over the past eight years. I was still a kid when I half-lifed, just a dorky little third grader, and I didn't really understand it at first. We moved away because people started treating us so differently. It wasn't as bad in Philadelphia, at least at first. I could deal with no one at my new school wanting to be friends with the kid who was going to kick it in high school. But then freshman year came and . . .

That was the worst year. For a lot of reasons.

I finish burying the bird and wipe my hands on my jeans. I pull my phone out of my back pocket. I've set the lock screen to be a countdown, and for a minute I just stare at it. Watch as the seconds tick by.

Another second, gone.

Tick.

Another.

What could I have done with that second? What *should* I have

10

done with it? Sometimes, in between the waves of fear and sadness and anger, there's guilt. I hate the guilt the most.

Death is going to be a hell of a lot easier than this crap. Easier than sitting around just waiting for the end.

Here's the thing about half-lifing: Nothing can kill you before your deathday. I could walk out in front of an 18-wheeler or tie myself to train tracks, and I wouldn't die. I'd be a mess, but I wouldn't be dead. Not until December 4. I shudder when I think about the cultlike groups that have popped up over the years or the weird phases in history when it became fashionable to thrill-seek. Cliff diving with no training, swimming with stingrays and alligators, drag racing. People say it's about the rush of adrenaline, or taking back control and defying death, but I've seen how it plays out too many times. The injuries are brutal. Limbs ripped from bodies, third-degree burns, paralysis. Excruciating pain is why most people don't screw around. We just live with the countdown.

I look at the spoon jutting out like a headstone over the bird's grave.

And that's when the thought hits: My parents are going to have to *bury* me.

For all the time I've spent waiting for my deathday to roll around, I don't know how that never occurred to me before.

My parents are guaranteed to grow old. My dad half-lifed two years ago, when he was forty-two, and eighty-four is a long way off. My mom hasn't even had hers yet, and the half-life is never wrong. One day, they'll make it to a birthday where they'll have spent more years without me than they spent with me.

My chin starts to wobble. God, not this again. I just want to make it through my last few weeks and die without hurting anyone. Is that too much to ask?

I glance up at the cabin. When I go back in, Mom will want to hug me, comfort me about the dead bird. Dad will argue my side every time Mom treats me like fine china. Maybe I'll hear her cry herself to sleep like she does every weekend when I stay at her place.

I press the heels of my hands to my eyes. I can't go back up there. I can't breathe in that house.

There in the woods, an idea starts to form.

I need to find a place to spend my final few days. That way they won't have to hear my last exhale or watch the light go out of my eyes.

I can't let them see me die. It'll break them.

I breathe in the smell of the forest. Wet bark and pine needles, the sweet pecan scent of decaying leaves.

I think I know just the place.

Instead of going back up to the house, I turn and head deeper into the woods.

september

I NEVER WANT to leave this room.

My hand is cramping from copying down isotopic formulas and genetic algorithms, but I don't care. I'm in the only place where I can let my guard down and actually breathe: the observation room overlooking the top-floor biochemistry lab at the Half-Life Institute.

The lab is a multimillion-dollar marvel: an enormous, high-ceilinged rotunda filled with genomic sequencers, liquid-handling systems, spectrophotometers, and clinical workstations. It's bathed in cool white light, but softer blue and purple sconces glow at equal intervals on the curved walls, making it look like the inside of a high-tech spaceship.

Thanks to years of obsessively hard work, I get to eat my lunch here every day, towering thirty stories over Carbon Junction as I witness scientific history happen.

I can't take my eyes off Dr. Emilia Egebe Jackson, the world's leading half-life scientist, as she strolls around the vaulted room in her pristine white lab coat. I've been an intern at the Institute for two months, and I'm still pinching myself that I can get this close to her brain.

I gather my hair and twist it into a heavy copper-colored rope that hangs down my back, all the way to my lowest vertebrae. In moments like this, I almost feel like the September I used to be. Whole and calm, my heart glowing with phosphorescent *rightness*. Everywhere else I go, I have to work so hard not to think about what I lost six months ago.

Who I lost.

Dr. Jackson approaches the famous whiteboard wall. I lean forward—I wonder if she'll find the mistake I noticed ten minutes ago. She stands there like a stationary particle suspended in a turbine-agitated kinetic field, assessing the formulas and molecular diagrams.

A minute later, she snaps up a dry-erase marker and corrects the error.

"Yes! I knew it," I whisper, even though I'm the only one in the observation box.

Dr. Jackson finds a blank space and starts writing. Sound can't penetrate the plate glass of this cube, but her whiteboard marker must be squeaking furiously. I copy down every number and symbol she writes. My eyes go wide when I see where she's going with it.

Everything Dr. Jackson does is revolutionary. She started as our director two months ago, and now the whole institute is abuzz, like it's been injected with $C_9H_{13}NO_3$—adrenaline. There's this collective feeling that we're getting close to really understanding the half-life. *Curing* it, maybe.

And that—curing the half-life—is what I'm here for. Two and a half years ago, it became my entire reason for existing.

A voice pierces the air-conditioned hum of the observation room. "September. I can't say I'm surprised to find you here."

I jolt upright in my chair. The safety of my lunch break shatters.

Annoying Percy stands in the doorway. He's the other advanced sciences intern. There's a lordly sneer on his face, and his hands are linked behind his back like some ducal heir.

Obviously his name isn't really Annoying Percy—it's worse. It's Percival Bassingthwaighte, I shit you not, and he's the bane of my existence.

Percy lifts his chin so he can look down his nose at me. "Aren't you supposed to be assisting our fearless leader in Intake?"

An electrostatic sizzle of *oh crap* lightnings through me. I stuff my notebooks into my messenger bag and leave the observation box. I groan when I hear Percy's heels clicking down the hallway behind me.

I swear it's like his personal mission to hover over me just so he can point out every single one of my mistakes. I guess it makes sense—I'm the competition. Percy and I have both applied for a spot in Carbon Junction University's biochemistry and genetics program, but they have a policy of only admitting six students per year, and they have to be from six different countries. In January, one of us will be getting a letter of acceptance from the Institute-affiliated university, and one of us won't.

I jab the button to call the elevator. On the ride down, I twist my hair up into a clip and brush a few crumbs from my lab coat. I have to make sure I look as professional as possible. I'll never beat Percy when it comes to being the textbook example of a serious scientist— cold, clinical, and emotionless—but he's not the one who won the National Young Scientist Award three years ago for research on a genetic variation linked to an increased risk of Alzheimer's disease. Plus, my ability to memorize formulas is kind of . . . freakish. Most scientists can't rattle off the chemical formulas for every substance they've ever read about, but I can. I can also recall every peer-reviewed paper I've read in near-perfect detail. Too bad this superpower only seems to apply to science—last year I barely passed English.

"Have you finished your half-life history presentation yet?" Percy asks. On top of assisting the scientists, we have to do monthly projects assigned by the Institute's Education Team.

"Just putting the finishing touches on it. You?"

"I turned it in yesterday," he says with a smirk.

This month's assignment was to make a slideshow on half-life history—the kind of stuff kids learn in fifth grade. Everyone knows that the Italian Renaissance thinkers like Leonardo da Vinci were the first to start collecting reliable data regarding the half-life, proving that the twinge—the seizure you get when you're halfway through your life—was directly related to deaths. Before that, there was poor record keeping around births and deaths. Of course, when British archaeologists started digging up mummies in Egypt, it quickly became apparent that the ancient Egyptians knew about the half-life too.

So as far as we know, it's been with humans forever. We've learned to live with the weight of death hanging over us.

Sometimes, when I'm in a crowded place, I imagine hundreds of clocks ticking above everyone's heads.

When the elevator stops, Percy and I take turns leaning our faces close to the retina scanner. The building doesn't let anybody wander around without authorization, not even the lead scientists. The scanner bleeps, and the doors slide open to let us out onto the second floor. We do six-week rotations with each department at the Institute, and I always knew Intake would be the toughest. It's where we admit members of the general public for our deathday studies.

My boss allows us to share exactly one square foot of her windowless office, so I dump my notebook and bag on top of Percy's briefcase (how many seventeen-year-olds own a *briefcase*?) and power walk down the long, curving hallway.

At the door to room I-37, I double-check that I've done up the buttons on my lab coat right. I don't need a repeat of last week.

Right before I go in, I close my eyes. *I'm a good scientist. I'm a good scientist.* Maybe if I repeat the mantra enough times, my boss will believe it too.

I knock twice and slip inside. The room's not much bigger than the hospital bed in the center, and the white walls are quilted—literally a padded cell. The patient in the bed looks exhausted. She's tiny and birdlike, and her heart-shaped face has gone blank with fear. She looks younger than me, even though I know she can't be—you have to be over eighteen to enroll for deathday services.

Next to her, on a rolling stool, sits my boss, Dr. Uta Juncker.

Dr. Juncker's gray-blond hair is tied at her nape in a small, tight bun, and the deep lines on her makeup-free face make her look perpetually disappointed. I've never seen her crack a smile.

Dr. Juncker nods at me, then turns back to the woman in the bed.

17

"Ms. Vásquez, this is one of my interns, September Harrington." Dr. Juncker's German accent isn't usually very noticeable, but it always rides roughly over my name, landing hard on the *gt* so it sounds like *Harrinkton*. "She'll be assisting me as I hook up your equipment and take more blood samples."

Ms. Vásquez winces. "More blood?"

"It's important to monitor changes closely, so we'll be taking blood every four hours today and every hour tomorrow," Dr. Juncker explains in her brusque, dispassionate way.

I grab one of the clipboards I prepared earlier this week and take my spot at the head of the hospital bed. I know the drill, and I'm good at it.

"Ms. Vásquez, can you scoot up a little for us?" I ask.

"You can call me Aubrey," she says with a weak smile.

"Sure," I say, but then I flick a glance to Dr. Juncker, who clearly doesn't approve.

While we work, Aubrey goes quiet, staring down at her hands. She's wearing a standard-issue Institute gown, a silver beaded bracelet, and her own worn pale-blue socks.

Sympathy blooms in my chest, heavy and oxygen depleting. This always happens if I look at the patients for too long.

Her vitals are perfect. The heart monitor and all the other machines we have hooked up to her blip along cheerfully. But she's going to die tomorrow, and there's nothing Dr. Juncker or I can do to stop it.

Fifteen years ago, the Institute's founder, Dr. Elias Blumenthal, made the first breakthrough discovery. He found out that when people weren't sick or deteriorating from old age, you could isolate them and put them on every form of life support imaginable, and they'd still die on their deathday. He hooked them up to all kinds of machines to figure out what was really happening in his padded rooms, and that's when he discovered that the half-life had a built-in backup—a spontaneous aneurysm that would rupture and kill the patient.

The aneurysm—always in a different part of the brain, always too sudden to treat—would kick in and finish the patient off. He tried to call it the Blumenthal effect, but everyone just calls it the kill switch.

Once they could *see* the problem on a brain scan, that meant that scientists could start trying to *fix* it. Suddenly Dr. Blumenthal was getting billions of dollars thrown at him from every country in the world. The towering Half-Life Institute was built in his hometown of Carbon Junction, and scientists came from all over to work here. For the past fifteen years, the Institute's been examining everything about those aneurysms and trialing treatments to stop them. Nothing has worked so far, but Dr. Jackson has some incredible new ideas, and it feels like we're close to a breakthrough.

Of course, it'll be too late for Aubrey Vásquez, age twenty, of San Antonio, Texas.

Dr. Juncker's adjusting the electrode on Aubrey's left arm when she notices the silver bracelet. My boss is nothing if not a stickler for the rules.

"I'm sorry, but I have to ask you to remove all jewelry," Dr. Juncker says with a tinge of annoyance.

Aubrey looks stricken. "But it's from my—" Her voice catches in her throat. "I really can't keep it on?"

"I'm afraid not, no." Dr. Juncker doesn't even spare her a glance.

Aubrey touches the bracelet, and her eyes start to fill with tears.

She glances at me then, hoping that I'll appeal the decision, I guess. There's something about that pleading look—*Make this right; fix this*—that feels strangely familiar.

"I can get you a bag," I hear myself say. It's weird, this sudden, nagging sense of nostalgia. Like some deeply buried instinct in me is stirring back to life. I fish out a small specimen bag from drawer 4C, trying to ignore the heat of Dr. Juncker's glare. I give Aubrey a smile. "We can clip it to the top of your bed. That way it'll stay with you when you go up to the next floor."

Her face crumples with gratitude. She slides the bracelet off and hands it to me. The beads are threaded on a stretchy band like something a kid would make. There are letters on them, but I can only see some of them without turning the bracelet.

STERS♥FOREV

No.

The ground tilts under me. It's as if the room is suddenly full of nitrous oxide—N_2O—slowing everything in my body to a crawl.

I know why that look felt so familiar.

It's the way a little sister looks at a big sister.

The instinct it tugged out of me is something I never thought I'd feel again. The last time I felt it was six months ago.

When *my* sister was still alive.

The clipboard slips out of my hands and clatters to the floor.

"I'm so sorry," I mumble, dropping down to fish it out from under the hospital bed. I'm grateful for the chance to hide my face. I'm shaking.

When I come back up, Dr. Juncker's staring at me like I'm a specimen under a microscope.

"Why don't you head back to my office, Ms. Harrington," she says, her voice slicing through the chaos in my body. "I'll be right behind you."

She doesn't have to tell me twice.

I make it ten feet down the hallway before I have to lean against the wall, sucking in clean breaths of pristine hallway air.

I need to get a grip on myself. Sometimes I can make it through whole days without thinking about her, if I bury myself in science. But then, all it takes is one small thing, a word, a bracelet, a *look*, and I lose the tenuous grip I have on keeping it all pressed down.

The door to I-37 opens. I jerk upright. Dr. Juncker closes the door behind her with a soft click.

Her cold blue eyes settle on me. "Ms. Harrington. You seemed rattled during the intake."

I want to shake my head—*No, I'm fine*—but I feel like someone's injected me with a venom that makes me unable to move. Strychnine comes to mind: $C_{21}H_{22}N_2O_2$.

"Our patients are emotionally vulnerable," she continues. "Our job is to get in, get the samples and the data we need, and get out."

Shame bombards me, dissolving me like a nucleus in mitosis. Being a scientist has been my dream since YouTube skipped from a simple volcano experiment to an advanced genetics lecture I shouldn't have understood as a ten-year-old.

Dr. Juncker frowns. "Many scientists here have had personal experiences with the half-life. Be sure not to bring your emotions into the room with you. They can only cloud the scientific lens."

I nod. I need to try harder. Pretend harder. What happened to my family isn't something you ever forget—I just have to smash it down and hope I can keep a lid on it. Normally I'm good at that. I don't know what's going on today.

"I'm due in the main lab," Dr. Juncker says, straightening her lab coat. There's not a wrinkle on it. "I'll see you tomorrow."

I hold my breath until she's in the elevator and the number above it starts ticking up, then I go to the office to collect my things.

"I assume the intake didn't go well?"

I jump. "Damn it, Percy."

I was hoping he'd be in the prep room. My cheeks burn as I grab my bag. I have to get out of here.

I'm almost to the door when he speaks.

"You know, Dr. Juncker's going to figure it out sooner or later."

My steps slow, dread sinking through me. "Figure what out?"

"That this," he says, waving at my lab coat, at my Institute badge, "isn't you. I know what you're really like."

For a second, I just sway on the spot, stunned.

"Goodnight, Percy," I say, as calmly as I can manage, even though inside I'm a mess.

Don't cry, don't cry.

As I hurry through the hallway, I text my two best friends, Dottie and Bo. Emergency. Meet me at the Ruins ASAP.

In the elevator, I rip off my lab coat and stuff it into my bag. *This isn't you.*

I grab my vintage orange lace-up boots from the staff locker room and shove my boring work flats into my bag. I let my hair down, pull on my favorite wine-red coat, and loop a chunky yellow scarf around my neck. For the last touch, I slide a tiny silver stud into my nose piercing. Halfway across the country, my mom is wearing an identical one—we bought them together at her favorite boho market. For one sharp moment, I swear I can smell the clary sage and jasmine notes of her perfume.

The way I dress when I'm not in this building is the only part of me left that feels like the *me* from before. The September who was obsessed with science in a simple way, the September who was bouncy and bright and fun.

The September who was a big sister.

I break out of the Institute and into the cold, crisp afternoon. I run down the flight of white marble steps to where the gleaming stone ends and Carbon Junction's trendy Main Street begins.

The house where I live with my grandma is a five-minute walk through town, but I turn and run in the other direction.

Into the woods.

flint

SOGGY BROWN LEAVES cling to my shoes as I trample through the forest. I'm starting to regret leaving my coat by the bird's grave, but at least all this walking is keeping my legs warm.

Overhead, an airplane sears through the sky with a ground-shaking *whoosh*. Air force by the sound of it, most likely an F-16. Curiosity sparks in my chest—I could so easily look up and confirm the exact model. I know them all. My grandpa's a pilot, and he took me to my first air show when I was four. Instead, I clench my hands and keep my eyes on the uneven forest floor. I shouldn't be far from the Ruins now.

The trees thin, and I'm suddenly spilling out onto a suburban street.

Shit. I thought I was heading deeper into the woods, not back toward town. I shake my head in frustration, then look around to get my bearings.

On either side of the road, there are neat two-story houses, each a slightly different shade of beige. Other than a squirrel running up the nearest tree and someone a few houses down raking leaves into a pile, it's quiet.

Wait—I recognize these houses. This is Steeplechase. My best friend used to live on this street. Still does, maybe.

I run my hands through my hair. My fingers are stiff from the cold. It's not below freezing out here, but it's certainly not comfortable.

I think if I take a left at the end of this road and duck back into the forest after I pass the auto shop, that'll get me to the Ruins.

The more I think about it, the Ruins could actually be the perfect hiding place. When I was a kid, no one ever went out there. I make a mental note to buy a sleeping bag and a cheap tent.

I start walking down Steeplechase, hands jammed deep in my pockets, my long legs eating up the pavement. We're coming up for Halloween, and on each porch, two or three carved jack-o'-lanterns grin at me. For a second, I'm smug—they'll be thrown out weeks before my expiry date. But I guess it's kind of pathetic to be comparing life spans with a rotting gourd.

I sort of hoped I wouldn't remember which exact house my best friend lived in, but muscle memory takes over as I approach it. I shouldn't be surprised—I came here hundreds of times as a kid.

My chest gets tighter as I get closer. I try to pass by the house without looking at it, but something stops me right at the bottom of the path to the front door. I stand stupidly in front of the house, staring.

Memories flood me: Two kids popping wheelies up and down this driveway, having Nerf gun fights in the backyard, eating every pizza roll we could find in the freezer.

I stand there so long I start to lose feeling in my lips.

And then. A face in the window.

Shit.

I turn and power walk away from the house, but the damage is done. A voice calls out from behind me, sounding thin in the clear, crisp air.

"Wait. Hey—dude! Wait!"

25

Part of me wants to duck into the nearest bush, but if I know my former best friend, that won't deter her a bit. And I'll end up looking ridiculous.

A hand grabs my elbow.

"Hey, creep—why were you staring at my house?"

I take a deep breath before turning around. My brain is feverishly working on a plausible story, something that would explain a weirdo staring at a house for an inappropriate amount of time. The other part knows it's hopeless.

I blink hard. Because even though it's been eight years, it's definitely Aerys.

She's short. I was always taller than her, but I've grown two feet since I was eight, and she has . . . not grown two feet. She's wearing baggy jeans and a T-shirt with the sleeves cut off, and she's in the middle of pulling on an oversized hoodie. Her straw-blond cap of hair is cut short, Peter Pan–style.

I grit my teeth, hoping she won't recognize me. "Sorry," I say. "I was just—"

Her mouth drops open. "Holy shit—*Flint*?"

I cough. "I'm not— You must have me confused with—"

"Oh, cut it out," she says, cheeks dimpling into a smile. "Your birthmark gave you away."

Self-consciously, my hand moves up to touch the single dark mole above my lip. I should have known someone in this town would recognize me. I just didn't expect it to happen less than an hour after getting here, or for it to be my childhood best friend. My shoulders slump in defeat.

"Why were you staring at the house like that?" she asks. She punches my arm, and there's real strength behind it. "And holy crap, you got tall! Wait." Her face falls. "You remember me, right?"

I sigh. "Of course I remember you, Aerys."

How could I forget her? We rode our bikes all over this town, made forts in the woods, carved the initials of the girls we liked into the bark of the elm in her backyard.

Aerys barrels into me, pulling me into a tight hug. She's like a little cannonball.

She claps my back locker-room-style, and I return the patting awkwardly. As a rule, I don't generally allow hugs.

Finally she steps back. "So? Spill—where have you been?" she asks.

"Philadelphia. I like your hair," I say.

"Yeah? Check out the back." She turns, showing me an edgy undercut that honestly looks so awesome.

"Badass," I say.

Her eyes twinkle, pleased. "Are your parents here too? How are they?" she asks.

"Uh—they split up. Not long after we moved."

"That sucks, man, I'm sorry."

I look away. "It is what it is. I've been living with my dad."

"Oh, really? I would have thought you'd stick with your mom—you always were such a mama's boy. So why'd you come back to Carbon Junction . . . oh."

Aaaand here we go.

She's doing the math.

Aerys knows about my half-life. She was with me the day I

27

twinged. We stayed in town for a few months afterward, but that was long enough for the news to rot through everything.

"You know what? I'm glad you came back," Aerys says, soldiering on bravely. "We have so much catching up to do! I've been working on a couple of dirt bikes in the garage—you can help me get them up and running. Remember that skate park where we used to go and pretend we were hard-core skaters?"

"The one where you broke your wrist showing off for Ellie Jenkins?"

"Still got the scars," she says, holding her arm up proudly. "And it must have worked, because we dated for a bit freshman year. Well, anyway, they have a sick dirt bike track out back now."

I blink.

"You seem bewildered," Aerys says. "Is this a lot? This is a lot."

"Sorry. I'm just—not used to talking this much."

"Why not? Don't you go to school?"

I shrug. "Not often, if I can help it."

"Oh. Seriously?"

"Seriously."

Last year, I logged a record low of fourteen days in class. They passed a law a few years back to loosen the attendance requirements for half-lifers whose deathday is under the age of twenty-one. I pretty much stopped going to school as soon as the bill was signed, because, again, what's the point?

Aerys looks confused. "Wait, so what do you actually do? Like, what are you into?"

I shrug again.

She whistles. "Okay. We definitely have to get you out on the town. So how long we got?"

"Six weeks," I mumble.

"Consider me your new wingwoman. Great timing, actually, because my girlfriend and I just broke up. I hereby vow to make your last six weeks kick serious ass. I'll be your best friend again in no time," Aerys chatters on. "I mean, unless you have one already? Or maybe you're dating someone?"

"Definitely not dating anyone."

"Okay, that makes it easier to plan things, I guess. Have anything in mind? You don't want to go down the thrill-seeker route, right?" she asks.

"Absolutely not," I say. "There are worse things than death."

"I hear that. What about a bucket list? You must have a bucket list, right?"

"Nope."

"What? Who doesn't make a bucket list?"

I shrug. When I was a kid, right after it happened, I sat down a few times to start one, but it felt too big to think about. The lists ended up being a few scrawled video game titles before I crumpled them up and trashed them.

The other thing about bucket lists is they start costing a lot. After seeing my parents argue over whether we could afford a trip to a water park or a nice meal out, I decided a bucket list was off the table.

Later on, once I started wanting big, life-milestone kinds of wants, I was old enough to know I'd never get to cross them off. At the end, I'd just be devastated about the ones I didn't get to do.

29

I shake my head. "Aerys . . . I don't get why you'd want to do this. I never even wrote to you after I moved like I said I would."

"We're good. You were dealing with some shit. And we were eight."

I'm stunned at how quick she is to forgive.

"Come inside," she says. "Mom would love to see you. Besides, how are you even out here without a jacket?" She crosses her arms against the chill as she turns back to her front door.

I almost follow her. My mom would be all about Aerys's live-life-to-the-fullest plan.

But *I* am not all about it.

"Aerys—I have to go." I don't have time for dirt bikes and pizza rolls and memories. She's a normal, peppy seventeen-year-old who's thinking about homework and girls and high school, and I am literally in the process of selecting a location to wait out my upcoming death. We're in totally different worlds right now.

I turn and start walking toward the end of the street.

"Flint?" Aerys calls out behind me. Now she's the bewildered one.

I don't answer. I can't.

I stomp through the forest, heart beating overtime in my effort to get away from town and people and *talking*.

The sun's past its peak now, slanting through the trees, and it's getting colder.

I think I see something ahead—a stone wall, or what's left of a wall.

The Ruins. I find the gap that must have once been the doorway, stepping over a patch of poison ivy and into the space.

The ghosts of the walls form a rectangular room. At one end, there are the remains of a fireplace. The roof's been gone for a hundred years or more. No one in Carbon Junction really knows what this was. A hunting lodge? Schoolhouse?

I swipe my boot over the ground, sending pebbles scattering. Then I sit with my back against the crumbling wall and drag a finger through the dirt. This is the place, then, I guess.

My mind wanders. When I come here on December 4 . . . what will end me? The cold, biting through me until I can't breathe? A bobcat or a black bear? Starvation? Or will I go the way people go when they book into the Institute for their deathday, like an off switch being flicked somewhere in my brain?

I wonder what they'll do with my body. I don't have a strong preference, and it's one thing that Mom and Dad haven't asked. Buried or cremated . . . I guess if I get mauled by a bear out here, I can go for half and half.

I chuckle at that. I close my eyes and tip my head back. I'm exhausted. I have a lot of trouble sleeping at night, for obvious reasons.

I try not to think of anything at all, but a line from Nabokov starts pulsing in my mind. *Life is just one small piece of light between two eternal darknesses.*

I must fall asleep, because the next thing I know, something's nudging my foot.

My brain jolts awake, but I keep my eyes squeezed shut, holding very still. I expect to see yellowed eyes, to smell the meaty breath of some animal that wants to maim me.

But when I peek through my lashes, it's not a bear or a bobcat or even a squirrel.

It's a girl.

I open my eyes fully and blink them clear. I must not have been out for long, because it's not quite dusk yet.

The girl stands over me with a worried look on her face, clutching the strap of an old leather bag. The first thing I notice is her hair. It's long—like down to her waist—and it's the rich, gleaming orange red of a brand-new penny.

She presses her hand to her heart. "Oh, thank god—you're alive. I was starting to freak out that I'd found a dead body."

I shift, groaning a little. "Not dead."

Yet, I almost add.

"Need a hand up?" she asks, offering one, her expression all open and friendly.

Irritation flashes through me. This girl is infringing on my *death spot*. What is with the universe today, throwing all these *people* at me? I just want to be left alone.

I ignore her outstretched hand. "Thanks for waking me up, but I'm gonna get going."

I stagger to my feet. God, everything in my body aches from the cold. It's seeped into my bones.

I sway.

The world spins, then goes black.

september

THE BOY'S SKIN is bloodlessly pale in the cold. He looks so out of place here, stark against the soft colors of nature. I'm about to ask his name when he starts to tip sideways, eyes rolling back in his head as he passes out.

I reach him just in time, shoving my wrists under his armpits, staggering under his weight. I stand there for a few seconds, stunned, my muscles straining to hold his limp body.

"Um," I say, but there's no one to hear. The forest swallows my voice.

God, he's cold, and *really* heavy, but I manage to lower him to the ground in an awkward scuffle. I kneel next to him. Stones dig into my knees, and the ground seeps cold, damp patches into my tights. What the heck was he thinking, coming out here in a T-shirt? I take off my scarf and lay it in a bright yellow zigzag over his bare arms, covering as much of his exposed skin as I can.

I press two fingers under his jaw to check his pulse. It's a little slow, but steady. *Orthostatic hypotension*, my brain supplies, pulling it straight from a medical textbook. It's a fancy way of saying your blood pressure is so low that going from sitting to standing too quickly makes you faint. He must have been sitting here for a long time. Plus, he's kind of astoundingly tall, which increases the odds of experiencing postural hypotension upon standing.

I check my phone. The signal is always spotty in the woods, and if this is more than just low blood pressure, we've got bigger problems. I shrug out of my coat and lay it on top of the scarf for good measure.

We're alone out here. I texted Dottie and Bo, but they're not coming—Bo has a late rehearsal, and Dottie's working an after-school shift at Rag House, the vintage clothing store on Main Street. They blew up my phone with solidarity emojis and promises to let me vent over dinner later. Not that I'll tell them what really happened in Intake. It'll be enough to complain about Percy and Dr. Juncker.

I'm resetting my cellular data for the fifth time, hoping to snag one bar of signal, when the boy finally stirs, blinking and frowning in confusion as he comes around.

"Oh, thank god," I say, dropping my phone to my side with a slump of relief. "Are you okay?"

"Peachy," he grumbles.

He peels my coat off his arms and shoves it in my direction, then splays one hand on the ground and starts to rise again.

"Hold on—you can't get up yet. You need to get your blood moving first."

He sinks back down. "I don't understand," he says. "Did I fall?" His voice is startlingly deep, and he sounds profoundly weary. Like the whole world's pressing down on him.

"You fainted," I say. "I caught you."

He raises an eyebrow, clearly not believing that I was able to support his weight.

"You stood up too fast, and your core temperature's probably too low. Start rolling your ankles and wrists, then take some deep breaths."

"What, are you a doctor?" he asks sarcastically.

"Not exactly."

"'Not exactly'? Great." He gives me a withering look and makes no move to do the exercises.

I roll my eyes. "Just do them, please? I can't haul you back to town if you pass out again, and I don't have a signal out here."

His eyes lock on mine, and the stubborn intensity in his glare almost shoves me back. This boy has *walls*.

Well. So do I.

I meet his stare head-on, unflinching.

After a few seconds, he bites out a *Fine* and starts wiggling his feet.

I scrape a few rocks out of the way and sit down next to him. As the grip of our little medical crisis loosens, I realize that the pressure in my chest from earlier has dissipated. I have myself under control again, everything pressed down where no one can see.

I study him out of the corner of my eye. The sleeves of his black T-shirt are rolled at his biceps like some old-school James Dean, and his black boots look kind of . . . piratical? They're ankle-high and have two silver buckles each, and I actually really dig them. There's a good chance they're from Rag House.

Dottie likes to assign music to people's personalities, and I'm guessing she'd say this boy is like a Billie Eilish song: devastating, melancholy, haunted. His hair is so dark it eats up the light, and there's so *much* of it. It reminds me of Vantablack, the substance scientists created out of carbon nanotubes to get the darkest possible shade of black.

It strikes me then how attractive he is, even if it's in an unconventional way.

I should probably at least know his name if I'm going to get him back to town alive. "I'm September, by the way," I offer.

He stares at me blankly for a second, then seems to remember himself. "Flint."

Even his name is stony and sharp edged. Suits him perfectly.

Whatever's hurting him, he's letting it. I can keep my own broken parts shielded from the world. Today I had a slipup, but usually I can keep it together. At the Institute, I make jaws drop with the amount of science I can fit in my brain, and everywhere else, I can smile and make people think I'm bright and happy and fun. No one in either half of my life would ever guess how hard I have to work to make it seem like I'm whole.

Flint stretches his arms. "Why are you even out here?"

I bristle. "My friends and I come here all the time. I think the better question is, why are *you* here?"

He stares out into the trees, and a muscle tenses in his jaw.

I narrow my eyes. Interesting. But if he doesn't want to share why I found him napping up against a two-hundred-year-old wall, I won't pry.

He shivers. It's only the smallest tremor, but our arms are touching from shoulder to elbow, so I feel every quaver of it.

We're both silent for a minute.

"What did you mean before," he asks after a while, "when you said you're not *exactly* a doctor?"

I hesitate. I'm dressed for meeting Dottie and Bo. Which September am I going to give this boy?

"I know a little bit about medicine. I'm an intern at the Half-Life Institute."

He stiffens visibly. "Oh."

"Not that that makes me at all qualified to treat you the way a doctor would. But I'm not like an HR intern or anything; I do actually work in biochemistry."

He nods, but he's looking down at his boots. It's clear he doesn't want to talk about this either. He's hard work, this one.

"Maybe you should eat something," I suggest. I dig into my bag and produce a few pieces of Halloween candy and a floppy, tasteless energy bar. He takes the energy bar and eats it in two bites. I hold my hand out to take the wrapper.

"You don't have to take my trash," he says, stuffing it into his own pocket.

I notice for the first time that there's a single dark mole above his top lip. I feel a fleeting but intense urge to reach out and touch it.

I clasp my hands together in my lap.

I'm weirdly . . . *aware* of this boy. Every second that passes feels ultravivid and important, and my brain keeps zooming in on him the way it usually only does with science.

I clear my throat and try to shake the feeling off. "We should get you out of the woods before dark. Come on, I'll help you up."

I offer my hand, expecting him to stubbornly refuse like before. Instead, he takes it.

His palm is huge. It swallows my hand completely.

He's wobbly for a second, but he soon steadies. He winds my scarf into a neat loop before handing it to me.

I want to tell him to keep it, because fresh goose bumps are already breaking out on his arms, but I get the feeling he won't take me up on it.

"Thank you," he says. "September." I wait for the inevitable joke, because most parents don't name their kids after months of the year, but it never comes.

He squints into the trees. "Do you know how to get back?" he asks. He takes a few steps, but then he has to grab for the broken wall. "Shit. Still dizzy."

"Take your time," I say. "Give the energy bar a minute to get your blood sugar up."

He perches on the low stone wall. "So . . . biochemistry," he says slowly. "Is that your thing?" He looks like he doesn't really want to be talking about it, but it's the only thing he knows about me.

"Half-life-specific biochemistry and genetics, yeah," I answer.

"Genetics. Like DNA?"

I nod, getting the zing of excitement I always get when I start thinking about science. "Our director, Dr. Jackson, thinks that the instructions that tell our bodies when to half-life might be coded into our DNA."

"That can't be all there is to it," Flint says. "How could DNA possibly know when someone was going to get in a car crash or get stabbed in an alley?"

It's a good question. Only 4 percent of deaths are accidental, though. The leading causes of death are heart disease, dementia, and stroke. With those, there could be a scientific explanation; maybe the body can actually predict its own failure years in advance. The accidents are harder to explain.

We have our theories at the Institute, of course: that people let their guard down in infinitesimal ways on their deathdays, making them more likely to break the speed limit or walk through a dangerous alley. Maybe something in the brain starts failing, causing them to take subtle risks they wouldn't have taken before.

I read last week that 94 percent of people think the half-life is something science will never understand. They think it's fate, or a higher power, something spiritual and inexplicable.

Deep down, there's a part of me that's terrified they're right. Even though I believe in the Institute with every fiber of my being, maybe there's something about the half-life that we might never be able to explain. Why do accidents even happen? Why don't we all just die kill switch deaths? How do our bodies know when we're exactly halfway through our lives? It's hard to admit that we simply don't know.

Yet.

Flint frowns. "So your boss thinks it's in our DNA. What does that even mean?"

I sit up straighter, inspired all over again by the hypothesis. "We think it could mean that deep inside every cell of our bodies, there's a little instruction card that says: 'When X happens, trigger the half-life. When Y happens, shut everything down.' If we can figure out what X and Y are, maybe we can stop *those* things from happening."

He tilts his head, studying me. "You're really into this, aren't you?"

"Yes. Very."

He's been listening so attentively, never taking that steady gaze off me. It's strange—I'm not sure that anyone's ever really *listened* to me like this before.

Flint tucks his hands into his pockets. "So, what, could X be something like if you eat two hundred bananas on April fourth, you'll half-life?" he asks.

I laugh. "Well, I mean, sure, but we would have noticed if everyone was eating—"

I go very still.

"Oh my god," I whisper. Could it be?

Flint looks confused. "What's up?"

"Say all of that again," I demand.

He laughs. "What, the thing about if you eat two hundred bananas, you'll twinge? Don't listen to me; I have no idea what I'm talking about."

My mind is going a million miles a minute, pushing at each part of the hypothesis that's starting to form in my mind, expecting it to fall apart. But it doesn't.

This . . . this could be it. It's starkly obvious, but the best science always is.

If Dr. Jackson is right, and it's in the DNA, and if I can prove *this* . . . it could change everything.

I hop to my feet and start pacing between the ruined stone walls.

"Please tell me you don't actually think half-lifing has to do with how many bananas we've eaten," Flint says in a tone that makes it clear that whatever burgeoning respect he had for my intelligence is fading.

"Please. I'm not an idiot."

It has nothing to do with bananas. But associating the X and Ys with a *measured level* of something in your body . . .

I'm in my zone, my mind humming, following each line of thought until I come up against a wall and have to turn back. Not for the first time, I think that a scientist testing hypotheses is not unlike a lab rat sniffing its way through a maze full of dead ends.

When I get like this, hours can pass by without me noticing. My mind becomes a cascade of symbols and formulas and chemicals and isotopes, but before long, the whiteboards in my head are full.

I stomp over to the half-crumbled fireplace at the other end of the Ruins. Dottie and Bo and I like to light fires out here on summer evenings, roasting marshmallows and filling the forest with laughter.

I kick my boot through the rubble until I unearth a chunk of charred, blackened wood. Ta-da—makeshift pencil. Thank you, carbon.

I press the sharp tip against the smoothest, biggest stone I can find.

I need to see this on a wall.

flint

I WATCH AS the girl draws on the stones with a rhythmic *scratch-scratch-scratch*.

I'm stunned speechless, mostly by the weirdness of the whole situation, because this girl I've just met (and subsequently fainted on) is now totally ignoring me—but also because it's clear that whatever she's writing is *advanced*.

I lean against one of the low stone walls, cross my arms over my chest, and watch her attack the wall with the fervor of an animated teacher at a chalkboard.

There's an eager, hungry look on her face. Every now and then, she shakes her head at something, rubs it out, and tries again on another stone.

There are long strings of letters and numbers, filled with Cs and Hs. Chemical formulas, maybe? On the first (and only) day of chemistry I attended this year, the teacher told us that most things in the universe were made of carbon, hydrogen, and oxygen.

There are honeycomb diagrams where letters are linked together with lines, pointy Greek-looking Es, and lists with the kind of long, unpronounceable words you find on pill bottles. There's nothing about bananas, thankfully.

None of it makes any sense to me. This girl is a freaky,

genius-level kind of smart. She'll probably be voted Most Likely to Win the Nobel Prize in her yearbook. If I still went to school, I'd be voted Most Likely to Depress People.

Before long, she's covered nearly every stone that's still standing. I worry that she's about to start writing on the pieces of fallen wall that are scattered over the forest floor, but she seems satisfied with her calculations. She drops the burnt piece of wood and dusts her fingers off. Then she pulls her phone out and starts snapping photos of the things she's written.

I clear my throat. "Are you sure you're just an intern?"

She jumps. "Oh my god, sorry. I forgot you were there."

I push myself off the wall and take a step closer, squinting at the largest stone. "What does all this even mean?"

Her eyes meet mine, and I notice for the first time that they're a light, clear amber.

"This," she says, gesturing at the formulas with a proud wave, "is going to help us beat the half-life."

A spark of something I haven't felt in eight years flickers in my heart.

Impossible. I thought I was dead there, blackened beyond repair. But I'm sure I felt it.

Hope.

"Well, at least I think it will," she says. "I have some research to do—a lot, actually—before I can be sure. But it's . . . I think it's actually a solid hypothesis."

Just as quickly as the spark of hope flared into existence in my chest, it burns to ash.

I grit my teeth. I'm an idiot. To think there's even a sliver of a chance that I'll make it past December 4 is pure stupidity. You can't *cure* death.

This girl might be brilliant, but she's still just an intern. What she's drawn on the walls looks fancy to me, but it could be the most basic science in the world. And even if the Institute's getting close to a cure, it'll be years before it goes through testing and gets approved by the FDA and all that.

"We need to get you out of here before you turn blue," September says, slicing into my thoughts. "Come on, town's this way."

She sets off through the trees without a backward glance, abandoning the wall of formulas like it's nothing. I leave every place with a small, silent goodbye, as if it's the last time I'll ever see it—because it usually is.

I stare after her stupidly, a blur of red-riding-hood scarlet against the autumn brown of the forest. Her pace falters when she realizes I'm not following.

She turns back. "You coming?" she asks. Her words are tinged with impatience.

I jerk into motion, catching up to her in a few long strides, and shove my hands into my pockets. Afternoon is tipping toward evening, and the gold light filtering down through the tree canopy is slowly going gray, like color draining from an old photo.

September holds out her hand, offering me something wrapped in clear cellophane.

"What's this?" I ask with a skeptical raise of my eyebrow.

"Butterscotch," she says.

"Didn't anyone teach you not to take candy from strangers?"

"Are we strangers?" she says, eyes dancing. I'm envious that she can be this buoyant and carefree. She nudges my arm, offering the candy again.

I can't let myself take it. I love butterscotch, but ever since I twinged, I only let myself pick at the edges of anything that tastes good.

"No thanks," I say.

"Suit yourself." She unwraps it and pops it into her mouth, and a warm caramel scent blooms through the cold smell of the forest.

Who even is this girl? Who carries around Werther's like a freaking grandpa?

I risk a sidelong glance at her. She's a whirl of color, and I don't know if it's the boots or the flared coat or the tiny silver nose stud glinting in the light, but there's something almost unbearably *cool* about her. Something that makes me feel like a freshman talking to a college girl. Her hair is perfectly straight, a shimmering curtain of copper that I want to run my hands through. When I was little, my grandpa used to make these amazing wooden toys for me, and my favorite was a P-47 Thunderbolt—a WWII plane—made of rich mahogany. The propeller and wings were made from the reddest wood he could find, burnished and lacquered to a shine. It used to catch the light just like September's hair does now.

She plows ahead with purpose, taking two steps for every one of mine. I get the impression she's still thinking about the equations she wrote on the wall. At one point, I'm sure she mutters "Tyrosine?" to herself. Whatever that is.

After my impromptu nap against the wall, the sudden change of pace is making me feel shaky. I'm about to ask her to slow down when suddenly, instead of more trees ahead, I see wider gaps of sky between the branches. We push through the last line of trees and out into the open air.

The sight in front of me catches me so off guard I nearly stumble.

We've come out on the edge of a hill east of Carbon Junction, and on the other side of town, streaked low on the horizon, is the most vivid sunset I've ever seen.

I force my eyes down immediately. I zero in on my scuffed shoes, on the spongy, decaying layer of leaves on the ground.

"Now that's a sunset," September whispers beside me.

"I bet you could tell me the exact pollutants that make it look like that, huh?" I ask, keeping my eyes glued to the ground.

"Well, atmospheric science isn't my thing, but I probably could take a stab at it." She hums thoughtfully. "Most of it has to do with the way sunlight scatters when it interacts with nitrogen and oxygen—" She breaks off. "Wait, why are you looking at your feet?"

"Rock stuck in my shoe," I lie. I'm about to bend down and pretend to fish it out, but she grabs my elbow and pulls me to her side.

"That can wait. Soak up this sunset with me, Flint."

"Nah, I'm good," I mumble, my eyes still cast down.

"What are you, allergic to pretty things?" She laughs, tugging again on my arm.

Well, this is it.

Whenever I meet someone new, there inevitably comes a time when I have to tell them my expiry date is right around the corner.

46

I open my mouth to tell September why exactly I can't look at this sunset, but then I raise my eyes to look at her.

Big mistake.

Because she's nearly as searing-bright and alive as the sky.

Everything I'm about to say fizzles on my tongue. I just stand there, gaping. And then, because she asked me to, because her eyes are alight with wonder, I look at the damn sunset.

It's the most beautiful thing I've ever seen.

A second ticks by.

Another.

Everything is still, and instead of the ever-present guilt that I'm wasting the seconds of my life, I feel like I'm part of something bigger than myself.

September's coat sleeve brushes against my bare arm. The wool is rough on my skin. I'm in the moment in a way that I never let myself be, and it's . . . nice.

When she turns her whiskey-warm eyes on me, I swear they make me feel a little drunk. The light on our hillside dims to the sort of blue that ghosts the hard edges of buildings into mist.

"I guess we should call it a night," I say, trying not to let my reluctance bleed into my voice.

She nods. "I need to get to the Institute. There are some things I need to check."

"Want me to walk you?" I ask.

I think the question surprises her nearly as much as it surprises me. I've known this girl for less than an hour, and she's already got me breaking my rules.

In the half-light, I hold my breath, waiting for her answer.

She pulls her coat tight. "Sure. I'd like that," she says.

As we walk together down the hill into Carbon Junction, the last of the twilight seeps out of the sky.

I'm afraid if I let her out of my sight, I'll never see anything as rich and bright and real ever again.

september

BY THE TIME Flint and I arrive at the bottom of the marble steps leading up to the Institute, the sky is dark.

He eyes the tower warily. I feel a piercing protectiveness for this place that's given me so much. I want to tell him that it's not so bad, but people have their reasons for fearing the Institute.

"So. This is it, then," Flint says.

I nod. "Thank you for saying that stupid thing about bananas."

"Thanks for making sure I didn't turn into a Popsicle."

He stands there, so still and solemn. It strikes me—something about whatever's hurting him seems so familiar. Like I know that pain *exactly*.

I shake the strangeness of that feeling away.

"Well. It was nice to meet you, September," he says.

For a moment, everything goes still. His dark eyes bore into mine. I almost think he's going to say something else, but then he lowers his eyes and takes a step back.

"Bye," I say quietly, and then I turn and head up the steps.

When I get to the top, I look back. Flint is trudging down Main Street, a lanky shadow with his hands shoved into his pockets. When he disappears around the corner of a building, it feels bizarrely like the moment when two magnets move far enough apart that you can feel the force between them vanish. But then I blink, and I'm left wondering if I even felt it at all.

I drag my attention back to the Institute. What I wrote on the walls of the Ruins is more important than one sad, serious boy.

In the gleaming foyer, I wave my badge at the two security guards on duty and hurry to the elevator. I'm hyperaware of my hair, which is wind tangled and wild, and my outfit, which isn't hiding under a lab coat like it usually is. I press my face close to the retina scanner and tap my keycard against the reader at the same time. The doors slide open.

Upstairs, I hurry through the Intake floor's silent, curved hallway. Aubrey Vásquez and the other patients who arrived today have been moved up to Observation, so all the rooms are empty and awaiting tomorrow's fresh wave of patients.

Motion-activated lights blink on as I make my way down the corridor. There's no one else here. Dr. Juncker's office is locked, but there's a small meeting room with a row of computers along the back wall. I drop into a chair and log in.

The CDC has a database called the NDI—the National Death Index—but that isn't comprehensive enough for the work we do here, so we have the Global Death Archive.

I glance over my shoulder, but the room is still dim and empty. Percy better not pop his head up now.

I open the database and adjust the search parameters. Science is easier when you know what you're looking for. The biggest breakthroughs are in realizing *what* you need to look for in the first place.

I'm interested in the few people who outlasted their prescribed deathday. It's never been by more than a handful of minutes, though. The longest one lived twenty-two minutes and forty-eight seconds past the end of their deathday. I wonder how that person felt—if they thought they'd beat the game, if they thought they were some sort of medical miracle, only for the lights to go out twenty-two minutes later.

The anomalies aren't anything new—we've known about them for years. But I've always had a gut feeling that they'd be a part of figuring out the half-life.

When the search finishes, a notification pops up on the page. *289 results.*

Two hundred eighty-nine anomalies. In science, every data set has a few outliers—things that don't act exactly as we expect them to. So even though dozens of tests were run on the dead bodies of these patients, we couldn't ever figure out why they made it past their deathdays. It was eventually concluded that they'd either lied or written down their half-life date wrong. Simple data-input error.

But maybe there's something linking them after all. Maybe we just weren't looking in the right place.

In the eerie silence of the lab, the light from the computer screen washes over my arms. I add another filter to the search.

Show results within: 300 miles. Deaths within: last 10 years.

The computer hums for one second. Two.

The list refreshes.

7 results found.

Bingo.

I can work with this. I comb through the information we have on file for these seven people. It's nowhere near enough for what I have to do. I'm going to need their full medical files. Technically that's the sort of thing I'm allowed to ask for on behalf of Dr. Juncker. I've made calls for her before, to medical archivists who scan and email the documents over for me to hand to Dr. Juncker.

I could do that again. Start making calls from here tomorrow morning. But they'll email the scans to my Institute address, and someone might ask why I've requested these without Dr. Juncker's permission. And no archivist is stupid enough to agree to send it to my personal email.

Besides . . . part of me wants to keep this close to my chest. I think of Percy, sticking his nose in my business. Then I'd have to explain it to Dr. Juncker too, and she'd take over from there, yanking my discovery out from under me.

My discovery.

If I'm right, there's no way the CJU admissions panel could turn me down. And I'd keep the promise I made to—

I press my eyes closed, refusing to let my sister's name surface in my mind.

I print out the info on the seven anomalies. In a stroke of bad luck, none of them came here for our deathday services, so we don't have extensive last-day statistics on them. But we do have the names of the hospitals where they died. Those hospitals will have fat manila folders languishing in a storage room or hard drives packed with digital records. And somewhere in those files, there will be one small thing that links these people. A psychotropic medication, maybe, or environmental exposure to a specific rare chemical. Some small thing that held off their deathday for a few minutes.

I run my fingertips over the names of the hospitals.

I have to get my hands on those files.

The next morning, I'm sitting at the breakfast table, hunched over a bowl of Froot Loops as I blearily try to wake up. Between the internship, the three classes I still have to attend at Carbon Junction High, and homework, I'm averaging about four hours of sleep a night. Last night was even worse. My brain was churning, trying to work out the logistics of how I can get the anomaly data. I'm kicking myself for not taking driver's ed last semester.

My grandma bustles into the kitchen with a mason jar of Diet Coke in her hand.

"Mornin', sunshine," she says, kissing my head. She smells like hairspray and perm chemicals, and her short, not-so-naturally blond hair is gelled into what she calls "rad grandma" spikes. This year there's one bright purple streak that matches her glasses. Last year it was hot pink.

My grandma is a home hairdresser, working out of what used to be the dining room. She's from North Carolina and the only person in town with a drawl, but she's a local favorite. Everyone in Carbon Junction over fifty (a frankly dwindling population) comes here to get their hair done at Miss Gigi's.

There's only one pea in the stack of mattresses that is my relationship with my grandma: As much as I love her, sometimes it annoys me that there's no shadow following her around. She's happy-go-lucky all the time. The holes left in us are the exact same shape, so why does she never seem to have to work to keep the memories of my sister from drowning her?

"Well, would you look at that," Gigi says, staring shamelessly through the back porch window as she sips from her mason jar. "Someone's finally moved into that monstrosity over on Gravel Ridge."

I finish my cereal and join her at the window. It's become our tradition to spy on the people across the creek. Our street is a row of squat houses left over from Carbon Junction's coal miner days, but Gravel Ridge has million-dollar mansions spaced far apart.

I squint through the trees. A guy in a plaid shirt chops wood on a stump on the back porch. He looks up when he sees a beetle-black Jeep pull into the driveway, waving to greet the person climbing out of the driver's seat.

My pulse stutters.

"No way," I whisper.

Because trotting up the back porch of the newest house on Gravel Ridge Road is a tall, thin figure dressed in all black.

"Quick, pass me the binoculars," I say to Gigi.

She perks up. "We got a cutie on our hands?"

I hold the binoculars up to my eyes. It's definitely Flint.

"I met that kid yesterday," I tell Gigi. "Down by that old house in the woods."

Flint tucks his car keys into his pocket, talks to the man for a minute, then leans over with his elbows on the porch rail, plowing his fingers through his Vantablack hair.

I drop the binoculars, suddenly very awake.

This could be the perfect solution. Sure, he's a little grumpy, but he has a car, which is more than I can say.

"I'm gonna go over there."

Gigi raises her eyebrows. "What, right now?"

"Sure, why not?"

"He must have made quite an impression on you yesterday," she teases, eyes twinkling.

"I'm just being a good neighbor, that's all."

"Mm-hmm. Whatever you say, honey. Take some banana bread," she says, turning to the pans sitting warm on the stove. Gigi bakes two loaves every day for her clients to snack on while she's covering their grays.

She hums as she wraps the loaf in foil, and fondness swells in me. Most of the time I can handle the fact that she's already half-lifed and I'm going to lose her in fourteen years. It still seems like a long time away. Gigi always says the one good thing about knowing your deathday is that she never puts anything off. She doesn't ever say, "I'll do that when I'm retired." Instead, she learns new hobbies, joins exercise groups, goes on road trips with her friends.

I'm on my way out the back door when I hear her chuckle to herself and mutter, "Good neighbor my foot."

I traipse through our backyard. No one around here has fences, and the fastest way to Flint's house is across the creek that winds through the miniature valley between our houses. The hike up the other side of the hill is hard, but eventually I get to the porch where I saw Flint leaning against the rail.

It's empty.

I trek around the side of the house to knock on the front door. The woman who answers isn't much taller than me. She's perfectly put together, her long hair waved in a way that appears effortless but I know takes a *lot* of effort, but when I peer closer, there are tired smudges under her eyes. This must be Flint's mom.

"Hi. I'm looking for Flint," I say. "Is he here?"

I feel about six years old asking like this, but her face just *lights up*.

"Oh! We weren't expecting anyone. Come on in, I'll go—"

"Mom?" Flint appears behind her. When he sees me, he stops. His eyes widen.

He and his mom exchange a look that seems to contain an entire debate. He must win, because she steps out of the way and floats back into the kitchen. Flint fills up the space in front of me, and I feel instantly jittery, like I've had too much caffeine. He seems even taller today than yesterday.

"What are you doing here?" he asks in a flat voice.

"I'm your neighbor," I chirp. "Well, not like your next-door neighbor. I live on Harker's Run—you know, across the creek out back? I can see your porch from mine. My house is the purple one. Purple is my grandma's favorite color."

Flint looks bewildered. I try to clamp down on this weird sugar-rush feeling in my body. It must be because of the cold.

Flint keeps the door cracked open only a foot, wedging his body in the gap like he doesn't want me to see inside.

I frown. Something's off here, but I can't think clearly enough to figure out what it is.

I try again. "I brought banana bread," I say, pushing it toward him.

"Um . . . thanks."

"You know, small town hospitality and all that."

He nods, then casts another glance back into his house.

That's when I put two and two together.

It's so obvious now—they're death tourists.

That's what we call people who come to Carbon Junction to enroll in the Institute's deathday services. If they're from out of town, sometimes they come early with their families and stay in a nice rental before one of them checks in with Dr. Juncker on the Intake floor.

One of Flint's parents is about to die.

It stabs me in the heart—his mom looked so friendly and excited, but she did look tired. And it would explain the pain radiating off Flint.

I don't know what to say. I just stand gaping on his front step like a fish.

"Let's take a walk," Flint says. He grabs the loaf from me and tosses it onto a shelf in the entryway, then slides out and shuts the door behind him. He doesn't even tell his mom—his probably *dying* mom—where he's going; he just takes off up the street.

I draw in a long, steadying breath, then trudge reluctantly after him.

flint

THE STREET IS steep, but I plow on. Up, up, up this mountainside road through the tall trees. I have to get September away from my house.

When I saw her at the door, my stomach dropped. My mom was about to invite her in, for god's sake, and it would have only been a matter of minutes before the whole me dying thing came up. I didn't tell her yesterday because I thought I'd never see her again. This complicates things. By a lot.

The road curves around the mountain. If I look back now, my house will be safely out of sight. Every extra foot of space between September and my mom loosens the pressure in my chest until I'm finally calm enough to slow my steps.

September catches up to me. We're both breathing fast, thanks to the pace I set.

"You seem to know your way around," she says. "I haven't seen you at school—do you go to the university?"

"No. I'm not here for long. Just in town because my parents are going through some stuff."

Please don't ask for more details.

She doesn't. She's silent for so long that I finally risk a sidelong glance at her. When she showed up on my doorstep, she was bouncy,

like she wanted to tell me something. Now she looks distracted—
and upset.

I stop walking. She does too, but she won't meet my eyes.

"Sorry for walking so fast," I say. "I just needed to get out of
there."

"It's okay," she says, but she wraps her arms around herself and
glances out into the trees.

"Thank you for the banana bread," I say as sincerely as I can.

She shrugs. "Just being a good neighbor."

There's something else, though. Something she was going to say
at the door, and I screwed it up by being me.

"Was that the only reason you came over?" I ask.

She rolls a pebble with the toe of her boot, then kicks it off the
road. "No. I actually came to ask you something." She takes a breath,
blows it out. "Okay. You know all those formulas I wrote on the
wall yesterday?"

"Yeah. No idea what they meant, by the way. In case you're
worried I'm going to sell your big breakthrough to the highest
bidder."

"That hadn't occurred to me, actually." She looks me up and
down, considering, but she must decide that I'm harmless. "I ran
some searches last night, looking for patient files to support my
research, but I need more detailed records than what were in the
Institute's database. Which means I need to visit the hospitals where
those patients—"

She breaks off, but I hear the word between us anyway. *Died*.

I stare out into the trees, something heavy forming in my stomach.

"And . . . what does all this have to do with me?" I ask.

She chews on her thumbnail again. "Well, I don't exactly have a license. So . . . I was wondering if you would drive me."

She raises her eyes and locks them on mine. In that moment, I see her determination rally. She *really* wants these files.

Her hair gleams copper gold in the morning light, and I'm a little mesmerized. But the fact that she wants *me* to drive her to all these places?

Not happening.

It would break my most important rule: Make no new connections. There is no way I can commit to spending that kind of time with someone. Especially not her.

"I can't drive you, September."

Her face crumples. So much for trying not to be a jackass.

I sigh. "Can't you ask your parents?"

A shadow passes over her face. Yesterday, she seemed so . . . uncomplicated. Peppy and energetic and sunny. The exact opposite of me. But today I can see there's something lurking behind that energy. Maybe she's not all hectic scientific formulas and butterscotch candy and bright colors.

I backpedal. "What about your friends—can't they drive you?"

She presses her lips together, and I can see the effort it takes to shove aside whatever caused that shadow. She recovers quickly, I'll give her that.

"Here's the thing," she starts. "The trips would have to be on the weekends because of school and my internship. I would ask Dottie or Bo—my friends—but Dottie works on the weekends to save up for college, and Bo has to be at rehearsals basically from dawn till dusk—he's codirecting the community theater musical this year. My grandma can't take me because she's a hairdresser and most of her work's on the weekend too, and we don't have a car, anyway, and . . ." She tapers off. "Yeah, that's all I got."

I pinch the bridge of my nose. "I'm sorry, September. But I really can't."

Her shoulders fall. "Okay. It's no big deal. I'll figure out how to get there."

We both go silent. The air between us feels scorched.

"I should get back," I mumble.

"Sure. Yeah, of course. Me too."

We turn and walk back the way we came. Right before we get to my place, September veers off to her garish purple house.

As I watch her go, I can't help feeling like I've just made the worst decision of my life.

The next morning, I drag myself into the kitchen, hoping to nurse a black coffee in the predawn silence, but my parents are already up.

"Did you call your brother?" my mom asks my dad in a low voice. She's already dressed and wearing makeup.

Dad grunts—his charming way of saying yes. "He's got his flights booked, but he's leaving the kids with Shelby."

"Well, that's good, I guess. They've only met Flint once, and they're a little young to handle the situation."

Her words fade as she clocks my entrance. She hastily gathers some papers into a stack, smiling a big guilty smile.

"Hey! You're up early. Want some breakfast? How do pancakes sound?"

I'd ask what they're being so suspicious about, but I already know.

They're planning my fucking funeral.

They asked me once if I wanted to help, but the idea of choosing songs and making PowerPoint slides with photos of me as a kid is quite possibly the worst thing I can imagine doing. A little pain's okay, but I'm not into torture.

I told them to plan the whole thing without me. I don't care what the ceremony's like. We've never been religious, but it can have a Catholic priest waving one of those smoking metal balls around as far as I'm concerned. I'll be dead.

The lump in my throat is back already. Fantastic. Sometimes I can squeeze in an hour or two of being awake before it comes back, but not today.

I've been through the darkest part of this journey. The months of crying, the anger, the denial, the bargaining. Turns out it's not a thing you can keep up for years. I'm not going to go curl up in my room about this. It just feels weird to know there's a family gathering on the horizon that I'm not invited to. Well, I'm the guest of honor, but I won't *really* be there, will I?

I slump at the counter as Mom starts pulling out the bowls and ingredients she needs for pancakes.

Dad slides onto the barstool next to me. "Sleep okay?"

"Like the dead."

Mom's mouth presses into a thin line, and Dad gives me a warning look.

"What do you two want to do today?" Mom asks. "I have a call with a client at one, but I think I can rearrange some things and spend the afternoon with you."

"Don't rearrange anything, Mom. I'll be okay."

Mom goes very still, staring at the mixing bowl.

"Flint."

I shrink.

"We're here because we want to do stuff together as a family. There's no point in me and your dad working all the time and not talking to you."

"Yeah, I know," I mumble.

I press my cheek to the cold countertop. A few inches away, a newspaper is folded so only one headline is visible. Apparently a TV actor has tried to kill himself for the third time. (And failed, for the third time.) "There's just no way out," he's quoted as saying, in bold lettering on the page. As if we didn't all know that already.

As I watch the coffee machine burble, it occurs to me: If I helped September out by driving her all over Pennsylvania, I wouldn't be around to see and hear shit like this.

september

ON WEDNESDAY EVENING, I tumble into the steamy heat of the wood-paneled restaurant that's my second-favorite place in the world, after the observation box at the Institute.

Stepping into Le Belgique's waffle house is like being transported directly to Belgium. Every surface is covered in dark wood, and candles flicker on the center of every table. The doughy scent of waffle batter hangs in the air, mingling with the smells of dark coffee and stewed fruit, and Lukas stands behind a U-shaped counter, working over three enormous cast-iron waffle presses.

"Hey, Lukas," I call over the noise of steam and sizzling dough.

He waves at me. His big arms flex as he deftly flips a huge, fat waffle onto a plate. "The troublemakers are in the back, as usual," he says in his thick Dutch accent.

Instead of one big eating area, there are themed rooms spread over two floors, plus lots of nooks and crannies. I sidle through the tables and head for our favorite booth in the Landscape Room, where paintings of the Belgian countryside hang in ornate frames.

Before I go in, I straighten my carefully curated outfit: a burnt-orange slouchy sweater and plaid cigarette pants. A stack of plastic Bakelite bracelets in matching fall colors *click-clack* at my wrists. I hike up my smile—Dottie and Bo only ever get to see fun, upbeat September.

Dottie jumps up right away, squealing. She gives the best hugs, and I let her squeeze me until I think I'm going to pop. She smells like magnolia perfume and vintage clothing. She must have come here straight from Rag House.

Dorothéa "Dottie" Reyes and I met on my first day at Carbon Junction High, a week after I moved here from Colorado to live with Gigi. I remember getting up that morning in a zombie haze, unsure of how I was going to play it. Back home, I carried my sister's death everywhere. Not by choice but because my whole school knew about it. In Carbon Junction, I could start over.

So I put on my favorite vintage dress, fringed leather ankle boots, and one of the boho cardigans my mom knits to sell in Denver craft markets. It was the cardigan that caught Dottie's eye. I didn't think I'd be able to muster even a hint of a smile that day, but then these two blazed into my life.

Tonight Dottie's wearing a black turtleneck and a polka-dotted rockabilly skirt cinched with a wide cherry-red pleather belt. A padded headband tops off her wavy black bob. Even though she's not religious, she always wears the delicate gold cross necklace that her Catholic grandmother gave her the first time Dottie visited her in Guadalajara.

"Loving. Your. Work," Dottie says, nodding approvingly at my outfit.

"Hey, sugarplum," Bo calls from his place at the table, where he's nursing a smoothie. He's got papers spread out all over his side of the table. Bo wants to move to New York City and be a producer for Broadway shows after graduation. He's already messing around with

65

stocks, trying to build his capital, and he's astonishingly good at it. He could definitely convince me to pour my measly savings into *Twilight: The Musical*, which is his dream project.

I slide into the booth next to Dottie. This—the three of us—is still new, and sometimes I'm not sure why they so readily absorbed me into the friendship they forged years ago, when they both moved to Carbon Junction just before sixth grade. But they've never once made me feel like a third wheel, even when I'm at my most guarded.

I ask them how the rest of their classes went while I was at my internship. Dottie holds up her phone, where a snail version of her (complete with eyeballs on long gooey stalks) screams, *It's Wednesday, my dudes*.

"This pretty much sums it up," she says.

I laugh. "What even is that filter?" I pick up my phone to find it in my own app. I'll have to show it to Maybelle; she'll love—

My heart wrenches sideways in my chest.

Maybelle.

It's one small moment, one missed step. But in it, my sister dies all over again.

The memories that I've gotten so good at smothering rise. When Maybelle discovered Snapchat on my phone, it instantly became our favorite thing to do together. During sister sleepovers, tucked into a blanket fort in our living room, we went through every available filter, making video after video. Us as vampires, as avocados, as talking potatoes.

"I am a po-tay-toe," she said one time, in her weird little four-year-old voice, and for some reason I couldn't stop laughing. She looked at me, head cocked, trying to figure out why I thought it was so funny. But then she realized it didn't matter—she could keep doing it, and I'd keep laughing.

She did things like that a lot. She had no idea how little time she had left, and she still kept trying to make us laugh—and beamed triumphantly every time she made us smile.

And it hits me that I can never take a picture with her again. Because my baby sister is in a coffin a thousand miles away, forever four years old.

I swallow and close out of Snapchat on my phone.

"Babe? You okay?" Dottie asks gently.

I blink and struggle to come back to myself. "Yeah, fine."

Dottie and Bo don't know about Maybelle. No one in Carbon Junction does, apart from Gigi.

There's an awkward silence, but Dottie doesn't press the issue. I love her for it. They know I shut down sometimes, and they're okay with it.

If I let them see the grief, we won't have this. And I need this.

"So, give us the dish," Dottie says. "Have you figured out a way to get your Top Secret Files?"

"I don't care about boring old files," Bo says. "Tell us more about Tall, Dark, and Sullen."

At the mention of Flint, something strange happens to the balance of the chemicals in my bloodstream. But I'm a scientist, and I can acknowledge that scientifically I might have been a little drawn to him and not let it throw me off.

"I haven't seen him again," I say, hoping I sound nonchalant.

Ever since Flint told me in very simple terms that he wouldn't drive me to get the files, he hasn't so much as stepped out onto his back porch.

Dottie sighs. "That's totally what a Billie Eilish song would do. Get you hooked, then ghost you."

"Maybe you should try asking him again," Bo says.

"I don't know. He was really not interested. And he was kind of grumpy. Although I did like his piratey boots." If there was a shimmer of anything else between us, it was just pheromones.

"Honestly, I think you need to march over there and ask him if he wants to make out," Bo says.

"I don't need a make-out buddy. I just need a ride."

"You want to ride *him*," Dottie says.

I roll my eyes. "Uh-huh, sure. There's definitely no way you can get out of your shifts?" I ask, trying to steer the conversation away from Flint, even though it must be the tenth time I've asked this week.

"I'm so sorry, babe. You know my managers insist on a freaking four-week notice to change the schedule. I can take you after that, though."

"I wish I could help," Bo adds, "but on top of all this paperwork, I'm coaching Troy Wittman to be Pippin's understudy."

"Coaching him on his kissing scenes," Dottie says behind a fake cough.

Bo glares at her. "Well, I mean, I have been helping him practice the kissing scenes, but I'm also coaching him on his lines, because I have a feeling the actor playing Pippin is going to freak out on opening night and refuse to go on."

"Why do you think he's going to freak?" I ask.

"Didn't you hear?" Dottie says. "Poor kid twinged last week."

My stomach lurches. "Shit."

We're quiet for a moment, but I know that we'll move on. We'll tuck our classmate's misery aside, because it's not us who have to face it. This happens every day, all over the world. Teenagers find out that they're going to die; children succumb to the kill switch.

Rage flares in me. It's not acceptable.

I have to get my hands on those anomaly files, and I can't wait for Dottie to drive me. Every day I wait is another win for the kill switch.

If no one can drive me, I'll hitchhike. On Saturday morning, I'll walk up to the highway, crook my thumb, and hope for the best.

I start making a mental list of what I need: pepper spray, cash, phone charger, energy bar—

My phone rings. The name on the screen makes me freeze.

Dad.

A brick of tungsten drops on my chest. I tap the red decline button.

"Everything okay?" Dottie asks.

"Yeah. Just my parents, but I talked to them last night, so it's no big deal."

I'm lying. I haven't talked to them in a week.

"Who wants to share a Dutch apple cinnamon waffle with me?" I ask brightly, desperate to change the subject.

"Me," Dottie says. "But only if we have ice cream and butterscotch drizzle on top."

I'm about to flag down a waiter when my phone rings again.

A spear of alarm pierces me—Dad never calls twice in a row. I have to take this.

"Sorry, guys, I'll be right back," I say, then I head to the wood-paneled hallway that leads to the restrooms. I answer with a shaky tap to the green *accept* button.

Dad's face fills the screen. He used to be a walking stereotype of what you'd see if you google *Man Hiking in the Rockies*. North Face jacket, a forgot-to-shave-for-a-few-days beard, and the athletically outdoorsy vibe of a person who sucks in lungfuls of fresh air daily and is bursting with gratitude for the planet he's been given to live on.

Dad's still got the beard and the North Face jackets, but now there are bags under his eyes, and his skin's pale like he hasn't been outdoors in months.

"Hey, Tember," he says. He sounds downtrodden.

"Hi, Dad. Is everything okay?"

My heart thuds. Please don't tell me he's lost his job. Or that Mom's gotten worse.

"Oh, same as usual, I guess," he says. "I thought the first call hadn't gone through."

I let out a breath.

"Just calling for the weekly check-in," he says. "School okay?"

His effort is so lackluster it hurts. I suspect Gigi has to guilt-trip him into checking on me.

"I managed to get an A on an essay about *The Scarlet Letter*," I say, trying to sound bright and uncomplicated. I don't want to give them anything else to worry about.

"Hey, that's great."

I wait to see if he asks about my internship, but he never does. We have our lines down pat.

"Are you getting any hiking in?" I ask.

He scratches at his chin. "Work's really busy. Putting in a lot of overtime."

They're relying on Dad's income now. Mom used to make clothing out of reclaimed materials to sell in Denver's New Age shops. It wasn't that profitable, but it was enough that Dad didn't have to work quite so much.

"I'd get your mom on, but she's taking a nap. Sorry, Tember. She did want to talk to you, though."

Sure. I haven't talked to my mom in weeks; I don't think she ever gets up from naps these days.

Most of the time I can compartmentalize, but when I'm talking to them, it's hard to ignore how worried about them I am. I wish they would pull through this. Handle things like I am.

"Oh, hey, I saw Dakota in the grocery store the other day," Dad says.

I blink. "Oh."

Dakota was my best friend from kindergarten to eighth grade. Her parents were outdoorsy too, so we spent a lot of time together, our two families hiking and camping all over Colorado.

But like everyone else, Dakota took a step back when she found out about Maybelle's half-life. I still ate lunch with my Science Club group, Boushra and Evelyn and Vijay, but we didn't ever really hang out outside of school, and they didn't make any effort to stay in touch after I moved here. Not that I've made any effort either.

I don't really know what to say to Dad about Dakota.

"Well, I'm really glad you're doing so well," Dad says after an awkward silence. "Call us whenever, okay?"

We say our scripted goodbyes and end the call.

I close my eyes and take a long, steadying breath. My parents weren't always like this. My childhood was full of pine trees and fresh air and nature, handmade clothes and bohemian crafts and the scent of sage and incense.

This is what happens when you let grief consume you. It's a timely reminder—I need to do a better job suppressing mine. Lately it keeps threatening to climb up my throat and crawl out of my mouth.

flint

I WAKE UP unusually late on Saturday morning.

The week has been a depressing montage of suck, but for a second, I'm blissfully checked out, floating in that moment that comes just before I remember how many days I have left.

Before I remember that I heard my mom sobbing through the wall last night.

Mom would hate it if she knew I could hear her. She's always so careful around me, but it's getting harder for her to keep it together. Even my dad, who's usually so gruff, has been downright chatty and pats me on the back every chance he gets.

Sometimes I wonder what it'd be like to *not* live with a countdown clock strapped to your life. My parents and I wouldn't be here doing this shit, that's for sure. I'd be in school, studying my life away for a future that was going to be ripped out from under me.

Would it be better to be destined to die at seventeen but not *know*? I'm not sure. But at least I wouldn't have to watch my parents process the fact that they're about to lose me.

I drape a hand over my eyes. *Jesus, Flint.* Enough with the pity party. I've already had my darkest hour, and it was exhausting. Being a miserable zombie is a lot easier.

I swing my feet out of bed. Mom wants to go apple picking today.

73

I nearly choked on my breakfast yesterday when she announced it. What am I, five? Apple picking, *god*.

For the hundredth time this week, I wonder if I should have said yes to September. At least I'd be fulfilling my plan to get away from my parents and spare them some pain.

I pry myself out of bed and shuffle into the kitchen for a bowl of cereal. From my perch at the breakfast bar, I dare a glance out the back window. All is quiet. Morning sunbeams slant through the trees.

And then I see a flash of copper.

September is hauling ass down her street. I guess she's on her way to her first hospital. I track her copper hair as it appears and disappears between the houses on Harker's Run. I can sense her stubborn determination even from here.

Wait a second—she's headed toward the highway. There aren't any other houses out that way.

I go to the window. "Where are you going?" I mutter, my words fogging up the glass.

A frizzle of electricity pierces my stomach. She's not going to hitchhike, is she? Surely she wouldn't be that stupid.

I should let it go. Let her hitchhike her way to these hospitals if that's what she wants to do; what difference does it make to me? We've spent, what, less than an hour together, total? I'm not responsible for her.

I park myself on the couch. I'm busy, anyway—I'm going apple picking today.

I cast a glance down the dark hallway that leads to the bedrooms where my parents are sleeping. I can almost feel their grief lurking in the shadows there.

I press my fingertips to my temples.

Ah, fuck it.

Fine. I'll help September, but only because it'll get me out of here for a few hours.

I grab the keys from the kitchen counter and fly out the door.

Five minutes later, I slow the Jeep, carefully steering onto the shoulder of the road. In my side mirror, the girl in the red coat hurries to my open window, prepared to ask a stranger if she can get a ride.

When she sees it's me, she breaks into the biggest, most perfect smile I've ever seen.

"Well, don't just stand there grinning," I grumble. "Get in."

She drops into the passenger seat and *glows*.

september

I GLANCE ACROSS the Jeep, beaming at Flint even though he looks immensely ticked. I can't deny the relief that melted through me when I saw it was him, when I realized I wouldn't have to spend a vigilant hour in a car with a stranger hoping they don't have nasty plans for me.

"Okay, but wait," I say. "Does this mean you can take me to the other hospitals too?"

He gives me a look that drips with disdain.

I backpedal. "Never mind, I can always hitchhike to the—"

"Yes, I'll take you, damn it."

"Really?"

"Yes, really," he says. "But I'm only doing this because hitch-hiking is not known to be the safest of pastimes."

I cover my mouth to smother my smile. We're on our way, me and this abnormally tall, sadly beautiful boy, and I'm going to get my data. I'll pour everything I have into proving this hypothesis, and if it actually works, the things coiled inside me will have no choice but to unwind. I can be the September I was before.

I'm contemplating my upcoming successes when Flint cuts in. "Am I even going the right way?"

I pull out my phone and type in our destination. "Yep. Merrybrook, ETA . . . forty-five minutes."

"And what exactly is in Merrybrook?" he asks.

"The Merrybrook Regional Hospital, of course."

"Naturally."

I haul my backpack up from between my feet and dig out a couple of butterscotches. "Want one?" I ask, popping mine into my mouth.

"No thanks."

I shrug, then wiggle deeper into the leather seat. It smells like nature in here, like sawdust and cedar. But beneath the woodsy smell, there's a thread of something else—the softest hint of black cherry.

On the center console, my arm brushes up against his. I swallow and will myself not to move away, because if it were anybody else, I don't think I'd even notice. I try to ignore how soft the black flannel of his shirt is on the back of my wrist.

Outside, the sky is the pale blue color of liquid oxygen. Bursts of orange and yellow are sponge-painted on the hills, making Pennsylvania look like a scene from an old Americana puzzle, all pumpkin picking and red barns and falling leaves. Autumn is my favorite time of year.

"So, how is this going to work?" Flint asks after a few miles of silence. "You're just going to waltz in and ask for top secret medical files?"

"Well, they're hardly top secret," I say. "*I* think these patients are special, but no one else knows that yet."

Flint rubs his chin. "I thought hospitals weren't allowed to share stuff without the patient's permission."

I wave the badge around my neck with the Institute logo. "I

request files like this all the time. If my boss, Dr. Juncker, wants something, hospitals legally have to give it to her."

"What about HIPAA?" he asks.

"Have you even read a newspaper in the last ten years? HIPAA was amended right after Dr. Blumenthal discovered the kill switch. The Institute is allowed to access patient files."

"They can just poke their fingers into anyone's business if they want to? That's creepy."

I shrug. "Maybe a little creepy, but the research is important."

"And even interns can get this stuff, on a whim?"

"Well, no . . . But whenever Dr. Juncker finds a correlation she wants to look into, I'm the peon who gets to call up the archives department to ask for the records to be emailed over."

He nods.

It's odd, talking to him about science things. Usually I keep the science part of myself separate from the upbeat, more colorful part of myself. With him, everything is mixed up.

He frowns. "Hold on—did you say email?"

Oops.

"Why aren't you doing that, then?" he asks, irritated.

I bite my thumbnail. "Well . . . I mean, Dr. Juncker hasn't exactly asked for these files."

"Ah . . . so you're going rogue."

I nod. "Scientists can get pretty cutthroat. If anyone else found out, they'd probably take over and pawn the hypothesis off as their own, and I'd be forgotten. Not that fame or anything like that matters to me."

He's silent for a moment.

"What does matter to you?"

I blink. "Um. Solving the half-life, of course."

He glances over. "Yeah, but why do *you* care so much?"

I swallow. He's getting a little too close to the nerve here.

"Who wouldn't want to know more about the half-life?" I ask, deflecting. "It's kind of an important part of being human."

He nods, his jaw muscles working, but he doesn't push it.

It's too quiet in here. I shift in my seat, peering at the console between us. "Do you want me to find something on the radio? Or I can plug my phone in; I have—"

"No music," he says.

"Okay, jeez," I mumble.

No music, no candy, no smiles. This boy is something else.

The Jeep rumbles over miles and miles of highway. We don't speak. My mind keeps grabbing for small-talk topics, but everything feels too perky and fake. I want desperately to brighten everything up, to be the easy-to-deal-with September everyone wants me to be. I'm afraid of getting caught in the aura emanating from the driver's seat. It's the kind of thing that, in large doses, could make the cords holding me together snap.

We sit in silence for so long that when I hear a noise from outside, I'm relieved. Finally, a reason to break the silence. I crane my neck and look up through the windshield. A helicopter chops its way through the bright blue sky.

"I wonder if there's a fire somewhere," I say. "Or a high-speed car chase or something—there's a news helicopter up there."

"It's not a news copter," Flint says, without taking his eyes off the road.

"How would you know? You didn't even look," I scoff, turning in my seat to scan the horizon for billows of smoke.

"It's a military helicopter."

"Right, and you can tell that just from hearing it?"

"Sure I can. I can also tell you that it's either a Sikorsky Pave Hawk or a Black Hawk," Flint says.

I gape at him. "How do you—"

He seems to realize he's opened up a whole avenue for conversation. "I don't want to talk about it," he snaps.

God, fine. I'm starting to think hitchhiking would have been the better plan after all.

Flint blows out a breath.

"Sorry," he says. "I know I'm . . . a lot." He scrubs one hand over his face in that rough way that boys do, rearranging his emotions. "Look, I'm going through some shit, but I'll try to be less of a—"

"Grump?"

"I was going to say asshole, but grump works."

He looks so sad for a moment—like a black hole pulling all the light out of the car. I keep my darkest pieces pressed down, hidden from the world, but he's drowning in his.

I have to hand it to him. He's way braver than me, to sit in his grief like this, wearing it without even a half-hearted attempt at faking happiness. I sort of wish I could do what he does.

I fiddle with one of my coat buttons. Maybe I could try it. What would it be like to let myself just . . . be?

I lean my head against the window and watch the lines of the road pass in jots.

Then I close my eyes.

I can feel it immediately—the tangle of emotions straining to take center stage, like one of the viruses that lurk in the dorsal root ganglions of your spine and come out on special occasions to wreak havoc throughout your body.

Slowly, ever so slowly, I lower my guard. Just a little.

For the first time, it feels . . . okay to be sitting with it. To be two sad people in a pine-scented Jeep. With Flint, it feels okay to let my mask slip.

I let a memory gurgle up, closer to the surface than I've allowed it in months.

In the beginning, when I was waiting for her, the anticipation felt like the sweetest adrenaline.

Sister.

At last, I'd be what I'd always wanted to be.

Gigi rushed me to the labor ward after school. I bounced through the halls, wearing a *Best Big Sister* shirt I'd found online. I was in seventh grade, and if anyone from school had seen me, I would have been mortified.

Mom stirred weakly in the hospital bed when I came in. I knew I should check on her, or at least feel worried, but my eyes skipped right over her. Dad was in a chair next to the bed, holding a blanket-lump.

That snapshot image would be with me forever: the first time I saw my sister. Her smushed little nose, a tuft of orange hair, blinky, disoriented little eyes. It was like nothing else in the world existed.

Maybelle.

They let me name her. I wanted us to both have month names, even though she wasn't born in May. I wasn't born in September either. Maybelle and September. Sisters should sound like they match.

I relax in the Jeep's seat. Maybe I can do this. Maybe this is what Gigi does, just lingers on the good moments. I can forget about the nights when exhausted rage had me pulling a pillow over my ears to shut out her incessant, colicky crying. I can forget how impatient I got for her to do more than drink milk and sleep and drool.

If I'd known what was coming, I would have been patient with her every second.

The clean feeling of just sitting with it acidifies, eating away at my stomach lining. And then the memories jolt forward by years.

A playground. A metal slide, shining hot in the sun. Panicked shouting.

And then: the worst day, the day where we stayed inside, cuddled together in a pile of blankets and pillows, reading stories through the throat-closing pain of trying not to cry. Waiting for the worst thing.

I snap my eyes open and grab at the edge of the seat. Shove the memories away. They hurt too much.

"September? Are you okay?" Flint's looking at me, concern etched onto his face.

I dredge up a smile. "Yep, just fine," I say brightly.

We drive for a mile. Two.

"You know, you don't have to do that," he says quietly.

"Do what?"

Flint pulls his eyes off the empty highway, his intense hazel stare boring into me. "Pretend you're okay when you're not. It's okay to be sad."

Something clutches in my chest.

"I . . . kind of do have to pretend, though. People don't like complicated."

Silence again.

He shifts in his seat. "Well. You don't have to do that with me."

Something about it makes me want to cry. Has anyone ever given me that kind of *permission*?

Before I can make sense of it, the robot voice of my phone's GPS tells us to exit the highway.

Turns out I'm not the best at navigating. Two missed turns and twenty minutes later, we pull into the parking lot next to the ugly gray cube that is the Merrybrook Regional Hospital.

I tug my lab coat out of my bag, then I change out of my boots and into a pair of heels I borrowed from Gigi. I twist my hair and stick a pencil through it to make me look a bit older. I hope no one will be able to tell I'm still in high school.

I've never asked for files this way before. It's technically kind of . . . illegal. But I have no choice.

I brace myself against the cold and open the door.

"Good luck," Flint says.

I pause, one leg out of the car. "Don't be silly. You're coming with me."

He grimaces. "That was not part of the deal, September."

"What are you going to do, sit out here and get so cold you faint again? Or leave the engine running and pump a bunch of crap into the air?"

He closes his eyes even as his brows rise, then he shakes his head by one exasperated millimeter.

"Fine," he says.

He stalks across the parking lot and into the building. Right before he ducks in, the sunlight catches on his night-black hair and makes it gleam.

flint

I FOLLOW SEPTEMBER and a hospital receptionist down a windowless basement hallway. This part of the hospital isn't for the living—it's for the dead. And their records.

I pinch the bridge of my nose. I can't believe September talked me into coming in here.

The receptionist drops us off at a shabby door labeled *Archives*. Inside, there's a scratched-up wooden desk, a hulking photocopier, and a row of carefully tended succulents. An energetic young Black woman named Eloise jumps to attention as soon as she sees us.

"Dr. Harrington, come on in! Not every day we get someone from the Half-Life Institute," she gushes, pushing her stylish clear-framed glasses up her nose.

Eloise asks for September's ID, but she's too busy asking questions about the Institute to give it more than a cursory glance—or notice that September's holding her thumb over the word *intern*. September tosses out terms that any normal person would need a dictionary to understand, and Eloise's eyes get bigger and more adoring with each one.

"I'm a biology grad student at Penn State," she says. "I love keeping up with what you guys are doing over there."

Wild. She's probably at least five years older than us, but

September's got this calm, cool dignity about her, acting like it's completely normal (and legal) for her to be asking for these files. She's nothing like she was at the Ruins. Even her smiles are different: toned-down, serene. She's not being unfriendly—just mesmerizingly *capable*.

Even with all the photocopying Eloise has to do, we're in and out in less than thirty minutes. After we climb back into the Jeep, I sit for a minute in shock, staring at the fat manila folder in September's lap.

"I can't believe that worked," I say.

"Right?" She laughs. "It's amazing what you can get away with if you pretend like you know what you're doing."

She smiles, radiant again, and the air feels suddenly cleaner and sharper in my lungs.

I can't figure her out, can't keep up with the chameleon way she shifts. On the drive here, there was this moment . . . I'm *sure* I saw something that looked like the misery I carry around every day. She covered it up quickly, though. I know exactly how much energy—and courage—that takes.

She leans forward in her seat, watching the town slide by outside the windows. "There's something really gorgeous about it, isn't there?" she says.

I raise an eyebrow. "About Merrybrook?"

"Yeah."

I frown. The sky is the bleak expanse of an overcast day, and what few trees Merrybrook didn't pave over crook their dark, leafless fingers against it.

"The light here seems stronger, even though everything's gray," she says. "It's like a lungful of winter air."

I'm taken aback by her ability to find something beautiful here. But before I can respond, she launches into a spiel about psychotropic medications, which apparently have something to do with her hypothesis. It all goes way over my head, but she's so animated and seems so happy to have a rapt audience, I don't even mind.

We still have fifteen minutes left of the drive when she tapers off. And because of the small, contented smile on her face and the way she's tapping her foot, I decide to walk back my earlier ruling on music. "We can listen to the radio if you want," I offer.

"Really?"

I nod and tap the button on the steering wheel to turn it on. I'm about to tell her she can choose the station when the DJ starts talking about today's news.

"Listen to this," a woman with a smoky voice says to her cohost. "Eleven first graders at a school in Iowa have half-lifed, putting all their deaths on the same date, suggesting that a bus turnover, school shooting, or other classroom-related disaster would have occurred on that date."

I punch the off button so hard it nearly breaks, but it's too late. We both heard it.

My throat goes tight. The news is full of headlines like that. "The Half-Life Registry Has Announced That Over 900 Peruvians Share a Deathday." Hurricanes, revolts, terrorist attacks, volcanic eruptions. We can see catastrophes coming a mile off, and we can get the people out of harm's way, but we can't stop them from dying.

Those kids in Iowa will get a quiet kill switch death at home instead of a bullet wound. And the authorities will close the whole school that day, so it'll prevent the non-life-threatening injuries of the other kids, I guess. Still, my chest aches for all of them.

The radio is off, but the word *half-life* seems to echo in the Jeep. I needed the reminder. September has no idea that the boy sitting next to her has a countdown over his head.

We ride the rest of the way in silence. I've never been so grateful to see the turnoff for Carbon Junction.

I pull up to her house and put the car in park.

"Thank you again for the ride," September says, uncertainty edging into her voice.

I scrape my thumbnail over the logo on the center of the steering wheel. "Yep. Glad you got your file."

She tugs her bag onto her lap and reaches for the door handle, then pauses. "Can you still drive me to the other hospitals?"

Shit. I told her I would.

"Yeah. No problem."

"I have to be at the Institute next weekend, so can we do the Saturday after that?"

"Sure. See you then."

I force myself not to look at her in the rearview mirror as I pull away from her house. By the time I swing the Jeep into the cabin's driveway, I'm so ready to get out of this car—September was only in here for a couple of hours, and all I can smell is caramel and cake and her *hair*.

I'm halfway up the path to the front door when I falter.

Shit. My parents. We were supposed to go to that orchard today.

I sidle up to the house, close enough so I can peep through the glass without being seen.

Mom and Dad are in the living room. They're sitting close together on the couch, their backs to the front door. Probably planning more super fun funeral stuff, or, if I'm lucky, they'll be fed up with me and are making plans to leave me here so they can go back to Philly.

There's no way around it. I've got to go in. I brace myself, then turn the handle.

"Flint!"

Mom and Dad jump up from the couch and flock to the door. My mom grabs my arms, inspecting me for damage.

"Are you okay?" she asks. "Where have you been?"

"I'm fine," I mumble.

Dad stands back a bit, arms crossed, frowning. "Kid, you gotta stop disappearing like this."

I brace myself, waiting for some kind of punishment. But what are they going to take from me that I haven't already taken from myself? They weren't too excited that my bird burial the day we got here turned into a two-hour disappearance, but they let it go, because, you know, the whole dying-kid thing.

But instead of lecturing me, Mom just sort of . . . wilts. Without another word, she turns and goes to her room.

I would have rather she yelled at me.

Dad sighs. "You're kind of breaking your mom's heart here."

"I know," I say miserably.

"I get it. And it's important to have time with people your age too. Just tell us when you're going out, okay?"

I nod.

Alone in my room, I strip off my shirt and ball it up. But right before I free-throw it into the laundry basket, I catch a curl of vanilla, caramel, cake.

God. My clothes smell like September.

I could kick myself for having a nice time with her today. She's even more interesting than I thought, and I . . . I just liked being with her.

The thought is so off-limits, so gut-wrenching, that I lean my head against the wall and close my eyes. *Shit, shit, shit.*

I need to shore up my defenses if I'm going to get through these trips with her.

flint

I'M IN MY room reading Dostoevsky two days later when I hear the doorbell ring.

My heart skips a beat. The last time it rang, it was September.

This time, though, it's Aerys who pops into my bedroom doorway, wearing a denim jacket with a jersey hood flopping out and a ball cap on backward.

"Uh, hi?" I say.

"Hey," she says brightly, like it's not weird at all that she's here.

"Why are you at my house?" I thought she got the hint when I stormed off the other day.

She flops onto my bed. "Saw your mom at the coffee shop on Main and she said you were staying here. Thought I'd come to see what you've been doing so far in ye olde Carbon Junction."

I put my book down. "Just marching toward my doom."

"I thought as much. For today's activity, I present two options: One—we can go to the new retro arcade in town, but if you need to ease into things a little slower, I brought . . . drumroll, please . . . *Kirby's Epic Yarn*!" She unzips her backpack and produces a spaghetti nest of cables—her old Nintendo Wii.

"Does that thing still work?" I ask.

"Sure it does. I think. What do you say? Want to go to the arcade?"

Over my dead body. "No arcades, Aerys."

"Wii it is."

She bounds off the bed and gets to work hooking the console up to the TV perched on the dresser in my room. When yarn-Kirby bounces onto the screen accompanied by cheerful, tinkling piano music, nostalgia floods me. Aerys smiles and hands me a controller, then triggers the opening sequence.

We shred the first two levels. I'm begrudgingly having a small amount of fun when she shifts beside me.

"So what's with you not having any friends in Philly?" she asks.

I shrug. I don't want to talk about anything related to my past, or half-lifing, but I also don't want to be a total dick. "Nobody wanted to be friends with a kid who's post," I say.

"And you couldn't find a friend anywhere else? Aren't there forums online and stuff?"

I snort. Nothing more depressing than a half-lifer forum. I've lurked on my fair share of them. Kept seeing people blink offline and then be gone forever.

"I guess I shouldn't judge," Aerys says. "Not like I had people to hang out with before you rolled back into town." She goes quiet.

It feels like I should say something, but I don't know what.

"Well, Carbon Junction sucked without you," she says eventually. "I hung out with Joey Mettiscue for a couple of years, but it wasn't the same."

I swallow. Back then, I was more upset about leaving Aerys behind than I was about the half-life. When you're eight, another eight years seems like a lifetime, but the loss of her felt immediate. I cried every night for weeks.

This is the first time I've really thought about how it must have felt for her.

She pauses the game and turns so she's facing me. "Hey, Flint? I know we're on a compressed schedule, but if you want to talk about anything . . . I'm here, okay?"

"Thanks," I mumble. "But I'm good."

There are things too depressing to tell your friends. Like what happened on the day I came to grips with the magnitude of what I'd be missing out on, all thanks to my eighth-grade math teacher.

He launched into a tirade after the entire class failed a quiz. *You may not think these grades are important, but they'll determine your classes in high school, which will affect your SAT and ACT scores, not to mention your GPA, which will affect your chance of getting into college, which will affect your career, and IT ALL STARTS NOW.*

I skipped the rest of school that day and got on my bike. My heart was beating hard, and something like panic was starting to take over. I ended up on a trail that dumped out into a huge, untended field: the flyover zone for the international airport. I went out there a lot back then, when I still called Grandpa every time I saw a plane I couldn't identify.

I locked my bike to the chain-link fence and lay out on the brittle, dying grass, breathing fast. A Boeing 747 roared down the runway, lifting off just before it got to the field, soaring huge right over my head. I felt like I could reach up and touch its belly.

That's when it hit me. Not only would I never go to college—I would never be a pilot.

From that first air show Grandpa took me to, I think I really believed I'd grow up and become an aviator. That it was my destiny or whatever.

Something broke in me that day. It was broken for the rest of that year, and for all of freshman year. All I remember is crying. Mom and Dad, overwhelmed by it, split up. They both needed a break from *me*. Had to divide up the grief.

And then one day, after months of feeling sorry for myself, I got mugged in an alley in Philly. They took my favorite leather jacket— one my grandpa had bought me. I walked home in the middle of January with a bleeding lip and a lump on my forehead, and I was on the verge of freezing solid.

And I thought, *Death will feel like a warm blanket after this.*

That's when I decided to live every day in a way that would make the end feel like a relief.

"Flint?"

I jerk out of the memory.

"Flint? Are you okay?" Aerys asks.

"I'm great."

"Are you sure? Because you look kind of . . . fucked-up."

"I think you might need to get used to that, because fucked-up is my default. Do you want to be the blue Kirby now?"

That stuns her into silence.

I don't get why she wants to have anything to do with me. We haven't talked in *eight* years. Wouldn't it have been easier to let me leave and never think about me again?

Still, I feel bad for wrecking the little bit of fun we were having.

"I met a girl in the woods last week," I say, trying to get us past the awkwardness. "Out by the Ruins. Right after I saw you."

Aerys's eyebrows shoot up. "A girl? Damn, Flint Larsen, you work fast."

"It's not like that," I protest.

"Sure it isn't. What's this girl's name?"

"September."

Her eyes widen. "Red hair, only wears clothes in fall colors, skin like a face-wash commercial?"

"Yeah."

"September Harrington. She's in my second-period English class. But, bro. She's, like . . . so hot."

I ignore that observation, focusing on getting my little yarn-Kirby to jump onto a tricky platform.

Aerys shoves my arm, and my Kirby falls to his death. Damn it.

"Do you *not* think she's hot?" Aerys asks.

"I don't really have time to pay attention to stuff like that."

"Bullshit. She's gorgeous and you know it. Hold up—do you have a crush on her?"

"Aerys. I'm dying in thirty-five days. I don't have time for a crush."

"But you think she's pretty."

"That's beside the point."

"You totally think she's pretty," she teases. "Did you tell her you're post?"

I swallow hard. For some reason, I feel like Aerys would *not* be cool with the fact that I didn't tell September my expiry date was right around the corner.

"Yeah," I say casually. It doesn't even sound like I'm lying.

"Damn. How'd she take it?"

I shrug.

In the game, Aerys's character jumps up to ring a bell, triggering the end of the level. While she waits for the next screen to load, she taps her chin. "You know . . . September and her gang hang out at the Belgian waffle place on Main a lot. We could totally coincidentally 'bump into her' there."

"Not happening, Aerys."

"All right, cool it, dream crusher. But we'll be revisiting this idea tomorrow."

Tomorrow? God.

I glance out my window at the purple house. I think of what it'd be like—sitting next to her eating waffles with her friends. Elbow whispering up against mine, smooth coppery hair flashing at the corner of my eye like it did in the Jeep.

No matter how much I might want it, I can't do more than drive September to these hospitals. I'm about to die, and if I have to leave someone else behind, the dying thing will be immensely worse. If something . . . started, we'd both end up destroyed.

The half-life destroys everything.

september

MY EYES BURN with exhaustion as I skim over yet another form. The medical records I got from Merrybrook are strewn across my desk, my bed, my bedroom floor. In every small wedge of time between school and the Institute, I've been combing through the folder and devouring research papers on neurochemistry. I still can't believe I got this file. I can't wait to see the look on Percy's face when he realizes his chances at being the best intern have scattered like particles in the Large Hadron Collider.

I've made an immense amount of progress, but there's still so much to do. I don't have a lot of time tonight because I'm going out with Dottie and Bo. I haven't seen much of them this week. On the surface, things between the three of us look the same: Every morning, as the sun breaks over Carbon Junction High, I wait on a bench until Dottie's ancient silver Corolla sputters into her designated parking place. We go in through the main doors with our arms linked, sending freshmen skittering out of the way. There are more popular people at CJH than us—cheerleaders and the swim team guys and the TikTok fashionistas—but everyone loves Dottie and Bo. And by extension, me.

The three of us have our morning locker tour down pat. All week, I kept up with their banter while we changed our textbooks over, but something felt off, like I was playing a part in a movie. I usually love the morning rush, because when I'm with Dottie and Bo, everyone thinks I'm blithely uncomplicated. Undamaged. But this week, it felt like my sister's death was clinging to me like a black veil. I can't tell if it's because I'm working on this hypothesis, thinking about the half-life more than ever, or if it's a by-product of being around Flint's grief.

I pull out my phone and open the group chat between me and Dottie and Bo. There hasn't been a new message since this morning, which is weird for us. I wonder briefly if they're texting each other outside of this chat. They were friends before I got here, and it'd be silly to think they haven't kept doing that.

Still. It stings.

Part of me wants to cancel on them tonight, but it's Bonfire Night, and we've been looking forward to it for weeks. It's an epic street party that started with some British expats who worked at the Institute, but over time it became a local tradition. There are huts selling hot apple cider and steaming-hot bratwursts, stages for live music, and lots of sketchy carnival rides.

Dottie's also organized one of her epic games of flashlight tag. She's always on the hunt for abandoned places—she's the one who introduced us to the Ruins. Pennsylvania is full of rotting old buildings, so there's never any shortage of locations. Dottie found a derelict resort for tonight's game, and we're expecting a big turnout.

I survey the piles of paper around my room. I have less than an hour before Bonfire Night starts, but I can get some work done. Mitsuki Adams's whole life is spread out in my bedroom, her records sorted into life phases: baby, toddler, child, teenager, adult. I know everything that ever happened to her. Well, medically, anyway.

Here are some things I know about Mitsuki: She was lactose intolerant as a child but grew out of it. She broke her arm in a mosh pit in the '80s. She battled a myriad of small issues like everyone does: stress ulcers, carpal tunnel, migraines. Her appendix burst when she was thirty-two. She wore glasses to correct astigmatism, and later on she had a benign tumor on her back removed. She half-lifed at the age of twenty-eight—youngish, but not unreasonable—and she died at fifty-six.

She's been reduced to a stack of forms. I'll never know what dreams she fought for, who she loved, what the best moment of her life was. I have piles of information, but I don't really know her at all.

I pick up the next page and spot another medicine prescribed to her only months before her death. I highlight the brand name, convert it to its chemical name, then break that down into a chemical formula. I uncap a Sharpie and add the new information to the lists on my bedroom wall. Gigi gave me permission to write directly on the paint, so now I've got my own makeshift whiteboard wall on the six-foot-wide space between my door and my desk.

I'm looking for anything that could have altered Mitsuki's internal chemistry. Medicines she took that could have crossed the blood-brain barrier. Their half-lives, rates of decay, known isotopes. I've read research paper after research paper, memorized the makeup of neurotransmitters, psychopharmaceuticals, environmental toxins, neuropeptides.

I set the very last paper down and flop onto my bed. With only one patient's file, I can't really get much further. I need another anomaly to see if anything matches.

My phone buzzes.

DOTTIE: BABE, WE'RE HERE!

I grab my coat and scarf and rush to the kitchen. I rifle through the drawers, looking for hand warmers, a flashlight, and some cash for the fair.

My phone buzzes again.

DOTTIE: Are you on your way? Hurry up! Bo brought his
little munchkin. He's soooo cute.

BO: Shut up, Dotz.

DOTTIE: You should bring Billie Eilish!!

BO: Ooh, yes, bring your boy! We need to inspect this
dashing specimen!

They send a cascade of eggplants, and I roll my eyes. Of course they want me to bring Flint. They haven't shut up about him all week.

He's not MY boy, I type, punching out the letters.

But right after I send it, I stop digging through the kitchen drawers and glance out across Maynard's Creek.

The cabin glows, all sharp triangles of light. I can see figures moving, but I think it's Flint's parents, because they're regular-sized people, not lanky Endermen.

I want to tell him that I've finished going through Mitsuki Adams's file. Every time I drop my research into conversation with Dottie and Bo, their eyes glaze over. But when I talked science to Flint, he zoned in on me in a way that made me feel so *heard*. The world seemed to come into sharper focus, every detail magnified and ultrasaturated.

I press my eyes shut for a moment against the sudden sugar-rush hum in my bloodstream.

FINE. I'll ask him, I type.

I jam my gear into my bag and head out. I'm halfway up his side of the creek when I hear the sliding door on the back porch swish open. A tall figure steps out.

"Please tell me you brought banana bread again," Flint says, his voice as dark as the night, gravelly and low. "My dad won't forgive you if you ring the front doorbell without it."

I hold out my empty hands. "Sorry, no snacks this time," I whisper. "I'd better lie low, then."

"Yes, you'd better."

We're quiet for a moment, him leaning on the rail of his porch, me staring up at him.

"Hold on," he says. "Let me come down."

And then he's right in front of me, and I'm struck again by how familiar his sadness feels. If it were anyone else, I'd say something cheerful, boring, normal. But instead, I think of what he said in the car. *You don't have to be like that with me.*

It feels good to let the mask slip a little. To spend a few minutes not trying to be all the things people expect of me.

He jams his hands into his pockets. "So . . . just coming over to check on me?" he asks.

I narrow my eyes, realization dawning. "You saw me coming," I say.

"Not sure if you noticed, but your hair is pretty bright."

Sure. It's bright. But it's not like it glows in the dark. If he saw me, it was because he was already looking toward my house.

For some reason, it makes my whole body want to curve into a smile.

"I came to ask if you want to come with me to Bonfire Night," I say, gesturing through the trees at the orange glow. "It's the annual—"

"I know what it is," he says. "I grew up here."

Oh. He grew up here? I tuck that piece of information away. He's told me so little about himself.

"My friends are there, waiting for me. We're going to ride a few of the rides, grab some food, then sneak off to play flashlight tag. I want you to come."

He blinks. "Why?"

I falter. "I'm . . . not sure."

But that's not true.

I look away—the words aching to climb out of my throat are too real to be able to look at him as I say them.

"Do you ever feel like . . ." I shake my head. It's too much.

He waits. Doesn't change the subject or rush me. I can feel his stare on me like a cloak.

"It's like . . . I love my friends," I say quietly, carefully. "But do you ever feel like other people just don't get it? Like nothing truly bad's ever happened to them, and they don't seem to notice that every second of every day is another moment that's gone forever?"

I drag up the courage to meet his eyes.

He stares at me for a long moment. "All the time," he says. Soft and low.

I nod.

Flint casts a glance back at his house. It must be hard, facing the loss of a parent. It's a different kind of loss than what I know. When our family was counting down, I know all of us wished it had been Dad or Mom. Not Maybelle. Anyone but Maybelle.

Fireworks boom somewhere on the other side of the valley. I can't see them, but the whistle of them going up and the applause-like crackle of them coming down reminds me that Bonfire Night is in full swing.

"I'd better get going," I say quietly. Big social outings don't really seem like his thing, and—

"I'll come with you," he says.

Oh. "Really?"

"Sure. Lead the way."

flint

THIS TIME I do tell my parents where I'm going.

It's only later, when September and I are picking our way through the trees, leaves crunching underfoot in the shadows cast by her heavy-duty flashlight, that I stop to think about why I said yes to this.

This week's been more horrendous than any other so far, the seconds ticking away just a little faster, the hours of sleep I'm getting each night shrinking, like my body is trying to tell me, *Don't sleep through this; there's not much time left.* As if I don't know that.

When I saw her stepping over the creek, I couldn't resist the temptation to feel just the tiniest bit alive.

The night is smoky and feels strangely heavy. The bonfire must be warming the whole valley, because I'm not even cold in my T-shirt and black hoodie.

As soon as we step onto Main Street, nostalgia floods me. Strings of patio lights drape from building to building, making it feel like a summer block party in the middle of winter.

There are people *everywhere*. Underneath the canopy of light, hundreds of faces glow, all smiles and warmth and wonder. Aerys is probably here too—we loved Bonfire Night when we were kids.

September and I merge into the crowd, pressed shoulder to shoulder with dozens of strangers. We pass a corner parking lot where food stalls designed to look like little German wood cabins stand in a circle. They're bright with heat, selling bratwurst, giant pretzels, doughnuts, stollen, mulled wine.

September stops there for a few moments, appreciating all the small wonders. There's not a trace of the scientist in her tonight. Her hair is down, long and wild, and instead of the tiny nose ring she was wearing when I met her, she's hooked a delicate gold loop through her piercing. I feel very uncool in comparison.

The air heats up as we get closer to the bonfire. The Half-Life Institute towers over Main Street like an indifferent god, permitting but never partaking in the revelry at its feet. At the bottom of its marble steps, the bonfire's flames lick up to the sky from a pile of old warehouse pallets and scrap wood.

September and I squeeze through until we're right at the bonfire's barrier. The wall of heat almost knocks me back, but the fire is mesmerizing. September tries to say something to me, but between the live music and the crackling roar of the fire, I can't hear her.

"What?!" I shout.

She puts a hand on my shoulder and stands on her tiptoes to bring her mouth right next to my ear.

"We're supposed to meet my friends in the general store parking lot," she shouts. "Ready?"

I nod. My stomach clenches at the thought of meeting her friends. It's not really something I have a lot of practice doing.

September grabs my hand and pulls me around the left edge of the bonfire barrier. She doesn't let go until she sees the knot of people chatting outside the general store. I hang back, not sure what to do with myself. My hand, now that she's not holding it, feels ten degrees colder than the rest of me.

September flings herself into the arms of a girl with silky black hair, brown skin, and retro cat-eye glasses, then she tugs me forward by the sleeve of my hoodie.

"Guys, this is Flint," she says. "Flint, this is Dottie, and this is Bo."

A guy in an immaculately tailored wool coat steps forward. "We've heard a lot about you, Flint," Bo says, his eyes twinkling with mischief.

I hold out my hand to shake his—is that what you're supposed to do?—but the girl next to him, Dottie, dissolves into giggles.

"Pssh, come in for a hug," Dottie says, and then she squeezes me so tightly she almost lifts me off the ground. "September says you were responsible for her light bulb moment."

"Maybe I said something stupid, but the science is all her. She's brilliant."

"She is." Dottie beams, pleased.

There are a dozen other kids in the parking lot, but none of them are really paying attention to us. September points at each one, naming them: Amira, Dex, Troy, Heather, Javier. The rest of the names blur under the streetlights. I feel more awkward than ever. I shove my hands into my pockets and stay pathetically close to September.

Dottie links arms with her. "You're, like, so fuckin' late, babe," she says. "We've got to roll out right this second, but I knew you'd want to stuff your face, so I brought you a bunch of snacks from the food stands."

The boy next to Bo scampers forward and hands September a grease-stained takeout container.

September lights up, hugging it to her chest. "You're a lifesaver!"

Before I know it, we're all piling into a crusty old VW van. I'm not gonna lie . . . it's gross inside. The orange seats are covered in what might be their original '70s upholstery, and it smells like stale Fritos.

As we pull out of the parking lot, the radio blares Lizzo, and the other seven people packed into the van start singing along, getting boisterous as hell. This is not what I expected high school parties to be like. But what do I know? I haven't had a friend since I was eight.

September and I are crammed into the back row with two other people, and every time we take a corner a little too tight, the momentum presses me up against the window—and presses September against me.

After just a few turns, I become *hyper*aware of this fact.

I start to crave the bends in the road, hoping for another press of her shoulder, her elbow, her hip against my own.

"I'm smashing your arm," she says suddenly, and I want to say, *It's fine, I'd let you turn me into roadkill if you wanted to*, but she tugs my left arm out from between us and pulls it over her head.

God. I've got my arm around her shoulder now, in a distinctly un-friend-like way.

She's so warm, radiating heat where she's pressed up against my rib cage. I grip the back of the seat so my hand doesn't get any ideas about drifting down to tangle in her hair.

After what seems like hours of exquisite torture, the van finally lurches to a stop.

Out the front window, shapes loom up from a wide clearing: the crumbling shell of the old resort. Every window is either broken or completely missing. To our left, there's a kitschy sign that might have once been painted in bright neons: *Penn Oasis Honeymooner's Resort*.

"Um, how dangerous is this, exactly?" I whisper.

"Pretty dangerous," September says. "We'll be okay, though; Dottie plans for everything."

More cars pull up after us. In total, there must be thirty or forty kids out here. I wonder how many of them sat with me on the rug during story time in elementary.

The drivers all leave their headlights on, pointing at the resort from different angles. I stick close to September after we climb out.

She looks up at me. "You okay? You seem a little out of your element."

"I'm fine. I just don't really get out much."

She, on the other hand, seems comfortable with all of this. When she turns back to the clusters of people milling around in the headlight beams, there's a steely, determined glint in her eye, and it makes me wonder if this—the friends and the game and the electricity of this night—is all a way to keep the dark in check.

Because there is dark there. The pain that flashed across her face when she asked me that question—*Do you ever feel like other people just don't get it?*—was serious.

We move from group to group to say hi. Curious eyes keep

sliding to me, then snapping away. I'm the only person they don't know, and I feel so out of place. I step even closer to September.

There's an invisible thread connecting us tonight, and I couldn't break away from her if I tried. She must feel it too, because after a while, she tucks her hand into the crook of my elbow and leans in close as we make the rounds.

A guy shouts, "Temmmmmberrrr!" like he's a lumberjack calling a tree down. September makes a show of rolling her eyes. "Like I haven't heard that one before, Dex," she says, smiling.

After a few minutes, Dottie breaks away from the group and stands in the brightest pool of headlights. She whistles a shrill note, and the noise dies down.

"Okay, losers, listen up!" Dottie shouts, clearly the evening's ringmaster and emcee.

It's an interesting mix of people out here, jocks and goths and theater kids like the boy who's holding Bo's hand, who September says is an understudy in some musical.

A lanky Black guy with a huge megawatt smile and a puffy neon-green coat is really playing off Dottie's energy, clapping and whistling after every statement.

"Ayy, Jonah! Let her talk," someone shouts.

Jonah? The name pinches inside my chest.

Oh shit. I know him. We were in the same class for first and second grade, and we used to love playing dodgeball together at recess.

My insides seize up, instantly cold with fear. It's been a long time, but he might recognize me.

I can't let that happen.

Dottie holds up a hat with a bunch of slips of paper. Someone does a drumroll on the hood of a car, and she draws out two names.

"For round one, the seekers are . . . Amira!" The crowd erupts, and a girl in a pastel-pink hijab dances up to Dottie, clearly stoked to be a seeker.

"And . . . Jonah!"

Jonah whoops and pumps a fist in the air as he jogs over to join Amira.

Great. Now I have two reasons to stay away from him.

"So for anyone who doesn't know the rules," Dottie shouts, "here's a quick recap. Rule one: Everyone has to pick a buddy, and you have to stick with them. The. Whole. Time."

I glance down at September. She's still got her hand tucked into the crook of my elbow.

"Be my buddy?" she asks, amber eyes lucid in the headlights.

"I was just about to ask you the same thing."

Dottie keeps talking. "Rule two: Do NOT go upstairs! I'm serious about this one, guys. The floors might cave in. Heather is our safety captain for tonight—she's nineteen, so technically we have an adult on-site. If you have any problems, call or text her, and she'll get you help."

An older girl in a Carbon Junction University sweatshirt waves from her tricked-out wheelchair next to a huge pickup truck. She takes a swig of her Venti coffee, looking completely at home.

"We'll set a timer for ten minutes," Dottie continues. "That's how long you have to hide. I'm texting everyone a rough map of the place now."

September digs out her phone and angles it to me so I can see.

"I'll give Jonah and Amira thirty minutes to seek. If you're caught, point your flashlight straight up and walk back to the cars. After their thirty minutes are up, I'm going to mark a location on the map. That will be home base, and it's where the golden idol awaits."

The crowd titters, teasingly repeating *Ooh golden idol*.

"If you can get to the golden idol before the seekers catch you, you win! Got all that?"

The crowd cheers. The excitement is fever-pitch now.

Jonah and Amira make a big show of clambering into the VW and putting on their blindfolds. Dottie gives the signal, and thirty kids take off running across the parking lot. September slides her hand out from my elbow but grabs my hand before I can miss the touch, and then we're running too.

Adrenaline floods me. The excitement of this night is so unlike the past eight years of my life it's laughable.

And then we get inside, and my jaw drops.

The resort lobby looks like a set from a zombie video game. The grand staircase is slumping like a destroyed wedding cake, wooden banisters splintered, moldy stains on the carpet.

September slows, shining her flashlight around. Graffiti smothers every wall, colors popping as the beam of light sweeps over them. One particularly poignant one reads *OUR GENERATION IS FUCKED!*

"Oh wow," September says. She steps close and traces the neon lines, taking it all in like it's the finest museum art. I'm struck again by how much courage it must take, to just stop and appreciate things, when I'm starting to understand that her life hasn't been all rainbows and unicorns.

The whispers and thumps and nervous giggles of the other teams fill the abandoned building. Hopefully all this racket will chase away any animals making their nests here.

September checks the map on her phone. "I usually like to get a feel for the layout, then go back to the best hiding place right before the ten minutes are up," she says.

"Sounds good to me."

We step gingerly down a hallway lined with doors, or rather, what used to be doors. Some are hanging on hinges, some are lying on the floor, some are totally MIA. The floor is covered with broken glass and dirt and god knows what else.

I peer into one of the rooms. "Is that a *heart-shaped* hot tub?" I ask.

September laughs. "Yup. Pennsylvania has loads of these. Didn't you know? Swinging sixties and all that. Apparently that's when America finally discovered sex."

I can't help it; the word *sex* sends a skitter through me.

"Huh," I manage to say.

September steps around a broken chair to peer into the tub. "You had to have a marriage certificate to even book. Hence the honeymoon part of the name."

"Aannnd there's even a mirror on the ceiling," I say.

Our eyes meet in the misty glass, and a flush of heat crawls up my neck at the implication.

I'm the first to look away, hoping desperately that she can't see my blood sparking in my veins. I'm acting like a blushing virgin, which, thanks to some pity hookups last year in Philadelphia, I am very much not.

Back out in the hallway, flashlight beams cross the air like lasers as the other teams search for their own hiding places. September's flashlight beam guides us through a weight room full of spiderwebs, through admin offices with overturned desks, and through one high-ceilinged room with soggy carpet and stacked chairs that reminds me of a school auditorium.

"Hey—maybe we should hide over there," I say, nodding to the stage at the end of the room. It's flanked by imitation Greek columns, the plaster chipped and only faintly reminiscent of the white it used to be.

"Could be a good place," she agrees.

I poke the moth-eaten velvet curtain with my boot, half expecting a swarm of vermin to pour out. When they don't, I pull the curtain aside to reveal a small stage with stacks of junk in the wings. In the corner, a grand piano slumps, missing keys like knocked-out teeth.

"Perfect," September whispers.

We tuck ourselves down on the floor between the piano and a sofa that looks kind of Egyptian. The resort goes still as we near the ten-minute mark. Throughout the building, flashlights click off one by one until all is quiet.

The cold swirls in, reclaiming the resort. The stage is velvet black, and, for a minute, the total lack of light makes me feel like I don't exist. But then my eyes adjust, and I can make out the limned blue edge of September's copper hair, the pale flash of her teeth.

In the distance, a car horn honks three times: the signal that Jonah and Amira are on the way.

"The game is afoot," September whispers.

My heart thumps.

Her arm is pressed against mine again. Hiding together, sharing the same keen mix of fear and adrenaline, is an even stronger bond than my arm around her shoulder, her hand on my elbow. Underneath the game's manufactured fear, I feel content. Happy.

In the darkness, September shifts.

"You okay?" she whispers.

"Yeah."

"Having fun?"

"Actually . . . yes."

I can only see the hint of her smile, but I know it's there. I can feel it.

I hear a crinkle of plastic. She presses something into my hand—one of her infamous butterscotches.

"Is there something I should know about?" I whisper. "You're constantly eating these. Are there addictive substances in them?"

She laughs quietly. "No substances. I just have an insatiable sweet tooth."

She's already sucking on her own candy, and the caramel smell of it twines with the cinnamon-sweet smell of *her*.

I unwrap mine and slip it into my mouth. It's just candy.

The only problem is . . . it's delicious. The butterscotch melts in my mouth like Christmas and winter and memories all rolled into one.

We relax into the darkness—until we hear voices on the other side of the curtain. Shit—Jonah and Amira.

I thought this would be the best hiding place in the joint, but the couch suddenly doesn't seem like the most effective shield. A few feet away, there's a vertical gap between two flat pieces of scenery. Without a word, I point to it. September nods, and we drop to the floor, crawling to the safer hiding spot.

Behind us, the curtains part, and a beam of light slices through.

"Ready or not, here we come," Amira sings in a truly creepy, childlike voice.

We squeeze into the gap just in time.

Their flashlights sweep over the piles of junk. September flinches away from the light. There's less space back here than I thought. It's like standing in a coffin, and we're trying to fit side by side, but her entire arm's still peeking out.

She looks at me, eyes wide and panicked. We've got two options here, and they hit both of us at once: She can either squeeze against me back to front . . . or front to front.

The air in my lungs turns into dizzying, intoxicating fumes.

She goes for front to front.

As she maneuvers herself in, I suck in a breath and press myself back to give her as much room as I can. I shut my eyes.

And then we're in, sandwiched together between the two sheets of plywood. Our legs are pressed together from knee to thigh. Every time one of us breathes, we shush against each other, phantom-light touches feathering over my chest, my arms, my stomach.

The only sign that it's affecting her as much as it is me is a nearly imperceptible change in her breathing. I press my lips together. I don't know where to put my hands.

Think about something, anything. Don't get lost in these sensations.

But her hair smells like autumn leaves and cinnamon and banana bread. She's like a holiday wrapped up in a girl, and I'm . . . *God*. I need to breathe.

I've just about got myself together when Jonah's flashlight beam rakes close again. My hand flies up to September's hip, urging her to stay still.

I can feel her heart beating against my sternum. It's getting unbearably warm, tucked in here, our body heat multiplying, but we don't dare move.

Finally, Jonah and Amira give up, their voices fading as they continue their search.

September starts to slide out of our hiding place, but for some stupid reason, my fingers tighten where they're resting on her hip in an unspoken plea. *Don't go yet.*

It's pitch-black, but somehow I know exactly where her mouth is in the dark. I can *feel* her there, her face tipped up to mine. Her lips are just a breath away, and somehow I know that what happens in the next moment will change everything.

september

EVERYWHERE FLINT'S TOUCHING me, I'm burning.

Each drag of air feels like denatured alcohol in my lungs, making it somehow both easier and more difficult to think.

I look up at him, my eyes wide in the dark. Is this really happening? *Experiment*, the scientist in me commands, yearning to test the parameters. *First test: Slide one hand up over his shoulder, slowly, to see how he responds.*

In the dark, his grip tightens on my hip.

My pulse is everywhere.

Second test: Lean into him; let his body hold the weight of yours.

He reacts instantly—and the rough snag of his breath is a match strike in my wrists.

I tilt up to him, going dizzy as the distance between our mouths closes.

But before I can get there, I hear a noise. A *scritch-scritch-scritch*, coming from the corner to my left. And then—the soft padding beat of tiny running paws.

When I feel the first rat scramble over my feet, I *shriek*.

Everything's chaos, both of us twisting awkwardly to get out of the tiny space. His shoulder catches my chin, and my elbow digs into his side.

I clap my hand hard over my mouth to keep quiet—another scream would have Jonah and Amira coming back for us. I'm so grossed out. Lab rats are one thing, but a swarm of dirty, potentially rabid rodents rushing over my *feet*?! No thanks.

The rats scurry away, and everything goes silent again.

"What the hell," I whisper.

"Seriously. What the hell," Flint whispers back.

I can't believe this. Did we just get thwarted by *rats?*

I turn on my flashlight. Suddenly I don't care if we get found—I can't be in the dark right now.

Flint drops onto the sofa and covers his face with his hands. I hesitate for a moment, then sit next to him. I bring my feet up, hugging my knees to my chest. I don't want to be touching the floor right now.

"You okay?" Flint asks. "They didn't bite you or anything, did they?"

"No. You?"

He shakes his head, then slumps back on the couch. As he does, the side of his leg brushes against mine, and my nerve endings crackle back to life.

You'd think the chaos would have rinsed away whatever hum was building in my body, but nope. It's still there.

All of this—the heat under my skin, the burning flush in my cheeks, the disordered jangle of my thoughts—it's just science. My brain oh-so-helpfully supplies an entire slideshow of research papers, academic journals, and textbook pages. The science of attraction. Pheromones. It's all just chemicals. Testosterone and estrogen creating the physical desire. Dopamine, norepinephrine, and sero-tonin creating attraction. $C_8H_{11}NO_2$, $C_8H_{11}NO_3$, $C_{10}H_{12}N_2O$. Even in this moment, my mind is fully capable of recalling the chemical formulas.

Beside me, Flint's silent. I'm aching to know if he's feeling this too.

Instalove might not be a thing, but insta*lust* is. Sometimes people get the terminology wrong—they say they're in love when it's just that first air-robbing punch of physical, chemical attraction. This is definitely lust. For it to be love, there'd need to be oxytocin too, to bond us.

Still . . . no science in the world could have prepared me for what's happening to my nerves. My *skin*. I can still feel the phantom burn on my hip where he steadied me.

My phone buzzes. It's Dottie, texting everyone the home base location: the indoor swimming pool. I hold my phone out so Flint can see, and if he notices the tremor in my hands, he doesn't say. There's a follow-up text too. *Only three teams left. Seekers on the prowl.*

"Do you want to go back to the parking lot?" Flint whispers in the dark. "Or are we still playing?"

The stage's heavy velvet curtain blankets the edges of his words and turns them into flat, hollow things. I can't figure out what he's thinking.

"Up to you," I say. I push my coat sleeves up to let the cold air bite at my wrists. I've got to get the swirling chemicals in my brain under control.

"The rats probably won't come back," he says. "Should we keep going?"

"I guess," I say. I force myself to think. "You remember how to get back to that big rec room? It's on the other side of that."

"All right. Let's go."

Flint takes the lead this time. I follow him down the dark hallways, my fingers aching to hook inside his elbow again or simply latch on to a handful of his hoodie. But I don't touch him, afraid that even the smallest contact will trigger another frenzied neurotransmitter rush.

He's a shadowy tower in front of me, solid and capable. Maybe touching me didn't affect him at all. Great. Now I feel foolish— what brain chemical is responsible for that?

Slowly, inch by inch, room by room, we claim ground. He's like a stealth ninja in a video game, peering around corners, slipping into hallways. We get closer and closer to the indoor pool, and so far no sign of the seekers. Then I hear small noises from other parts of the resort. Scrabbles and whispers and accidental flickers of light. The other two teams.

We sneak into one of the changing rooms leading to the pool. I stumble, about to land palm-down on shattered mirror shards. But Flint catches me, a fistful of my coat in one hand, the other hand burning a new path of heat onto my ribs.

"I got you," he murmurs, and his voice is so low and gruff in my ear that I shiver.

That can't be *just* science. It has to be more than just chemicals, because I don't think any of this would be happening if not for his vintage boots, the soft Vantablack of his hair, the sadness he carries around him like a cloak. The way he keeps his eyes trained so intently on mine whenever I'm talking.

Flint peers around a corner, beckoning for me to join him.

We've made it to the pool. Night reaches in through the broken windows, but the moonlight's no match for the brightness of the pool itself. It glows, the tiles still pale blue after so many years, even though they're cracked and the grout's moldy. There's no water in the pool, of course, except for one green puddle in the corner that probably boasts its own complicated microbiome.

At the bottom of the deep end, surreally, there's a single, intact pool lounger. On it, the golden idol glints.

An errant flashlight beam arcs over the ceiling.

Flint presses me back into the shadows.

Jonah and Amira emerge from the opposite changing room, guarding the path to the pool. No way we're making it to the idol with them patrolling like this.

But then a muffled crash comes from our distant left—one of the other teams. Jonah's and Amira's flashlights swivel to investigate.

"Now," Flint hisses.

We bolt from our hiding place. Debris crunches underfoot as we run. He jumps down into the pool, then turns back to offer me a hand, eyes glittering with determination.

I land hard, a lot harder than he did. The sound echoes like a drum in the empty pool.

Amira shouts from the hall.

"Shit! They heard us," Flint says.

We run down the slope toward the deep end, skidding on broken tiles and mildew.

We touch the golden statue at the same time.

Amira and Jonah rush back in, flashlights bouncing, but it's done. We've won.

Flint collapses onto the pool lounger, exhaling his adrenaline with what might be the first real laugh I've heard from him.

I'm clenching the trophy like it's the cure for the half-life. This time it's a golden goat with *Greatest of All Time* etched on the base. I chuckle and pass it to Flint to see.

He pushes his hair back from his forehead.

And . . . he smiles.

And oh my god, his *smile*. One of his canine teeth is too small and too sharp, and it makes him look a little boyish. He's always so grim and serious, but this? This is so endearing my heart feels like it might explode.

It hits me then—this is the first time I've seen him smile.

The rest of the night is a blur. We play two more rounds, but Flint and I get caught early both times. There's not another opportunity to cram ourselves into cupboards or closets, and I can't help feeling a sinking disappointment.

In between the games, he doesn't leave my side. I'm still fighting down the storm of chemicals, still a little high on black cherry fumes. It's weird, how intensely awake I feel around Flint, compared to other guys I've liked—at one point, we run into Bryson Oliveira, who I dated for a few weeks over the summer, and the contrast knocks me sideways. Bryson was fun, and easy to be with, always in a basketball jersey and a tufty mess of teddy-bear-brown hair, and I decided to go for it because it was part of my new Carbon Junction persona, and I was trying to keep up with Dottie and Bo. Bizarrely, I feel more buzzy just sitting next to Flint in the back of a van—and Bryson and I hooked up a few times.

When the van dumps us out into the general store parking lot in the small hours of the morning, I drag in the first real breath I've taken since we left the resort. The crowds have gone home. The fire marshals circle the glowering remains of the bonfire, tending to the embers until they're ashes and carbon. A few volunteers amble around, picking up trash.

We say goodnight to Dottie and Bo. This time, Flint's easier with the hugs, and he even works in a deadpan joke. I can tell Dottie and Bo like him, even if they haven't had a chance to talk to him tonight.

Dottie envelops me in a hug. "Updates needed ASAP. I feel like we haven't talked all week."

I swallow hard—she's noticed me distancing myself from them, then. "ASAP," I agree, hoping she doesn't notice the hesitance in my voice.

And then it's just me and Flint.

We don't say anything, just turn in unison and start walking toward Gravel Ridge. It feels comfortable, like we do this all the time: September and Flint leaving a party together.

There's a high concentration of suspended particulate matter in the air, thanks to the bonfire. The beams of the streetlights pushing through the smog look eerily cinematic.

As the energy of Bonfire Night fades, I start to feel my hypothesis tug at me again. It's late, but I'm alert, so I can spend an hour or two streamlining my collected data and prepping the next phase.

We stop outside Gigi's house.

I hug my arms around myself against the cold. "Thanks for being on my team tonight," I say.

Flint nods. "Thanks for inviting me," he says, his voice scratchy and deep from the late hour. "It was . . . actually pretty fun. I usually don't let myself enjoy stuff."

We're silent for a few moments.

I swallow. "Flint? You know when you said it was okay for me to be sad sometimes? Maybe it's okay *not* to be sad sometimes too."

He blinks and looks off into the night. "Maybe," he says, shoving his hands into his pockets.

He turns to go, then stops. Looks back.

"Goodnight, September," he says softly.

I watch him disappear into the trees, darkness blending into darkness.

flint

WHEN I LET myself into the house at 2:15, my heart is pounding thick in my chest. I'm not used to letting myself want things, and I *very much* wanted to kiss September. I press a hand over my ribs until I have my thoughts under control.

Something rumbles in the dark—a purring snore. Dad is a lump on the couch, asleep under a blanket.

I frown. He wouldn't have put that blanket on himself. Mom must have tucked him in. In a flash, I can picture her switching off the screen and laying a blanket over him. I can't tell if it's something I've seen before, a blurred memory from when I was little, or if it's all in my head.

The pressure in my chest morphs into a different kind of ache.

Two plates rest on the coffee table, crumbs casting long shadows. Looks like pecan pie—Mom's favorite. Dad makes killer pies, and he must have made one for her.

They're getting along better than I'd expected them to.

In my bedroom, I switch on a lamp and sigh out the day.

Tonight was . . . incredible. For a few hours, I forgot I was dying. That's something I never expected with four weeks left on the clock.

I start to tug my phone out of my back pocket to charge it, but,

125

just for tonight, I don't want to see the countdown timer on the lock screen.

So instead, I fall asleep in my hoodie and my jeans, with my phone in my pocket. I imagine the life draining from it as the batteries run down, until it's just a hunk of cold, dead metal.

When Aerys shows up on my doorstep two days after Bonfire Night, there's only a fleeting jab of irritation—*Why is she here again?*—before I resign myself to another hangout.

I don't know how she talks me into going into town, but before I know it, we're meandering up and down the aisles of Carbon Junction's three-story general store. It smells woodsy and inviting, like pine and the rubber of brand-new rain boots.

"Have you left your house at all since I last saw you?" Aerys asks.

"This might shock you, but yes, actually. I went to a flea market with my mom yesterday."

"For real? Look at you, swanning all over Pennsylvania like a damn socialite."

I swallow. I'm not sure I'm ready to tell her about Bonfire Night—about what almost happened there between me and September. Every time I think about that moment in our hiding spot, I get dizzy, dropping like a Cessna in an engine-failure free fall.

I did the flea market thing mainly to make up for bailing on Mom's apple-picking plans, and it must have worked, because she was chatty and bright as we drove over to the next valley. We spent hours combing through rows and rows of musty old stuff to source furniture for her clients, and I even found a few things to spend last year's Christmas money on. Not like I'll need the cash when I'm dead.

I told myself it was okay to indulge just a little, like with the butterscotch on Bonfire Night. Maybe I can spend more time with my parents and Aerys—not enough so that it makes my deathday more painful for all of us, but a few small things here and there can't cause too much damage, right?

Aerys pauses to try on a pair of cycling gloves. "Remember that time we tried to do parkour outside the dentist's office and you busted up both of your knees?"

I grimace, remembering the blood and the bits of gravel stuck in my skin. "Yeah, I remember. I still have the scars."

She puts the gloves back. "Man, we did an embarrassing amount of planking back then."

It catches me off guard, and I bark out a laugh. "Way too much planking," I agree.

I breathe through the dull pinch of nostalgia. We had some good times, Aerys and me.

As we turn down another aisle, it feels like she wants me to offer up another snippet of our childhood in return. I can think of a few, like when we tried to re-create our favorite pop star's dance routine, or when we built a giant maze out of cardboard boxes in her back-yard, or when we rode our bikes all the way out to Philipsburg to get ice cream and had to call our parents to come get us.

I'm not sure if these strolls down memory lane are more for her benefit or mine. It's not that I don't want to remember those things; they don't bother me as much as a lot of other topics (like my nonexistent future, or whether or not they'll put me in a suit to bury me). It's just . . . won't talking about this stuff hurt *her* more? Why strengthen a bond before you sever it?

"Oh, hey," she says. "Are you still into airplanes? Do you still go to air shows?"

This is one of the topics I do avoid.

I haven't been to an air show since the day I half-lifed.

A memory flashes: a perfect blue sky, six airplanes hovering in a delta formation. I can almost smell the fresh-cut grass, the hot asphalt, and the jet fuel. Feel my small hand in my grandpa's huge leathery one, my fingertips sticky with powdered sugar, wearing stupid little overalls and a baseball cap with the air force logo on them.

Air shows only remind me of the headache. The seizure. The day all my dreaming ended.

And my grandpa . . . the last time we were together, before things got weird—before *I* got weird and asked for space—he pulled a fast one on me. He said we were going out for lunch, but instead he took me to the regional airport where he teaches flight lessons. He'd arranged for me to go up with Jen Polaris, this famous stunt pilot. I know he was just trying to cheer me up. Pull me out of my dark spiral. And for thirty blissful minutes, it worked—it was heavenly up there, doing loops and barrel rolls and inversions and stall turns.

But when the landing gear hit the runway at the end of it . . . coming back to reality was the worst feeling ever.

Coming down from Bonfire Night with September is starting to feel a little bit like that.

Aerys waves at someone our age in the next aisle, chirping a friendly *hi*. The guy says hi back, but it sounds so grudging that I get secondhand embarrassment from the interaction. Something's clearly up.

I guess this friendship thing has to be a two-way street.

"So, um, what happened with that girlfriend?" I ask. "The one you said you broke up with recently?"

"Oh—Darcy. She was amazing. We were pretty wrapped up in each other for like two years. But I sort of zoomed my whole life in on her, and my other friendships fell away. When we broke up, I kind of didn't have anything to catch me, like no one to eat lunch with or anything. It's cool, though. I'll be out of here soon—I applied to Penn State. It'll be nice to meet a whole bunch of new people."

I should have invited her to Bonfire Night. My heart feels sore for her, but I don't know what to say beyond *"Penn State will be cool."*

She seems okay with that, staring blankly at some fishing rods, hopefully imagining her brighter, friend-filled future away from this town.

I haven't thought much about my plan for my own last day in Carbon Junction. With a reluctant ache, I remind myself that I have to dip out soon.

While Aerys tries on some jeans in the changing room, I wander over to an elaborate camping tent display. I circle the platform, eyeing up the smaller tents. I don't know where I'm going to go yet. The Ruins are off the table. September and her friends go out there, and I can't risk being found, especially by her. I guess I'll just start walking west, up Gravel Ridge Mountain and down the other side. I'll need a tent and a sleeping bag. A camping lantern and batteries. Some food and water, and a bag to put them all in, I guess.

"Whatcha looking at these for?" Aerys says.

I jump. "Jesus, sneak up on me much?"

"Dude, we should totally go camping!" Her eyes light up. "Remember that time we set up that tarp fort in my backyard and slept out there for a week, pretending we were stranded on a deadly island surrounded by sharks?"

"Yeah, but it was summer. No way am I going camping in this weather."

"Says the boy who never wears a coat."

"No camping," I say, then I plunge down another aisle, leading her away from the tent display.

"Uh, Flint? You're not going to do anything impulsive, are you?"

I stiffen. "Impulsive? Like what?"

"I don't know. You're not, like . . . planning to go out with a bang, are you? Did you hear last week about that cult that all jumped off the Empire Tower on their collective deathday?"

"I didn't hear about that, no," I mumble.

"Took police forever to scrape 'em all off the sidewalk. It's been all over the news. *Kids* had to see that shit."

Christ.

"So you're not going to do anything like that, right?" Aerys prods.

"No! God, no."

"Okay, good." Mollified, she drops the subject.

And then, at the end of the aisle, I see a flash of copper. My heart pulses hard in my chest, a strong, stuttering kick. Aerys hasn't noticed. I wander down the aisle and pick up a candle, pretending to smell it as I lean out.

It's not September.

The way my heart dipped when I realized it wasn't her is . . . problematic. Whatever this is—it can't be happening. I'm on a deadline. Literally.

I know I should call off the other trips to the hospitals. But September's so desperate to get these files, and even though I know they won't save me, I can't stand in the way of them maybe saving someone else.

I can handle a few more hours in the car with her. I just need to make sure I don't forget about my countdown or my plans for my last day.

We check out, then Aerys hugs me goodbye on the sidewalk outside. I watch until she rounds a corner and disappears from sight, and then I go back inside and buy the hunter-green tent.

september

THE LAB HUMS around me as I jab at the buttons on the mass spectrometer, but my mind is miles away. Specifically, on the interesting mole above a certain someone's lip and what almost happened between us on that pitch-black stage.

I haven't been able to stop thinking about it. Woozy heat keeps swamping me at the most inopportune moments: in the middle of intake interviews, during dinner with Gigi, in second-period English. The way he touched me, the breathless, oxygen-rich anticipation that hung between us like—

Beep.

The mass spectrometer bleats angrily at me. *Beep, beep.*

Crap. I must have inputted something wrong. I rub my eyes. Maybe I shouldn't have stayed up so late last night, streamlining how I'm deriving and compiling my data. I don't regret it—every minute of work on my hypothesis is valuable. Today, another ten Intake floor patients moved upstairs to die, and that's just a tiny fraction of how many people the kill switch is touching every day.

Percy appears at my side, holding another tray of samples he's prepared for me to run through the mass spectrometer.

"Nice jewelry," he says casually.

Oh shit. My hand flies up to my nose, to the gold hoop that's still in. What's wrong with me today? I never forget to take out my nose ring before work.

Percy's smugness continues to radiate as he sits back down at his station, where he's handling glass vials and blood samples from intake patients.

I cast a critical eye over his work. "Shouldn't you be using a 522 PP tube for those? Fewer paramagnetic impurities."

"I didn't think it necessary," he retorts. "These samples aren't that precious."

On a normal day, this would turn into a Ping-Pong match of us bickering over the optimal tube, but we have too much work to do. And it's not helping that every time I think about Flint, my brain dumps another dose of room-tilting chemicals on me.

Out of the corner of my eye, I see Dr. Juncker's phone light up with an incoming call. She's been in and out of the lab today and keeps leaving it lying faceup on the table.

I'm about to glance away, but then the call ends, and it returns to her lock screen. I know I shouldn't be looking at the photo she's chosen, but it's right there.

The picture is of her and a ruggedly handsome Nordic man. Their smiling faces are smushed together; their crow's-feet are crinkled deep with happiness.

I frown. Something tugs at my memory. That face—

The door to the lab opens, and I snap my eyes back to my work.

Dr. Juncker walks in, flipping through a thick report. She doesn't even look as she grabs her phone and slides it into her lab coat pocket.

I hunch over my paperwork, writing down numbers that make no sense in an attempt to look busy.

After a while, Dr. Juncker tucks the report into a filing cabinet and peers over Percy's shoulder. She nods in satisfaction—I guess he's using the right tubes after all. Then she hovers on my side of the table, checking the spectrometer, eyeballing all its different components.

"Mein gott," she says suddenly. "Ms. Harrington, this is not correct."

What? I haven't been giving this my full attention, but I'm sure I did everything right—

With a sudden, sinking feeling, I see my mistake.

It's bad.

"Percy, come. Take over the spectroscopy," she says, panic and disappointment seeping into her voice—and into my bloodstream.

He jumps up right away, the little weasel. Eagerly stepping into my role.

"The entire data set is ruined," Dr. Juncker says.

I never mess up like this. And this wouldn't have happened if I could have kept my mind on the task. I've been so preoccupied with Flint and my research, I forgot for a moment that I have to slay this internship and that Percy and I are vying for the biochem spot at CJU.

I *cannot* lose to him.

I do my best to make up for the mistake, but Dr. Juncker's disappointment in me doesn't lift. When she finally dismisses us for the day, I collapse onto a bench in the lobby and pull out my phone.

Something's been tugging at my mind all afternoon, even through my mortified panic. There was something weird about that photo on Dr. Juncker's lock screen.

I researched her before I applied for the internship, but I was focusing on her scientific achievements. This time, I tap *Uta Juncker husband* into the search box.

The first hit is exactly what I was afraid I'd find.

An obituary.

I look around, making sure no one's watching me, then I tap on the link.

Magnus Juncker's birthday and deathday are listed. I do the math in a split second. He was only thirty-eight years old. Which means he half-lifed at nineteen.

She had to have known when she married him.

I let the phone drop onto the bench next to me. I knew she was a great scientist, but my respect for her skyrockets. I've never seen her bring a shred of emotion into the Institute. She's keeping a lid on it, the way I should be doing whenever I'm in this building. *Emotions can only cloud the scientific lens.*

She knows there's no room for the dark places here.

I stand in the cafeteria line at school, trying to pinpoint when my life started wobbling like an unbalanced centrifuge machine.

Was it the bracelet with Aubrey Vásquez? Or is it all because I met Flint—is his ever-present grief coaxing my own out? I blink, and it takes an extra millisecond to drag my eyes open again. Maybe it's all just because I'm sleep-deprived from trying to prove this hypothesis.

I can't pull back on my research, so . . . maybe I need to pull back on spending time with Flint? My body instantly rebels at the idea.

I get to the front of the line and swipe my student ID. I turn with my tray of cardboard pizza and soggy broccoli and spot Dottie and Bo at our usual table. But when I get close, my steps falter. Bo's head is bent over his food, and Dottie is rubbing a hand soothingly up and down his back.

"Hey, guys," I say, warily sliding into a chair across from them.

Bo raises his head, looking tired and stressed. "Hey, sugarplum," he says. "Don't mind me, just failed another math test."

I watch as Dottie takes his hand and squeezes it, murmuring about how they just need to find him a tutor like they talked about, how they'll make sure he aces his next test. The world seems to shrink around them, and I suddenly feel outside of this friendship. Discomfort crawls all over me, and I don't know what to say, or where to put my hands, or if I should start eating or not.

Bo gathers himself, beaming a grateful look at Dottie. For a moment, I think, *Wouldn't that be nice*, to be able to fall apart in front of someone and know that they'll be okay with it.

But a dead sister's a little different than bad grades.

"September? Are you okay?" Dottie asks. I must have been staring into space.

"I'm just tired," I say. "I was up late."

"Homework or science?"

"Science. Always science."

"You know what you two need? Waffles," Dottie says. "Should we meet at eight after I get off work?"

My stomach flips nervously. "I'm not sure I can come, guys. I've got so much work to do."

At least they have the grace to look disappointed.

"Okay. But we need to do one soon. You still haven't caught us up on this whole Flint thing."

I keep wanting to share things with them, but whenever I start talking about him, I get stuck in these traps where what I'm about to say only makes sense if you know I have a dead sister. It was easy not to mention Maybelle before, because I had it under control. Now, as things get messier inside me, tendrils of memories and pain escaping more and more often, it's harder to pretend I'm cheerful and okay.

When the bell rings, Dottie wraps me in one of her tight hugs. "I miss you, babes," she says.

My eyes sting. "I miss you too," I murmur. I'm glad she can't see my face.

"Hang in there. Once you're done with this research, we'll have you back."

But it's not the research. I don't have the heart to tell them . . . I don't think it'll ever be the same again.

I don't think *I'll* ever be the same.

I come home to find Gigi sitting on a pillow on the living room floor with photo albums spread out all around her.

She pulls a photo out of the crinkly plastic, then lays it under a desk lamp and takes a picture of it with her phone.

"Thought it was about time I digitized these," she says.

I frown. "You know there are services that do that for you, right?"

Gigi waves a hand dismissively. "Cost an arm and a leg." She closes one album and reaches for another. "You want to grab a cushion and come have a look? This album's from when I came to visit y'all for your big science fair a few years ago."

I take a sharp step back. "I'm good."

She smiles, flipping through the pages. "I remember when you were real little, you'd sit and stare at the pictures of your parents for hours."

I skirt the edge of the living room. It's not the pictures of my parents I don't want to see. There are pictures of *her* in there.

As I watch Gigi blithely flick through the albums, envy curdles in my chest. I don't know how she does this. I'm in way better shape than my parents, but it seems like Gigi can look at loss straight in the face and not flinch.

I hang up my coat and spot a package wrapped in brown paper and old-school twine. My name is written on a small card on the front.

"Gigi? What's this?"

"Oh—package for you. Found it on the front porch this morning. And your dad's been trying to get ahold of you too, honey."

"I'll call him later, Gigi. I have a ton of stuff going on right now."

"I told him as much. Maybe sometime tomorrow, though, 'kay?"

"Fine. Not that he cares what I even say on those calls," I mutter.

Gigi stops photo sorting and looks up, suddenly all concerned. "Your parents will get better," she says gently.

When? I want to ask. Because the weirdest thing is—I thought we were going to be okay. After Maybelle half-lifed, maybe Mom slept a little more than before, maybe Dad worked more, but it felt like we were holding it together. I was already deep-diving into genetics before, but it became an obsession that I spent every hour outside of school on.

My parents had been clear on one thing: None of us were ever to talk about Maybelle's situation in front of her. But then we sort of just . . . ended up never talking about it at all. We acted like it wasn't coming.

I get why we couldn't tell her. I agreed with the decision. She wouldn't have understood, and it would have only made her short life worse. So we all pretended she'd live forever. We taught her nursery rhymes and how to count to ten and how to write her name, even though she'd never need to be able to do those things.

So when my parents both completely lost it after she died, it was a shock. I think I expected them to wake up the next day and carry on as if she'd never existed.

"September?" Gigi sets down her photos and starts to stand.

"No—keep working on your albums, Gigi. I have a ton of homework." I smile to show her I'm fine, and then I flee, feeling like I've swallowed something huge and it's about to claw its way out of my chest.

In my room, I switch on my lamp and collapse into my desk chair. My lists of neurotransmitters and psychopharmaceuticals and neuropeptides are strewn over my desk.

I turn the mysterious package over in my hands. I slide the card out and unfold it.

September,

Saw this and thought Dottie might like it. And look—they even had books for Bo.

—Flint

I rip into the brown paper and pull out a vintage hard-sided makeup case, about the size of a lunch box. It's covered with vibrant cherry-print fabric.

Oh *wow*. Dottie will love this. She's obsessed with cherries, and anything from the 1950s, as evidenced by the outfits she assembles from Rag House.

Underneath the cherry-print case, there are three worn paperbacks. *How to Become a Producer. How to Make Money in Showbiz. Producing for Theater.*

Flint got things for my friends. And these aren't arbitrary picks—these are things Dottie and Bo will actually love. If they were different gifts, or if he'd written something else, it'd be kind of weird, and I'd be searching for a motive. But this seems . . . genuinely kind.

Pheromones and physical attraction are one thing. I think what I'm feeling now is something else.

flint

I CLIMB INTO the Jeep on Saturday morning. Fog hangs in the air, swirling and thick, and it feels like I'm the only one in the world awake.

Surprisingly this week hasn't been that bad. There have even been a couple of mornings where my first thought wasn't about how many hours I have left. Instead, my first thoughts were of September, accompanied by a rush of light-headedness.

I pull up to the curb outside September's house. She's sitting on her front step in her signature dark red coat, scrawling something in a notebook. She doesn't spring up right away; instead, she raises one finger—*Give me a minute*—and keeps writing. I think back to the symbols and numbers she scratched onto the wall at the Ruins, and I wonder if that's what she sees in her head all the time.

My phone vibrates with a text. It's Aerys, saying, Have fun today—and don't do anything I wouldn't do!

I flush and click my screen off just as September opens the passenger-side door.

"Morning," she says, hiking herself up into the seat. She smiles at me, soft and shy, and there's something about it that cracks my heart in half.

It's clear that I'm going to need some firm reminders today. I force myself to think about the tent I bought from the general store, the one that's still stuffed in the trunk, under the false bottom where the spare tire hides.

September draws two thermoses out of her bag. "Coffee?" she asks.

"Uh, sure."

I take a sip. It's hot and laced with an outrageous amount of sugary creamer. It stuns me for a second—I haven't tasted anything as rich and sweet as this in . . . so long.

I pass the thermos back to her, and there's something so *normal* about the transaction, so comfortable. It's only our second trip, but I can suddenly see us doing this every weekend, a flickering future of road trips and dinners and games of flashlight tag stretching out in front of us—

A future I don't have.

"We're headed out to the boonies today," she says, cutting into my thoughts. "Low Wickam—two hours away. Is that okay? Not too far?"

"It's fine," I say, pushing through the tangle in my throat.

I cleared the trip with my parents this time, and they're both trying to get some work done today so they can take a day off on Monday.

For the first half hour, September and I are quiet. The world is waking up, and we are too, drinking our coffee and blinking away the night.

"Sorry I've been quiet," she says finally. "I'm not really a morning person."

"It's okay. I don't mind quiet."

"Oh," she says, turning in her seat. "Thank you for the gifts, by the way. Dottie's been carrying her cherry bag around school all week, and Bo was highlighting passages from one of the books at lunch yesterday."

"Glad they like them," I say gruffly.

"Seriously, it was really sweet of you."

I swallow, nodding awkwardly. I don't get a lot of thank-yous, and I'm not sure what to do with it.

"I still can't believe we won flashlight tag," she says, tugging her fingers through her hair. "You have to be my buddy for next month's game—Dottie wants to do it at a Christmas tree farm."

December. Christmas.

"So . . . what do you say? You in?" September asks, turning in her seat, a soft, unsuspecting smile on her face.

I won't be *alive* for Christmas.

I have to tell her.

It suddenly feels unspeakably wrong that I didn't tell her that afternoon at the Ruins. In my defense, I didn't see this coming—I thought I'd never see her again.

Telling her now will be a mess, but I have to do it.

I prepare the words in my mind, loading them on my tongue.

"September?" I croak. "There's something I need to—"

She shifts in her seat, turning to give me her full attention, and her arm brushes mine again on the center console. She took off her coat, so it's bare skin on bare skin.

At her touch, my mind goes blank.

"Flint?" she prompts.

"Huh?"

"Were you going to say something?"

"I—yeah, but I forgot what," I lie.

"It'll come back to you," she says, obliviously turning back to gaze out her window and sip from her thermos.

I'll tell her today, I promise myself.

It has to be today.

"It was actually great that you got those things for Dottie and Bo," September says after a while. "Things have been . . . a little weird between us lately."

"Weird how?"

"I guess I've been more subdued. I'm thinking about stuff more than I usually do. You know, like that feeling we talked about the other night, about time running out." She takes an unsteady breath. "There's something I don't want to tell them. Something that happened, before I came here. I feel like if I tell them, I might lose them. Not lose them totally, like they won't run screaming or anything, but that it'll never be as clean and simple as what we have now."

I nod, weighing my next words carefully.

"You never know," I say cautiously, thinking about Aerys. "I think people can handle more than you might expect of them."

The road hums under our tires.

"In my experience," I add carefully, "I've found that pretending to be okay is harder than just letting yourself wallow in it."

"Yeah," she says, picking at a seam on her skirt. "You are really not wrong about it being harder."

I wonder what she meant—*Something that happened, before I came*

144

here. But I get the feeling she doesn't even let herself think about the specifics.

"I don't know if you should be taking advice from me, though," I say. "I'm not the easiest person to be around. Or so I'm told."

"I think you're easy to be around," she says quietly.

I swallow hard, and we sit with those thoughts until we see a rusty sign that says *Low Wickam—16 miles*.

We pull off the highway and onto a narrow road riddled with potholes. The farther we cut into the countryside, the more run-down things get. Every few miles there's a steepled one-room church, and we pass dozens of slumping mobile homes set up on cinder blocks, Confederate flags waving next to collections of yard junk.

Up ahead, a peeling billboard catches my eye.

If it's your deathday
And you need someone to talk to,
Call the half-life hotline at 484-555-0169
Or visit us at www.thehalf-lifeinstitute.com/hotline

How nice. A reminder of death, even here.

And then suddenly we're passing through what must be the heart of Low Wickam: a shabby strip mall across from another shabby strip mall. That's it. That's the town.

We take the next turnoff. The Jeep grumbles over loose gravel to a small clinic shielded by towering trees.

September does her whole costume change, exactly like last time.

I can't help but wonder if this goes deeper than just wanting to look professional.

"September? You know that your clothes won't make you less of a good scientist, right?"

She looks down at her lab coat, an expression I can't decipher flitting across her face. "Sure. Um, yeah, I know," she mumbles, getting out.

I follow her to the clinic door. It's locked, but there's movement inside. September knocks, and a second later, a stout woman with tortoiseshell glasses shuffles over.

She cracks the door open a few inches. Her eyes are flinty and cold.

"You're not from around here," she says. "No appointments available, though. Dr. Deke's out at County General on an emergency call. What do you want?"

I step aside to let September work her magic.

"I'm from the Half-Life Institute," September says, cool and professional and every inch the scientist. "We need some files on a patient of yours. It shouldn't take long."

She flashes her badge at the woman, then starts to tuck it back inside her lab coat. But this time we aren't dealing with a friendly college student like Eloise in Merrybrook.

"Hold on, girl. Don't put that away just yet. Let me see." The woman leans close, squinting at September's badge.

"You're an intern," she says. "I ain't giving you the files."

September's smile stretches tight, but it doesn't waver. "Haven't you been contacted by the Institute for something like this before?"

"Sure have, and they usually do it by phone or email, so this all

146

smells a little fishy to me." She x-rays September with dull, suspicious eyes. "'Course, if you're so desperate to get these records today, I can call your boss to check."

"My boss isn't working today, unfortunately," September says coolly. I have to hand it to her; she sounds just the right amount of inconvenienced, not rattled at all. "I'll have her call you on Monday."

"Mm-hmm. You have a nice day," the woman says. The insincerity is so sour it curdles the air around us.

September speed walks back to the Jeep. I can almost feel her rattling, about to lose her composure. I pull out of the parking lot, and sure enough, she cracks as soon as the clinic is out of sight.

"Shit," she says. "What if she really does call Dr. Juncker?"

"Who?"

"My boss. Dr. Juncker. She can't find out I'm doing this. I'll get fired." She crosses and uncrosses her legs. Pumps her knees up and down. Bites her thumbnail. She's freaking out.

"I need that file," she says, her breathing getting more chaotic by the second.

"September—"

"What if she really calls? This is bad, Flint. This is really, really bad."

"She probably won't call," I say.

"We didn't even get the file," September says, and she's so wound up now, nervous worry pouring off her. She drops her head between her knees.

The solution slides into my mind as easy as smoke.

"Hey. September. Stop."

147

She doesn't hear me.

"September," I say, more firmly. "I'll steal them for you."

That gets her attention. "Flint, that's ridiculous. You can't do that."

I turn on my blinker and slow down to make a left turn. "There was a sign on the door that said they're closed for an hour-long lunch break at one. I bet that lady likes to leave for it. I say we stake out the joint, wait until she pulls out onto the main road, then I'll break in and get the file."

"Flint—that's . . . we really can't do that. It's a terrible idea."

The way she's looking at me, though, eyes sharp and glimmering with interest, suggests otherwise. She wants that file.

"I promise I won't get caught," I say. "No one will ever know I was in there."

She's quiet for a minute, still nibbling on her thumbnail.

"Are you sure?"

I nod. I didn't break all my personal rules to drive her out here just so we could come back empty-handed. And it doesn't matter if I get caught. What are they gonna do, throw me in the slammer in their stupid one-horse-town sheriff's office? Happy holidays to them when my dead body starts to stink up the place.

I have nothing to lose, and September—and maybe the world— has a lot to gain.

I turn the Jeep around and drive us back toward the clinic. I find a hidden spot to park, and then we wait.

At 12:59, the woman comes out and locks the door behind her. She doesn't spot us.

I give it five minutes to make sure she's not coming back, then I get out. There's a security camera trained on the clinic's front door, so I head carefully around the back.

No cameras here. I hesitate for a moment—*This is the stupidest idea I've ever had*—then I grab a rock and sling it through a window on the back of the building. I reach through the hole, careful to avoid the jagged edges of glass, and flip the lock from inside. I pause for a second to listen for the beep of an alarm system, but the clinic is silent.

Once I'm in, it doesn't take long to find the file September's looking for. *Marvin Ferret.* It's thinner than the one from Merrybrook, so it doesn't take much time to run it through the ancient photocopier. I sneak a glance at the last page—guy died in a knife fight, of all things. Who puts themselves in a position to be in a knife fight on their deathday? It shouldn't surprise me, though—there used to be reality TV shows where people got to choose their own death from a range of wild options. Not long after that, a law was passed against showing real deaths on-screen.

When I'm done photocopying, I place the file back where I found it and run back to the Jeep. We peel out at 1:16, long before the receptionist will return from lunch.

Adrenaline blurs the next fifteen minutes into an edgy, ultra-bright montage. I just *drive*, struggling to stay under the speed limit, casting glances at my rearview. September twists in her seat, watching behind us too.

"Holy shit. I can't believe you just did that," she says once we're far enough away from the clinic to breathe.

For the first time ever, with this electric chaos flowing through my veins, I think I might understand why people who half-life young do stupid shit.

September flips through the file, giddy with our victory. "This is amazing, Flint. Thank you so much."

Without taking her eyes off the report, she reaches out absently to squeeze my leg, just above my knee. Her touch glitters through me. It's even better than the adrenaline.

september

I LEAN MY head against the window, letting the afternoon sun paint fireworks behind my closed eyelids. I'm exhausted—I must be crashing after the chaos of Flint stealing the file.

I drift, warm in the sunlight. And then I'm dreaming.

Can you call it dreaming when it's a memory? Because what I'm seeing now is so detailed—and fully faithful to the day it happened. A day I try so hard not to remember.

The sun shines in a perfect blue sky, glinting off the dented metal slide at our neighborhood playground.

"Tember, look!" a voice calls.

Maybelle.

I'm sitting on the swing next to hers, but my phone pinged a minute ago with a newsletter from the National Institutes of Health, and I stopped swinging to read it.

"Tember," Maybelle says again, whining now.

"Just a second," I say. I've lost my place in the newsletter—I have to go back and read part of it again.

I wish I'd just looked.

Dad lifts Maybelle out of her swing, and she totters over to the slide. She calls for me again, pointing for me to stand at the bottom to catch her. I grit my teeth but slide my phone into my pocket.

In the dream, she's two-year-old Maybelle, with huge blue eyes and curly copper hair that matches mine. She's becoming more of a person now, finally. Before she was born, I filled a notebook with a list of the sister stuff we'd do together: building forts and having sleepovers, spa days and road trips when we got older. I still want to do all of that, but it's taking a long time for her to get to the point where I can even really interact with her.

"You got her?" Dad asks, and I nod, in position.

I'm looking up at her when it happens.

Her eyes go glassy and unfocused. A little shudder ripples through her small body. And then she starts seizing.

I move first, straight up the slide, my shoes squeaking on the metal. I get there before she goes down. I hold her head in my hands as she shakes. Dad's there, pinning her legs, her arms.

Not her not her not her anyone but her. Please.

And then it's over. Maybelle blinks awake, confused. She doesn't know what just happened. She doesn't know what the half-life is or what the word *death* really means.

But I know.

She cries on the walk home because we're too stunned to talk to her. Dad carries her, and the expression on his face is the most terrifying thing I've seen in my life. Maybelle's eyes are wide and locked on mine, flooded with tears and confusion, pleading for me to help her understand, to explain why Daddy's acting weird, but I can't speak.

Mom didn't believe us when we got home. For days, she tried to convince us that we were wrong about what we saw. We weren't.

My heart constricts. I can't breathe. *Maybelle.*

Two years old. We'd only ever get four years of her.

All of those things I'd written in my notebook—gone in an instant.

A voice slices into the dream, saying my name, but it's not right. This voice doesn't belong here.

"September?"

The dream tilts. My body slumps forward as real life pulls me back. I blink open my eyes, and I'm not at the park anymore; I'm in a car, the front seat of a car, and—

Flint.

The Jeep is stopped. We're pulled over on the side of the highway. A car whizzes past us, honking angrily. Flint stares, his eyes boring into me with worry, panic, fear.

"I pulled over," he says. "You were breathing really hard. And—crying."

I touch my cheeks. They're wet.

I never cried. Not when she half-lifed, and not when she died. There were times that I wanted to, but I had to hold my parents together. I think I was afraid that once I started, I'd never stop.

I stare at my damp fingertips. I cried, and I wasn't even awake for it.

It felt so real.

The tears are fighting to spill out all over again. The sob is in my throat, ready to unleash.

No.

If I break down now, I won't be able to prove my hypothesis.

I pull away from the sympathy written all over Flint's face. "Stop—stop *looking* at me like that."

"September, whatever happened, you can—"

"It was just a bad dream," I say firmly.

Flint's silent for a long moment, studying me. "A bad dream."

"Yeah. I can't even remember all of it," I lie.

Flint nods, but his stare is so piercing I have to look away.

I dump my stuff on the kitchen table when I get home. I have a stack of group chat messages from Dottie and Bo, but I don't have the energy to respond.

Where did that dream come from? My memories of Maybelle are getting dangerously close to the surface, and the masks I rely on are getting harder to hoist back into place.

She's gone.

Thick sorrow climbs up my chest, until I might scream with it.

Somewhere in the house, a door opens, followed by voices. Gigi and one of her clients.

"All right, honey, I'll see you in two weeks for a touch-up, okay?" I hear her say.

I shake my head fiercely, just in time to dislodge the darkness. Gigi bustles into the kitchen in her black hairdresser's apron.

She knows something's wrong as soon as she sees me. "Tember, what is it?"

I hoist up the fake smile. "Nothing. Your day going okay?"

She studies me for a second. I can't look her in the eye. It'll make me fall apart.

We're supposed to act like we're fine. From the moment I moved in, that was our unspoken plan. To act like we didn't just have something devastating happen.

"Is this about your sister?" Gigi says softly.

The room goes painfully still.

Gigi reaches out to take my limp hand. "You know if you ever need to talk to anyone about Maybelle, you can let me know, right?"

But the way she says Maybelle's name, without a hitch, without a trace of heartbreak—it lights an angry flame in my stomach. Maybe I'm not like Gigi at all. Her smile isn't a mask. Her friendliness to her clients is warm and real, not a tool she's using to hide something else.

It makes no sense. I know she loved Maybelle, but Gigi doesn't seem to have anything like this festering wound I have on my heart. Every day, I bandage it, but it refuses to heal. Sometimes wounds need to air, but I know better: I can't take the gauze off, or I'll bleed to death. I know that, the same way I know that you can describe exponential decay with $N(t) = N_0 e^{kt}$, that the melting point of Mercury is -37.89 degrees Fahrenheit, that the force of gravity on Earth is 9.807 meters per second squared.

My parents don't even bother with gauze. They're constantly picking at the ragged edges of their wounds. They still live in that same house in Colorado. They've kept Maybelle's room just as it was on the day she died. Her kid-sized bed is there, dust gathering on her pillow, on the trio of stuffed pigs in the corner. Her dirty clothes are still in the laundry basket. Her last bedtime story on the arm of the rocking chair, her baby spoons in the cutlery drawer, her sippy cups in the cupboard, her—

I suppress a scream.

I'm here, in Pennsylvania, because I couldn't bear to be there.

"Tember?" Gigi's eyes are full of sympathy. Pity.

I stiffen. Why does it seem like her wound has already scabbed over and shined into a scar?

I suck in a steadying breath. I'm not my parents. They're a disaster over Maybelle, and I can't afford to be. Today another floor of patients at the Institute died who this hypothesis might have been able to save.

I lost my sister, but it's not going to happen to anyone else. I'm going to work on this hypothesis, or the next, or the next, or whatever it takes, until no one ever has to lose their Maybelle to the half-life again.

september

MARVIN FERRET'S RECORDS take over my life.

Sharpie in hand, I fill another wall of my bedroom with equations, subtheories, and half-life calculations.

Every isotope of an element has a half-life. A measurable, predictable rate of decay. The one most people have heard of is carbon-14, because that's what's measured in carbon dating, but they probably wouldn't know its half-life is 5,730 years. I can tell you that the half-life of Astatine-213 is less than a microsecond, which means hardly anyone's ever seen it. I can tell you that the half-life of Tellurium-128 is over 160 trillion times greater than the age of the *universe*. You name the element, I can tell you what its half-life is. In some non-scientific, weirdly spiritual place, I wonder if I'm the perfect person for this research, for this moment in history.

The chemical half-life, the human half-life . . . there's a connection between the two, I know it.

I tap my phone. *Midnight.* I mumble a curse. I've been poring over Marvin's file for hours, and I feel like I've made no progress. Why haven't I found a connection between Mitsuki Adams and Marvin Ferret yet? Sure, there are some similarities, medicines they both took, but none of the elements in them would have broken down into anything that can cross the blood-brain barrier.

I trudge through the moonlit stillness of the house. In the kitchen, I make a cup of coffee—I can get another couple of hours of work in and still wake up in time for school. Probably. I turn back to my room, and that's when I notice the square of yellow light shining through the trees.

Flint.

I pick up my coat and slide the back door open.

There's something different about the air tonight—something heavier. Barometric pressure, I tell myself, or the full moon. Through the trees, Flint's living room light still blazes. If it's him, and not his parents, he won't know I'm here—my house is dark.

I bite my lip.

I don't know what makes me do it, but I wave my hand so the old motion-detector light snicks on. Weak light floods over the worn deck. I wait, listening hard.

A minute passes. And then—I see him. His ink-black silhouette is so familiar to me now. I know his loping gait, the hands-shoved-into-pockets shape of him. I watch as Flint picks his way through the trees, over the creek, and up the slope to my house.

There's a moment when he stops being a shadow and becomes a boy.

He pauses, hovering just outside the shallow pool of my porch light. Is this really the same boy I spent two entire days in a car with? Our acquaintanceship, or whatever this is, is strange. Sometimes I feel unbearably close to him, but then I remember that I hardly know him.

He stares, gaze unwavering, his soft Vantablack hair eating up the moonlight. God, maybe I'm still asleep. I'm afraid to speak, for fear it'll break the dream, but someone has to say something.

"Do you want to come inside?" I ask, my voice hushed.

He looks at my house, considering. He shakes his head no and holds out a hand instead.

I hesitate for a moment—then I take it.

Flint leads us down to the edge of the creek that runs between our houses. It feels like we're sleepwalking. Everything seems blurrier than it should be, the sounds of the forest hushed, the bubbling rush of the water soft at the edges. Even the leaves are quiet underfoot tonight.

Flint lets go of my hand and sits on a felled tree trunk. I sit next to him, close enough that our shoulders touch.

For a while, we just watch the water.

"I couldn't sleep," he says finally, quietly. The rolling timbre of his voice is like a warm fire in a cozy cabin.

"Same," I say. "I haven't had a good night's sleep in . . . in a long time."

The fog of sorrow that's always surrounding him seems to throb and darken. I wonder if I leaned a little closer, if it would be quieter inside it. If it would feel like letting go.

It still feels so familiar, that darkness, even though he's on the other side of his grief. He's facing his loss, and mine is in my past.

"Hey," I whisper.

He turns his head, settles that intense stare on me.

"I want you to know . . . It's really nice, never feeling like I have to pretend to be bright and bubbly with you. I used to be bright and bubbly all the time, genuinely, but lately it's just been an act."

"I'm glad," he says, low and serious like always.

I can't tear my eyes away.

"I wanted to help you, the other day in the car," Flint says carefully. "I wish you would have let me."

I open my mouth to respond, but there's something about the night, and the way he carries his own grief, that makes me give him a little more.

"You know the thing I don't want to tell Dottie and Bo?" I ask, choosing my words carefully. He nods. "Well, where I used to live, people knew. When they found out, they distanced themselves from me almost immediately."

"I know the feeling," he says. "It's like poison, isn't it? It seeps into everything around you."

I nod. "I had a best friend there. We'd been inseparable since kindergarten. After she found out, she just . . . stopped talking to me."

"Some people can't handle it. Or they just don't want to handle it."

He's quiet for a long moment. "September?"

"Mmm?"

"I can handle it," he says softly.

His calm, steady look almost has me telling him that I used to have a sister.

Almost has me telling him how she half-lifed. How she died.

Flint's eyes stay locked on mine. I unpeel the bandages, ready to show him the raw edges of the wound that losing Maybelle left on me.

But I forgot how heavily it's still bleeding.

"I can't," I choke out. "I'm sorry, I can't."

He reaches out, but my defenses are already back up. My hands don't get the message, though, and they latch on to his, clenching tight.

"It doesn't have to be me that you talk to about it," he says, with a gentleness that almost breaks me. "But trying to avoid it—whatever it is—it'll just eat you alive."

I can't speak.

I look down at our hands, and it makes me desperate for something I can't define.

After he loses his mom, he'll have the same wound as me, and maybe then we can make something out of this. Maybe he can be the thing I hold on to when I go dark, and I can be that for him.

"I can't," I whisper. "Not yet."

"I understand," he murmurs.

And, because he's always surrounded by that cloud of grief, for the first time in my life, I think that maybe someone actually does.

flint

SEPTEMBER'S SHIVERING. WHATEVER this is that she's carrying, she's going to have to deal with it—and soon. It's about to shatter her.

After a while, her grip on my hand loosens, but she doesn't pull it away. I think we're just going to pretend it's normal to be sitting here in the middle of the night holding hands. Which is fine with me—I don't want to let go either.

"You came out of nowhere," she says, shaking her head in disbelief. "I'm not like this with anyone else."

I give her a wry, half-hearted smile. "I came from Philadelphia."

She lets out a weak laugh. "You know what I mean."

"I've been thinking the same thing about you, you know," I say.

I certainly didn't expect . . . whatever this is, in my last few weeks alive.

September looks down. "I didn't come out of nowhere either. I moved in with Gigi when I got my internship. I'm from Colorado."

"Huh. I can see it." It seems so fitting, like she was sculpted out of sunset-soaked mountains and the crisp autumn air there.

She shivers again. "I seriously don't know how you can stand to be out here without a jacket."

I turn her hands over in mine, about to sandwich them to warm them up—and notice that the lacy sleeves poking out from under her coat are black.

"You never wear black," I say.

She shrugs. "First time for everything."

Something flinches in me. God—is even being near me leaching the color out of this girl?

I untangle my hands from hers, feeling suddenly hopeless. In twenty days, I have to pack up my camping gear and set off into these woods, leaving everything behind me so I can die without traumatizing anyone. Including her.

"Hey," she says softly. "What's happening? You're going all . . . gray and serious again."

"Nothing's happening," I mutter.

The touch of her fingertips under my chin is gentle, but it gives me a mild electric shock nonetheless. But instead of turning my face toward hers, she guides my chin up so I'm looking at the night sky.

"Sometimes it's easier to surrender to it," she says. "But sometimes you just have to ignore it and *be* here. Look."

The stars are cold above us. It's a beauty bigger than anything in our small, earthbound lives.

I breathe, and the night air feels clean in my lungs.

What is it about this girl that makes it possible to slow down? To look and listen and *enjoy*? For eight years, I've been nothing but control. I've kept myself from eating my favorite foods, listening to my favorite music, reading anything but the most depressing Russian literature. She's taking a wrecking ball to the boy I was when I rolled into Carbon Junction.

The longer we look up at the moon, the more grateful I feel to be here. Grateful is dangerous—the more I love the world, the more I'll miss it when I go.

"Something feels weird about tonight," September says. "I thought it was the moon, but now . . . I don't know."

We turn away from the sky at the same time, and our eyes meet.

For a long, breathless moment, we're locked in it.

Then, as if in a trance, she lifts her hand. Her first touch is light. Just a brush on my forehead as she tucks my hair aside. The moment feels as fragile as a butterfly landing on a fingertip.

Slowly, ever so carefully, she rakes her fingers through my hair.

I can barely keep my eyes open. It feels *incredible*.

Her stare throbs with a question. *What's happening here?*

I can't give her an answer. All I know is that the cold is gone.

Most of the time, I can act like a normal person around her— well, a normal *me*—but we keep having these moments where I just get swamped with . . . this. Like at the abandoned resort, pressed up against each other in the dark.

Her fingers comb through my hair one more time. Sparks crackle over my head and down my spine, an almost unbearable pressure blooming in me.

She pulls away, but she doesn't go far. She leans her head on my shoulder, and I stay very still, marveling at the rush of heat coursing through my body.

"I should go back inside before I fall asleep on your shoulder," she says, a note of reluctance in her whisper-soft voice. "Every time I close my eyes, I see half-life calculations on the backs of my eyelids."

I glance up at the cabin. "I think I'll stay out here a little longer."

A cold breeze sweeps down over the creek, and this time it's me who shivers. Beside me, September starts wriggling, and then something heavy's being placed on my shoulders.

She's taken off her coat and draped it on me.

"September—"

"You can give it back tomorrow. Night, Flint," she says, the faintest smile on her lips.

I watch her weave through the trees and climb up her porch steps. She turns back and gives a small wave, and then she goes inside.

The forest stills, and I wait for the burn inside me to cool.

I drop my face into my hands. I came to Carbon Junction thinking I could just . . . check out. Disengage. Things are not going according to plan.

Even with September's coat around my shoulders, it's too cold to stay out here. I sigh and stand up.

When I slip back into the cabin, the living room is empty. I switch all the lights off, lock all the doors. In my room, I check my stockpile of camping supplies.

Twenty days left.

I fall asleep with September's coat in my arms, my nose tucked into the collar, because it smells like her.

september

"DIFFERENT PLAN TODAY," Dr. Juncker announces as Percy and I convene in her office. "Mr. Bassingthwaighte, you're to assist the doctors on the third floor. Ms. Harrington, two things: I need you to call Cedars-Sinai and have them send over all files on a patient named Araminta Kovak. Then, at four o'clock, I'm presenting to Institute staff in preparation for peer review—you can assist me there. Meet me in the lecture hall after you've made the call, please."

She picks up her laptop and is gone before we can ask for more details.

Percy's pissed, which is convenient—when he's mad, he doesn't bother me. Presentations in the lecture hall are a big deal, almost as big as being a key speaker at a biomedical conference. How did I not clock that this was happening today? Oh well, at least I'll get to watch it, unlike Percy.

I boot up the computer and sigh. I'm perpetually exhausted these days. Last night, I found a few surface connections between Marvin and Mitsuki—like courses of antibiotics, standard childhood vaccinations—but nothing that would affect them in biologically significant ways long-term.

I type the name Dr. Juncker gave me into the Global Death Archive. *Araminta Kovak.*

Birthday, deathday, okay—wait—what's this?

She's an anomaly.

A giddy bolt of adrenaline surges through me. I pick up the office phone and punch in the number we have on record as the direct line to Cedars-Sinai's archival department.

The phone call takes less than five minutes. Cedars-Sinai has one of the most sophisticated digital archives around, and I imagine they get asked for Araminta Kovak's file a lot, seeing as she's an anomaly. She didn't show up in my search because I'd narrowed it down to within three hundred miles—Cedars-Sinai is in Los Angeles. Two minutes after I hang up the call, the plucky ding of my internship email goes off.

There it is—a 183-page PDF attachment.

For a minute I can only sit there and stare at it, stunned.

This is a *huge* stroke of luck. All I have to do is forward this PDF to my personal email, then delete the record that I sent it to myself.

How did this land right in my lap? I'm in disbelief. I have an entire new anomaly file. I've been struggling to link the Mitsuki and Marvin files, and a third data set for comparison will make a huge difference. I can't wait to tell Flint; he's going to—

I freeze.

Does this mean . . . we don't need to drive out to any more hospitals? I can't figure out how I feel about that. But the more files, the more data I have to work with.

My decision doesn't have anything to do with how it felt to run my fingers through Flint's hair, or how something sparked in my stomach when our eyes met and held. Something changed between us out there in the woods. I felt like the real me. I was messy, with no part of me neatly in its compartmentalized box. I'm still reeling.

I press my eyes closed, trying to shake off the rush of chemicals hitting my bloodstream. It's becoming clear to me that I really cannot think about him while I'm at work.

I lock the computer and head downstairs. The lecture hall on the Institute's ground floor is huge, complete with tiered seating and vaulted ceiling, and it's humming with excitement. I take my place at a small desk to the side of the podium, ready to pop up with whatever Dr. Juncker needs during the presentation. She nods brusquely at me, takes a few minutes to brief me on the handouts I'll be in charge of passing around, then stands near the door, greeting her colleagues as they file in.

Two minutes before she's supposed to start speaking, her phone rings.

Something about the way she answers makes me sit up and take notice. She goes very still, then turns her back to the room. I'm the only person who can see her face and hear her respond in German. The call is short, and even though I can't understand a word of it, I can read her body language. Something's seriously shaken her.

When she hangs up the phone, her hands are unsteady. She brushes a single stoic tear away from the corner of her eye.

I'm mortified. I glance at the audience—won't they lose respect for her if they see this?

But I don't have to worry. I watch as Dr. Juncker steels herself, turns back to the podium, and leans into the mic. When she launches into her lecture, her voice is as composed as ever. She clicks her presentation from slide to slide, reporting her findings to a roomful of the smartest scientists in the world. I'm the only one who sees how, behind the podium, she's clenching her phone in a death grip.

Dr. Juncker's presentation is a huge success, and I end up staying at the Institute until eight helping her. She leans on me more than she ever has before, treating me like a real assistant and relying on me to distribute her materials. She even lets me field some questions from the other scientists milling around waiting for a turn to speak to her.

When I finally slide off my lab coat and push out through the Institute's glass doors, it's dark. Carbon Junction twinkles below me. I check my phone, but I don't have any messages, and I don't even have any English homework tonight. I breathe in, and the air is cold and clean, almost purely nitrogen and oxygen. I've got a fresh anomaly file to work on.

I'm halfway down Main, power walking toward home, when I see the familiar peeling paintwork of Dottie's ancient silver Corolla. She must have just left work. She turned out from a side street and is heading away from me. I speed up, hoping she'll catch the next red light or see me in her rearview. I'm bursting with the anomaly news, even though the person I'm really aching to tell is Flint.

I'm about to pull out my phone to call Dottie when the Corolla swerves into a parking spot in front of the Liberty—the art deco cinema that only shows indie films.

I frown. Maybe she's picking up dinner from the restaurant next door?

But then the passenger door opens, and Bo gets out. I stop dead in my tracks.

Dottie locks her car, and they convene on the sidewalk. I can hear their laughter, more familiar to me than my own, carrying through the cold air.

I dig out my phone. Maybe I missed the text.

But there's still nothing.

They didn't invite me.

They walk up to the Liberty's glass ticket booth, bouncing on their toes in the cold.

I did this, I realize, with a strychnine numbness seeping through me. $C_{21}H_{22}N_2O_2$. I've been so wrapped up in my internship and my research and Flint, they assumed I'd be busy.

Or maybe this is because of the chasm that's been widening between us, the crack that opened when words started rising from deep inside me that I couldn't say.

I could take a step toward them. I could tell them everything. I could say, *I'm sorry I've been weird; I thought I was good with the whole dead-sister business but turns out not.*

Bo turns around as Dottie's paying for her ticket, blowing on his hands to warm them and watching the cars pass by, and the urge to duck into an alley to hide is strong.

I lean against the nearest wall. It's suddenly hard to breathe.

Maybe I'm overreacting. It's not a big deal. They were friends before I got here. Maybe they do stuff like this all the time without me.

I just thought we were a trio.

I watch them from far away, thanking the ticket seller, and the distance between us feels insurmountable.

The group chat lights up my phone at eleven thirty, while I'm combing through the Araminta PDF.

DOTTIE: Hey, are we waffling tomorrow?

My bruised heart just wants to ignore it. Ghost them, even though they took me under their wing when I moved here, broken and alone, no questions asked.

But if I ignore them, I'm not sure I'll ever be able to salvage the bright, uncomplicated friendship I had with them.

SEPTEMBER: Sure.

And then I get an idea.

SEPTEMBER: Can I bring Flint?

Having him there might keep me occupied enough not to slip into something dark. He's got a monopoly on that, and I'll look bright in comparison.

BO: ABSOLUTELY yes.

BO: To both waffling and bringing Flint.

DOTTIE: Yes. And I cannot believe you still haven't caught us up. Are you guys hanging out a lot?

SEPTEMBER: A little.

It's the truth. We've only seen each other a handful of times. We just tend to spend hours together on those occasions.

No one types anything for a few minutes, and I realize that the way I answered her question was pretty terse.

SEPTEMBER: Sorry, working on science stuff. But more soon.

I add a few hearts to soften it, then put my phone down.

I was going to do a bit more work, but instead I turn off my desk lamp and crawl into bed.

september

I'M TUCKED INTO the corner of our regular booth at Le Belgique. Bo's sitting next to me, and Dottie's across from us, but I can't dig my way into their conversation, and neither of them mentions the movie they went to last night, which for some reason feels even worse.

My leg jackhammers under the table as we wait for Flint, anticipation winding me up tight.

I hear the ting of the bell over the door, and then there he is, stepping out of the rain and into the restaurant. I feel instantly alive, a mess of chemistry wrapped in skin.

Dottie and Bo clock him a second later.

"Holy mother of god," Bo says, and I elbow him before he wolf whistles or does something equally embarrassing.

At the door, Flint nods, acknowledging us, then makes his way to our table.

We all stand, a weird little welcoming party.

"Girl, you've got it so bad," Dottie squeals. "You've been totally checked out since we got here, but you lit up like a Broadway marquee when he came in!"

"Shut up," I mutter, just in time, because Flint's here, towering over us. We do a round of hellos and hugs next to the table. When Flint shuffles in front of me, I almost step back and say an

173

awkward *hey*, but it'd be weird if I didn't give him a hug. So I launch myself up onto my tiptoes, and Flint's arms slide around my waist.

We both hold on for a second longer than is probably socially acceptable.

Bo grabs Flint's arm. "You're sitting next to me, mister. Us bros need to spend some bro time together, right?"

The term *bro* sounds ludicrous coming from Bo, but Flint just swallows, his Adam's apple bobbing, and says, "Sure."

"Okay, so I have to tell you that your boots kick serious ass," Dottie says to Flint as we all settle in our seats. "You should come by Rag House; I can work you up an outfit to go with them." She rubs her chin. "Might be tough, though. You seem much older than your years."

Flint raises an eyebrow. "Saying someone's older than their years just means they ran out of dopamine early."

Bo barks out a laugh. "That's dark. But I kind of love it."

The conversation plows on, and Flint holds up astoundingly well without any help from me.

And then, across the aisle from us, a family of four slides into a booth.

It had to be two girls. Sisters.

The older sister is on her phone, and for the entire two minutes that I watch them, she doesn't acknowledge her younger sister at all. The little girl is in a grass-stained baseball uniform and cleats, playing with her silverware like she wishes someone would pay a shred of attention to her.

The dyspnea hits first—the shortness of breath—making me instantly dizzy, and I know what's next, the—

Under the table, Flint covers my knee with his palm.

I go very, very still.

He squeezes, a gentle pressure, and I stop spiraling. I can focus again. Above the table, he's looking at me. It feels like steady ground, like I was being swept downstream but then caught hold of an immovable boulder.

That's the thing about his sadness. It's quiet and still and constant. It's exactly what I need right now. My own grief feels like chaos, like something too messy and enormous for me to handle.

Flint keeps his hand on my knee for a few minutes, his palm warm through my tights, until I can pick up my end of my conversation with Dottie and Bo. That's when his hand slides away.

Bo launches into an update on *Pippin*. He was right; the kid who half-lifed dropped out. My heart aches for that boy. Then Bo casually drops that his *boyfriend*, Troy, will be taking on the lead role, and we all erupt into cheers and congratulations.

After a few minutes, Dottie peers across the table. "Whatcha doing over there?" she asks Flint.

Flint flushes, then produces a beautiful paper airplane folded from the menu. I cock my head—this is the second aviation-related thing with him.

"That looks advanced," Bo says. "Will it fly?"

Flint scoffs. "Of course it'll fly." He lifts his arm, wrist poised, taking aim. The airplane soars over the heads at the next table, banks left in the updraft over the waffle makers, and lands on a table where a middle-aged couple is drearily forking food into their mouths. They freeze when the airplane lands on the man's stack of waffles. They look around, baffled, as the man picks the plane out of his maple syrup.

We dissolve into silent giggles, trying not to look suspicious.

"Will you make me one?" Dottie asks like an eager kid.

"Sure," Flint says, and he folds another menu into a different style of paper airplane, origami skill level. Where did he learn this?

Finally, when Dottie and Bo get going on some other conversation, Flint looks over at me.

You okay? he mouths.

I nod.

And then, under the table, Flint's knee brushes against mine.

My eyes flick up to his. Surprise flashes over his face—unlike the hand on my knee earlier, he hadn't meant to do that.

He shifts, and the contact is lost.

I'm not ready to let it go. I edge forward on my seat.

When my knee finds his, he pierces me with a stare so intense it feels more real than where our bodies are touching.

After one stuttering moment, he leans in, and his knee slides up the outside of my leg. I can feel the roughness of his jeans through my tights. The sensation drags through every nerve in my body.

I shift a glance to Dottie and Bo, but they're like kids at Christmas, using the restaurant crayons to color in the paper airplane. They have no idea what's going on under the table just inches away from them.

When Flint adds his other leg, catching my legs between his and pressing, I nearly dissolve.

Dottie chooses that moment to notice. "Are you feeling okay, babes?" she asks.

I'm so flustered I can barely answer. "Fine. Just fine."

The waiter comes over, finally, and Flint and I draw apart, but he keeps my feet sandwiched between his. When it's his turn to order, he asks if he can have another glass of water and a piece of toast.

We all gawk at him. You cannot ask for a piece of toast at Le Belgique.

"I'll order for him," I say, cutting in. Flint starts to protest, but I hold up a hand. "No arguments. You'll like this, I promise."

While we wait for our food, a thought nags at me. Ordering toast and water . . . the way he bristles every time I offer him a butterscotch—is he intentionally depriving himself of sensations? It's kind of like . . . he's punishing himself for something? That can't be right.

When the stack of Dutch apple cinnamon waffles comes, piled with stewed apples and scoops of ice cream and drizzled with toffee sauce, he stares down at it with a defeated look.

When he takes his first bite, I know I have him.

"Good?" I ask.

He savors his bite, looking like he might die of pleasure.

He leans across the table, and Dottie and Bo and the rest of the restaurant may as well not be there for how focused we are on each other.

"Don't think I won't get you back for this," he says, his dark eyes boring into me, pinning me against my seat.

I'm burning up. *Can't wait*, I think.

As I watch him devour the waffles, I realize . . . I want more of this. I don't want our friendship—or whatever this is—to end after I finish my research.

flint

AFTER THE NIGHT at Le Belgique, one thing becomes very clear:
I'm a mess for September Harrington.

I keep having these weird giddy rushes, and I wonder if it's something that happens when you're getting close to the end or if it's just
September.

I'm starting to get antsy, cooped up in this house. What did
September say down by the creek? *Sometimes you just have to ignore it
and be here.* Maybe I can let myself enjoy a few small things and still
handle my death.

If I were to let myself have a little fun . . . what would that
involve?

An idea strikes. I sit on the edge of my bed and text Aerys.

> FLINT: Hey. Want to hang out after school?

My thumb hovers over the send button. Every instinct I've had in
the last eight years tells me this is a bad idea.

Screw it. I hit send.

Her response comes back in seconds.

> AERYS: YES!!! School gets out at 2:45, want to pick me
> up? ALSO I'M REALLY HAPPY ABOUT THIS.

A second text comes through a minute later.

> AERYS: Proud of you, you miserable old hermit.

I smirk, then grab my keys. For the first time, I'm going to be the one to go to her, instead of the other way around. There's just one place I need to visit first.

I pull into a visitor spot at Carbon Junction High at 2:42.

Even brick walls can't muffle the shriek of the school bell, and seconds later, a million kids in a million coats spill from every orifice of the building.

I scan for a head of bright copper hair, even though I know September leaves early to go to the Institute.

Aerys bounds up to the Jeep's passenger door and raps on the window, startling me.

"Have you finally seen the light?" she asks as she climbs in. "Are we about to go on an epic party road trip?"

"No road trip, unfortunately, but I got something for us to do this afternoon." I nod at the back seat.

Aerys tugs on one of the brown paper bags. She reaches in and pulls out the first box—a video game that she wanted for Christmas eight years ago but didn't get, and the console to play it on.

"No way!" She cranes around to look at the three other bags on the back seat. "Are those all games?"

"Yep. Well, that and a metric shit-ton of old-school candy. Still got those beanbags in your basement?"

"Hell yes."

Half an hour later, as we're getting everything set up, she asks about developments with September, and I tell her about Low Wickam, the conversation by the creek, and dinner at the waffle house. Her reactions are a little skewed—she still thinks September knows about my half-life.

I'm a lot better at the games now than I was when I was eight. My hands are busy, and the smell of the basement is oddly comforting, and Aerys is bobbing her head to the music.

This is . . . really nice.

"Hey, Aerys?"

"Mm?"

"I'm glad we're doing this."

"Me too," she says.

"Hey, pause it for a sec," I say. When I'm sure I have her attention, I speak again. "You know the day I left Carbon Junction? I cried on my Action Man's head when we passed your house on the way out of town. It permanently messed up the fuzziness of it."

She swallows and looks down. "Thank you for finally telling me something real," she says quietly.

We play in contented silence for a while, and I'm more at peace than I've been in a long time. Maybe this whole *living* thing isn't such a bad idea after all.

Aerys hums. "So now that you're fun and all—"

"I wouldn't go that far," I say.

She rolls her eyes. "Now that you're *bearable*, there's a big party on Friday up at the Castle. We should go."

I sigh. "I don't know, Aer. Parties aren't really my scene."

"If it helps sway the decision, a certain trio *always* shows up at these."

My stupid lungs do something funny at the mention of September. Maybe if she's there, then I could handle—

Wait. There's no way I can go to that party. If the two of them meet—if they realize they both know me—I'm screwed.

"I'll think about it," I lie.

I make sure to get home before my parents clock off work, and I've got an entire meal's worth of fried chicken and mashed potatoes in tow.

I drop the car keys on the shelf by the door.

"Guys? I'm back," I call.

No one answers.

"Mom?"

Still nothing. My voice echoes through the house.

I'm thinking maybe they went out to eat when I hear the faint sound of laughter. I go to the back porch window.

My parents are here after all, in the woods beyond the back porch. Dad's chopping firewood on the stump. He splits another log, then steps back and says something that makes Mom, who's leaning against a tree, smile. Most of her smiles are sad these days, watered down, but this one's not quite so weak.

Dad brushes wood chips off the stump, then lays the ax down. He steps forward to rub Mom's arm, in sort of a comforting way. And then he winds his arm around her waist and kisses her.

I look away, embarrassed by the sweetness.

I'm happy for them, I am. I'm happy that they'll have a life after me.

I can't stop staring at September's house.

I'm sitting at the breakfast bar, looking out over the back porch.

It's been two days since dinner at the waffle house. Impatience crawls under my skin—we're supposed to be going to another hospital tomorrow morning, but I'm not sure I can wait that long to see her.

Damn it. I'll just go over for five minutes—I want to see how the research is going.

At least that's what I tell myself as I'm stepping over the creek and scaling the rise to the purple house.

I rap my knuckles on the cold glass. There's a sizzle of *WTF am I doing here*, but a minute later, a sleepy September slides open the door, rubbing her eyes.

"Hi," I say.

"Hi."

Something swells in the air between us. God, whenever I'm around her, I feel like I'm trying to solve a math problem while on a roller coaster.

"I just came to see how the research was going," I blurt.

"It's . . . going." She casts a glance down the hallway behind her. "You can come see if you want."

I hesitate. *Five minutes*, I tell myself.

"Sure," I say.

She leads me down the hallway and into her bedroom. Stepping over the threshold into the messy, cozy space that is all September makes my heart stutter.

Once we're in, she points at the wall behind me.

"Holy shit," I say.

The wall is entirely covered with the same sorts of things she drew on the stones at the Ruins.

She shifts a few sticky notes around. "I stayed up most of last night combing through Araminta's records. No connections yet between Mitsuki and Marvin, but I'm hoping this third one's the key."

"Hold on—third one? Who's Araminta?" I ask.

"Oh—um, Dr. Juncker asked me to get her a patient file the other day, and it turned out to be an anomaly case. I forwarded the PDF to myself, which is maybe a little bit illegal, but it's all good because now we have three data sets instead of two." She looks up at me, something like guilt tempering her obvious excitement at getting another anomaly file.

"That's . . . great news." I swallow, then cringe at how loud it sounds in the silence. "I guess you have all the information you need, then, right?"

She looks down. "I'm not sure. I was actually kind of thinking . . . four files is better than three, right?"

She lifts her eyes and looks right at me. Maybe it's stupid, but the fragile hope in her expression makes me wonder if our trips have been entirely about getting the files. Maybe she's as open to another excuse to spend a day together as I am.

I nod slowly. "Four is definitely better than three. So . . . still on for tomorrow?"

She smiles. "Yes."

Something unknots in me—our next trip is still in the cards.

I point at the equations on the wall. "Anything good yet?"

"No, not really. And I've been coming at it from every angle. And I'm about to fail English because I can't shake my brain out of science mode during school." She collapses onto her bed.

"Maybe you need an actual break—like outside of this room," I say. And, because Aerys mentioned it yesterday and it's still fresh in my mind, I say, "Maybe you should go to that big party at the Castle tonight."

She shakes her head. "I have too much work to do. I mean, just think—people are dying today, tomorrow, the next day. Every delay on my part is someone's *actual* life."

"I know," I say.

Trust me, I know.

She considers it. Glances at her formula wall and grimaces again.

"Fine. I'll go change," she says. She pushes off her bed. She's about to breeze past me to her closet, but then she stops and touches my shoulder.

A frame from our moonlight scene the other night—her hands in my hair, our bodies unbearably close—seems to crystallize in the air between us, then vanish.

"You're not wearing black," she says softly.

I look down. I'm wearing a gray shirt, and she's right, it looks weird. I snagged it off the rack last night when I went to pick up some groceries with my mom. If Mom thought it was imprudent to buy a new shirt so close to my deathday, she didn't say anything. *Maybe they'll bury me in it,* the old, morbid side of me thinks.

September blinks like she's shaking out of a dream, then she disappears into the bathroom across the hall. I'm alone in her room. The space feels awkward without her, and it takes quite a lot of effort

185

to steer my thoughts away from the fact that she is *changing* across the hallway.

I rub my hand over my jaw.

So much for five minutes, you absolute idiot.

Going to the Castle is a terrible idea. But ever since I met September, I seem to be fond of throwing myself headfirst into terrible ideas.

flint

FROM THE OUTSIDE, the Castle looks foreboding and silent, but if you strain your ears, you can hear a beat. A pulse, thumping through the ground. Music. I stick close to September, and we pick our way through grasses that have grown winter dry and brittle. I feel metal shapes underneath my boots: bolts, rails, pieces of long-lost broken machinery, who knows. We follow some others to an iron-plated door around the back of the power plant. A guy wearing a Carbon Junction University sweatshirt pops out, waving us in frantically. "In, in, quick."

We pile inside in a chaotic crush. Once we're all crammed into the tiny hallway, he pulls the door shut with a bang. The room we're in looks straight out of a horror movie, but before I can worry too much about how dangerous this is, September snags my hand and pulls me down a winding cinder-block corridor. Someone's laid rope lights on the floor, running down each side, and it feels so much like a Halloween haunted house that I shudder. But then the first corridor empties into a vast room with exposed beams and iron braces holding up the ceiling. The unsettling, creepy feeling blooms into awe.

Suddenly I want to explore every inch of this place, get lost in the maze of it. It smells like cold and rust. There are rows and rows of colossal machines, squat tanklike things for god knows what, with chutes winding around them that look like metal tube slides at playgrounds. The tanks are mounted on cracking cement slabs, and safety railings that used to be coated in bright colors are now peeling and rusted. There are bolts and rivets bigger than my wrist holding the machines together.

As we navigate through the Castle, September touches me in a dozen small ways, directing me. I've been touch starved for so long, I think I'm addicted to the way she moves when she's around me, how we knock together in time and space.

As we follow the rope light trail, the music gets louder and louder until we emerge into a cavernous room. The ceiling is so far above my head I wonder if it's even there. In the middle of the room, there's a gigantic metal turbine sunk half into the floor. Around it, students from CJU and the high school are talking, dancing, flirting, and drinking. Strobing lights pulse over the crowd.

As we weave through, dozens of people call out to September. We're connected by that invisible something again. When we're not holding hands, her fingers skim at my elbow, or my hand hovers at the small of her back. My blood is heating up, liquid pleasure with each graze of her fingertips.

"September!" It's Dottie, screaming over the music.

We make our way to her. "What's shakin', Tall, Dark, and Sullen?" she says.

"Not much," I say. "I'd smile, but then I'd be a traitor to the nickname."

Dottie laughs, a bright peal of bells. "Hey, listen—I found some incredible shirts for you at Rag House. You should come in and try them on. I went for all black, but maybe I should have diversified—look at you, wearing gray!"

September leans in. "You guys talk; I'll get us something to drink."

I want to tell her not to leave me. I do genuinely like Dottie, but I don't really feel right when I'm not with September.

Dottie and I sit on the turbine platform, and she launches into a story about work, shouting over the music. I try to hold up my half of the conversation, but I can't seem to keep my eyes from drifting back to September, who's still working her way through the crowd like a celebrity.

"For someone who hasn't lived here very long, she sure seems like the queen of the joint," I say.

"Well, our girl is sparkling, isn't she?"

"Radiant," I agree. And intensely clever, and determined, and resilient. How she can go from the girl I watched unravel after a nightmare to this bright, seemingly carefree one blows my mind.

September tosses her head back and laughs at whatever the person she's talking to is saying, and a smile tugs at the corner of my mouth.

My stomach flips. Oh Christ.

This isn't just physical attraction.

"You okay over there?" Dottie asks. "You've gone all still."

"Yeah, fine. I just think I might be a little in love with your best friend." It comes out flat, because I'm stunned by the realization.

Dottie gives my hand a sympathetic pat. "I think maybe more than a little."

"Yeah. Shit."

September makes her way back to us, careful not to spill the three plastic cups she's carrying. I offer her my seat, but she waves me off. "I'd rather stand. I'm boiling." She peels off her coat.

The DJ murmurs into his microphone, and the party anthem melts into something angsty and slow, sung by a gritty-voiced girl.

"Dance with me," September says.

"Excuse me?"

"Quick, dance with me." She grabs my hand and tugs me away from Dottie without a backward glance. Once we're firmly in the middle of a group of people hanging on each other, she loops her arms around my neck. I brace myself, then bring my arms around her waist.

We sway to the beat, and I'm suddenly hyperaware that our bodies are only three inches apart. I focus on a clock on the wall opposite us, swallowing hard. I've never danced with a girl, and I'm sort of petrified right now.

"Relax, Flint," she says gently. "It's just me."

I look down, cocking an eyebrow. "You seem quite at home at this kegger. I didn't think scientists were party animals."

"You've probably figured out by now that I'm not your average scientist," she says. Her fingers tangle idly in the ends of my hair, her fingertips rubbing softly on my neck. My head swims.

My own hands move before I can think about it, my thumbs skimming up the velvet of her dress. She makes the smallest noise at that, and my eyes almost roll back in my head.

Someone knocks into us, jolting us into another couple.

"There are so many people in here," I say wearily. It's a lot for someone who's used to being alone with his parents all day.

September shifts in my arms. "Let's go exploring, then. Come with me."

I nod, even though the last thing I want is to untangle my body from hers.

She leads me through the crowd and deeper into the factory. There are more nooks and crannies in this place than I ever thought possible. Everywhere we look, there are clusters of friends laughing or drinking, or couples stealing a minute of privacy.

We notice the sliver of moonlight at the top of a staircase at the same time. We climb the steps and push a heavy door open on a room with rows of gauges and dials and instruments. The power plant's control room, I'm guessing.

I follow September inside, both of us marveling at all the gadgets. The cold light from the sky filters in through a broken window at the far end of the room.

"Better?" she asks.

"Yes," I say, but it's not, because we're not touching anymore. I'd suffer crowds ten times that size if it meant I could have my hands on her hips again.

"You know," she says slowly, "just because we're not down there, it doesn't mean we have to stop dancing."

A thrill leaps low in my stomach. "You make an excellent point."

We step into each other at the same time. She looks up, right into my eyes, and the hum that's always been there between us swells louder. Her hand slides to my shoulder, and when the rest of her body grazes up against mine, a tremor runs through me.

She takes my hand in hers, so we're dancing Disney-movie-ballroom-style. The music from the turbine room throbs right through the cement walls, although the words are blurry now.

Her eyes burn into me, that clear, intense amber. Her voice is soft: half-embarrassed, half-amused. "I'm glad we got out of there. I think I was about to do something unseemly."

She takes her eyes off mine then—but only to watch her own fingers as they work through my hair, just like they did the other night by the creek. Sparks shower through my nerves, as hot and fast as the ones thrown from an arc welder. She rubs her thumb over my cheek, glancing it over the mole above my lip. "You're beautiful," she whispers.

I close my eyes. I never thought I'd be touched like this. I'm aching for more of her hands on me, more of this moment, more of this girl.

Then, with her thumb still resting at the corner of my mouth, September rises up and touches her lips to mine in a feather-soft, tentative press.

At first the kiss is sweet. And gentle. And slow. Languidly chasing the tingling rush of each slide of her mouth and mine. Our mouths were already slightly open from the awestruck reality of being so close, and it makes our lips interlock in the most exquisite, tender way.

And then she closes softly around my bottom lip, and all it takes is the tiniest edgy dig of her teeth, the smallest tug, to make everything in me go molten and *hungry*.

I'm the one who deepens the kiss. I'm the one who presses my palm to the small of her back, who drags her up to me for more.

Her hands flutter as they map my shoulders, my chest. "God, Flint," she whispers, in a quick, gasping breath between kisses. "We should have done this weeks ago."

I'd answer, but I'm already busy running my fingers through her hair, cupping the back of her neck so I can catch her mouth for another kiss.

We move together like wildfire. I never want to stop, because I've never in my life felt anything as good as this.

When we finally pull apart, the edges of the world are soft. I don't have to think about anything else but the humming and the happiness and *her*.

"We should get back to the party," she whispers.

"Do we have to?" I murmur.

"We can always sneak off again later," she says, pressing a smile into my shoulder.

Back in the turbine room, it feels like we're wearing a flashing sign that says *We Just Made Out*. I pat down my hair, but there's nothing I can do about the kiss-smudged mess of my mouth. We weave our way to Dottie, who, after one glance at our interlocked hands, grins widely. I flush and offer to get us some more drinks.

As I make my way to where the kegs are lined up, I don't even care that thirty people jostle me. I keep my eyes trained on September as I make my way back, staggered all over again by how stunning she is.

But then someone walks up to join them, and a needle of *Oh shit* lances through my gut.

I stand frozen, watching the train wreck in slow motion.

Because, through the crisscross of lights, through the throngs of people moshing, September is talking to *Aerys*.

Just like that, the dream I've been walking through shatters and falls to my feet in pieces.

Shit, *shit, shit, shit*.

This is it. The secret that I never intended to keep from September, the thing that started out as something like a white lie, that grew and grew and grew, is about to come out. And it's going to level us both.

Someone shoves past me, and beer spills over my fingers, but it breaks me out of my deadlock. And then suddenly I'm angry. What the hell was I thinking? Kissing her upstairs, like I had any right? Hoping that for just a few days I could pretend I wasn't about to die?

My breath starts coming in shallow bursts. I'm standing stock-still in the middle of an illegal kegger holding three overflowing cups of lukewarm beer, and I'm Freaking. The. Fuck. Out.

I ditch the beers. Push through people to get across the room, praying I can get there in time to stop this disaster from playing out. Every step toward them has dread building in my chest. I know from experience that it takes people about thirty seconds before they start discussing the fact that I've half-lifed.

Aerys clocks me, and she's so surprised to see me she stops in the middle of her sentence to Dottie.

"Flint—you're here." Hurt flickers over her face—a good friend would have told her he'd decided to come—but she holds out her fist for a bump anyway.

"Are you having fun?" she shouts over the music.

I nod, too petrified to speak.

September opens her mouth. Cocks her head at me, then at Aerys.

I know what's coming: *Do you guys know each other?* Not in a weird jealous way, just a friendly small-talk way.

I can't let that question come out.

I'm a split second away from just *running* (which won't look suspicious at all—great plan, Flint) when Dottie saves me.

"Aerys, have you seen that room with that huge slide thing?" she asks.

"Oh, yeah, the coal chute? It's so creepy, but cool. I heard Aidan Nguyen got a cut from a loose screw last year and needed twenty stitches, though, so no way am I going down it. Has anyone tried it tonight?"

My heart is thudding off the rails. I drop my mouth to September's ear. "Can we get out of here?" I whisper. "I'm not feeling very well."

It's the weakest excuse in the world, but she believes it, her face suddenly awash with concern.

"Sure, of course." She nudges into Aerys and Dottie's conversation. "Sorry, guys—we're gonna duck out for some air. Be right back."

Dottie grins. "Have a nice time," she says, tossing us a saucy wink.

I tug September away, beelining for the door that leads to the claustrophobic corridors of the power plant. I shouldn't be holding her hand, but I am, and that makes me the worst person in the history of all time. But letting go would be a small, immediate cruelty, a renunciation of what we just did, and I can't bear that. Not yet.

I'm so stupid. I should have never let things go this far. How did it come to this? I was just supposed to be taking her to a few hospitals.

And one broken rule led to another, and now I don't know where all my boundaries went.

I'm mad. Burning mad, at myself but at the universe too. It's not fair. Tears prick at the corners of my eyes. How could life throw her at me *now*? With six weeks left, I had to meet *her*?

It's bullshit. I want more time.

We push out through the heavy iron door we came in through, and September leads me over to a stack of rusted railway sleepers and sits me down. "Was it the beer?"

"Could have been the beer," I say, even though I hardly drank any. "I'm just a little dizzy. I'm really sorry, September, but I think I just want to go home."

Disappointment flashes on her face. "Sure, of course. I'd better get back to work, anyway."

"Actually . . ." I say, avoiding her eyes, "maybe we should postpone that trip tomorrow."

"Oh—okay."

"There's no rush now that you have a third file, right?" I ask. "How about next Saturday?"

"No, you're right. No rush. Next Saturday, sure."

She's hurt. I hate this. I want to lift her chin and tell her that I loved every second of what happened in that room upstairs, but I can't.

What if this is what I leave her with?

No what-ifs—that *is* what I'm going to leave her with. This is what she'll think about after I'm gone.

Oh god.

It's going to rip me to shreds, leaving her.

september

FLINT LEANS FORWARD on the pile of rusty metal in the factory yard and drops his head into his hands.

I feel numb. Off-kilter. My brain is trying to process the sudden change in the energy of our night—from the noise and the lights and the *kissing* to the cold silence—but I can't figure out what happened.

Flint does look paler than usual, but I'm worried he's more than "feeling sick." This isn't how people are supposed to act after their first kiss—especially not after a kiss as knee-bucklingly incredible as *that*.

My stomach sinks. Does he regret it? Is that why he doesn't want to go to another hospital tomorrow?

I hug my arms around myself. "Let's get you home," I say, hoping my voice doesn't betray my confused hurt.

We're silent as we cross the factory yard. Our new awkwardness hangs in the air like vapor. I didn't think the night would end like this, and humiliation starts to creep up my cheeks in a hot flush. I tell myself it's just my blood vessels dilating, giving me the extra fight-or-flight energy—because that's kind of what I want to do now. Flee.

And then the rhythmic crush of his boots on the ground abruptly stops, and he snags my hand. The momentum has my body ricocheting back to him, and then he's murmuring my name and *I'm sorry*, and before I know it, he's kissing me again.

It's a hard, desperate press, but it has me melting. I can't help myself—I meet him with the same rough enthusiasm, grabbing his shoulders so we don't fall over.

He pulls back, eyes searching mine, full of apology and the sweet, dark brand of sadness that belongs only to him.

"I'm sorry I made us leave," he whispers. "Please don't think it's you."

His thumb strokes along the edge of my cheek, and I have to close my eyes to the slow, swelling happiness.

"I thought you were regretting what happened," I say.

"No. Not at all, September. I'd kiss you every minute for the rest of time if I could."

My heart folds over on itself.

And then we're kissing again.

This kiss pulls me under, swirling soft and slow; the next one drags me up gasping, bruising and hot. I savor every wave of heat that burns through my body. I'm in love with the science of it, the neurons firing, the nerve endings crackling, the way this boy can make me feel things I've never felt before. It's the most powerful antidote to outrunning the shadows, more powerful even than scrawling formulas on whiteboards or watching my heroes in the lab at the Institute, because my mind is spinning, and there's simply no corner for shadows to lurk in all of this *sensation*.

His hands travel, and fireworks of serotonin, dopamine,

norepinephrine explode in my mind and rain down as incandescent starbursts. For the first time in my life, the Cs and Hs and Ns, and Os swim. I couldn't tell you the chemical formula for anything right now even if you paid me a million dollars.

We don't stop until a group of partiers slams out through the iron door, laughing into the night, and it reminds us that we're outside and in the cold. We untangle, but he doesn't let go of my hand for the entire walk to Gravel Ridge.

For the first time in weeks, I don't work on my research when I get home. I climb into bed without even changing into pajamas.

When everything's quiet, I run my fingertips over the velvet at the collar of my dress, right where Flint's jaw grazed as he kissed my neck. I bury my nose in the fabric at my wrist and smell mostly rust and cold, but here—just here, there's a vein of black cherry. I've kissed plenty of other boys and enjoyed it, but *that* . . . Even Bryson Oliveira doesn't hold a candle to that. It makes me wonder what it would be like, to go further with Flint.

I lie in the dark, smiling so hard my cheeks start to ache.

flint

15 DAYS, 18 HOURS, 20 MINUTES

DAWN BREAKS AS I plow down the sidewalk toward Aerys's house. I think I got a grand total of two hours of sleep after September walked me home from the Castle. Mom took one look at me this morning and said she wants me to talk to a counselor. Counseling—what a waste of everyone's time and money. I have fifteen days left, and after that, nothing I ever said or did or thought will ever matter. It won't matter that I was "sad" before I died.

Fuck.

I kick at a few acorn shells, sending them skipping up someone's driveway. There's some stupid-ass cartoon turkey in the middle of a wreath on the front door, and it pisses me off even more. How can people make shit like that when life is so fragile and short and pointless? I want to scream at them to do something better with their time.

I sink to the curb, head in my hands. Breathe. Don't cry, not out here. There are cars crowded in every driveway, families in town for the big meal next week. How many of them are watching a boy have a breakdown on the sidewalk?

I used to love Thanksgiving. But after I half-lifed, it was too close to December 4, the annual reminder of my deathday. Thanksgiving meant that the first number on my countdown was about to tick over. Seven to six. Six to five. Until the *years* section on the clock was gone altogether.

I stare down into the gutter until the lump in my throat loosens.

Shit at home is getting real. The phone calls my mom takes to her bedroom to answer are coming fast and thick now. Distant but concerned family members. Friends she hasn't spoken to in years.

Every moment in that house is like walking on eggshells. After Mom made me breakfast, she stood behind my chair and pressed a kiss to the top of my head—for an entire minute. Under any other circumstance, it'd be weird. It made my eyes well up with tears.

God. I have to get myself under control and do what I came over here to do. I push off the curb and walk until I'm standing in front of Aerys's house.

When I left the party last night, she was deep in conversation with Dottie. I have to know—did my half-life come up? Did Aerys tell Dottie how many days I have left? Did Dottie tell September? I'm too afraid to go to September's house to find out firsthand, so I'm getting my information the coward's way.

I press the doorbell, over and over, and clack the decorative brass door knocker too.

Silence.

I mutter a curse and shove my hands into my pockets, bouncing on the balls of my feet. I know it's early, but this can't wait. I'm about to freak out when the dead bolt clicks and the door opens.

Aerys's usually perfectly shaped hair is sticking out at all angles. When she sees it's me, she crosses her arms over her chest, which sets alarm bells off in my head.

"I know it's early," I sputter before she can speak. "I just wanted to see if you had fun last night at the party."

"I had a pretty good time." She frowns. "But there was *one* thing that kind of threw me. I was talking to Dottie Reyes, and the more we talked, the more it seemed like there was a big hole in the middle of our conversation. It took me a while, but I finally realized what she *wasn't* saying. She never brought up the expiration date on whatever's going on with you and September."

She shifts uneasily, as if she doesn't want to believe what she already suspects. "Flint . . . please tell me you weren't lying when you said you told September."

Time seems to slow. Her eyes lock on mine, desperate for an easy explanation to spill out, but I can only shrink under the force of her hope.

"I can't tell you that," I finally whisper. "I never told September."

Aerys takes a step back. "Holy shit, Flint."

I don't say anything. I feel so small.

She reaches up to tug at her hair. It's clear that her feelings about this mirror mine—I loathe me too.

I swallow. "Aerys, I have to know. Did you say anything to Dottie?"

"God, Flint. If I had, do you really think you'd be here groveling? September would be at your house ripping you a new one."

"Point taken." A heavy silence settles between us. "I fucked up. So bad, Aerys."

"No shit, Sherlock."

"What do I do now?" I ask, feeling so helpless. She looks at me like I'm an idiot.

202

"Um, you fucking tell her?"

"Won't it be better if she just never finds out?"

Aerys's eyes burn. "So let me get this straight. You want her to think you just ghosted her?"

"Isn't that better than the alternative?" My voice cracks with panic, with desperation. If I disappear, she'll just wonder. I'll be a snag in her past, something that feels a little embarrassing when she runs her memory over it. A tiny, forgettable nick to her confidence. But if I tell her I'm dying in fifteen days, I risk becoming a whole lot more than a snag in her past.

"Aerys, I can't. Please don't tell Dottie. Don't tell September."

She drills a finger into my chest. "You tell her, Flint Larsen. You tell her, or I will."

september

I FLING MYSELF onto my bed and stare at the blank ceiling.

My mind's been on fire, chugging through possibility after possibility. Mitsuki, Marvin, Araminta. There's got to be something here.

I drag myself up and pull another sheet from Araminta's 183-page PDF, which I printed in the school library when no one was looking.

The first sizzle of real worry came yesterday evening, but I brushed it aside. There were still some avenues to explore. Some formulas to solve, some variables to plug in.

But now the worry has turned into a creeping despair.

There's no link. I've combed through all three files, and there's nothing that Mitsuki Adams, Marvin Ferret, and Araminta Kovak all share. Nothing that would suggest any substance they ingested over the entire course of their lives was any different from the millions of people who died on time.

There should have been something. Some obscure medicine, something that had the power to cross the blood-brain barrier, that would have slightly boosted a specific element in their bodies, the element that their half-life chromosome was watching to trigger their deathday. I thought it would be the amphetamines Marvin was addicted to, or the medicine that Araminta was prescribed for her bipolar disorder.

All those trips were for nothing. All the slightly illegal things Flint and I did were for nothing. I swear I can feel my cortisol levels rising, $C_{21}H_{30}O_5$ dumping stress directly into my veins.

I've let so much slip so I could work on this hypothesis. I might be able to squeeze out a C in English, but it's a long shot. And my work at the Institute has been pitifully average, and Dr. Juncker certainly hasn't been impressed. My dream of getting the spot at CJU is further away than it's ever been.

There should have been something. A reason. The half-life *has* to be something science can explain; otherwise it's just this amorphous, mysterious thing that took my sister from me for no reason.

I go over it all one more time, but after another hour with the data, I know for sure.

My hypothesis is wrong.

The next morning, I trudge up the marble steps to the Institute in a blur of exhaustion and shattered hope. I have no idea how I'm going to work today. I'm numb inside. My hypothesis has fallen apart in my hands, all my grand plans vanishing into thin air.

And I haven't seen Flint since the party. I sent a text—the first one I've ever sent him since he gave me his number on the walk to the Castle in case we got separated at the party—but he didn't reply. Last night I stared across the creek, waving to click the porch light on, but nothing. I wanted to tell him, because he's the only one who seems to get it, and he's gone dark on me.

The security guard and the receptionist barely look at me when I shuffle through the Institute's front doors. *Happy day-before-Thanksgiving to you too*, I think bitterly.

I shake it off. This isn't me—I need sleep.

Tomorrow's a national holiday, but the Intake floor never rests. Dr. Juncker thought it would be a good chance to get Percy and me in for a few full days. We've had it planned for weeks, and before I started running all over Pennsylvania with Flint, I was excited about it. Now I just want to crawl home and sleep for a week.

When I walk into Dr. Juncker's office, Percy is already there, standing at attention with his hands behind his back. His lab coat is impossibly crisp and white. Buttoned up properly, as always. But something's off. He looks even more annoying than usual, if that's possible. A feeling of wrongness settles in my stomach.

Dr. Juncker is on the phone. "No, I appreciate you telling me. Thank you. It will be dealt with."

She hangs up but doesn't turn around. Just presses her fingers to her temples. The room is very still. Very silent.

"Percy, please step out of the office for a moment," she says. "And close the door."

Something like fear spreads through my veins, and my mouth goes dry.

She knows.

Somehow, she knows.

Percy takes his time, collecting a clipboard and a pen, and his mouth curves in a smirk as he passes me.

The door clicks shut.

Dr. Juncker swivels her chair around.

"September. I've been informed of an incident involving you. A violation of Institute procedures."

My blood goes cold.

"Did you, or did you not, travel to Low Wickam to obtain a patient file for a Mr. Marvin Ferret, claiming I had requested it?"

The world goes into hyper-sharp focus.

"I . . . yes. I did," I say.

"I'd hoped the information wasn't true," she says. "Do you have any explanation for this?"

I shake my head no. Dazed. Spinning. Sick.

"Unfortunately, this is a serious breach of the contract you signed when you started working here. Your internship is therefore terminated, with all clearances immediately revoked. You can leave the building with only your personal belongings. Human Resources will be in contact to get the details of the infraction and to inform you if the Institute will be taking legal action." She shakes her head and shows a tiny moment of humanity. "I didn't ever think I'd have to have a conversation like this with you."

"I'm sorry," I whisper. "I'm so sorry."

"Percy will escort you to security, and you can hand over your badge. Your retina scan has already been disabled." She sighs. "September, you know this means I can't give your application to Carbon Junction University a favorable review."

That almost breaks me.

Everything in me throbs as I turn from the room. Percy is waiting outside the door as promised, but I walk past him without a word,

207

zombie-like in my focus to get out of this building without falling apart. I hear him scamper to catch up to me.

How, how, how? The question pounds with my every step down the terrifyingly clean hallway. How did Dr. Juncker find out about my trip to Low Wickam?

That horrible woman at the clinic.

I should have known she'd call. I don't know why it took her more than a week to report me, but it doesn't matter—the damage is done now.

Percy surges ahead and pushes the button to call the elevator. He tilts his chin up, looking smug.

Realization dawns.

I grab his arm, yanking so he has to face me in the hallway.

"Did you take the call, Percy?"

"I assume you're referring to the call from the clinic in Low Wickam a few days ago? Yes. Dr. Juncker returned the call this morning, after consulting with Human Resources."

Tears prick at my eyes. Of course. I knew he was a weasel, but this is low.

"You know what, Percy?" I take a moment, until I'm sure my words won't shake when they come out. "If the roles had been reversed, I wouldn't have thrown you under the bus."

For a split second, I see him falter, but then he straightens. "When the woman from the clinic called, I felt it was my duty to check the log to see if any of the doctors had asked for files on Marvin Ferret, which no one had. I took the inquiry to Dr. Juncker, which I felt was the proper course of action."

"Of course you did," I say woodenly. The lousy rat. I should be angry, but I'm disconnected. Floating.

I jab the button for the elevator again. Where the hell is it?

"Wait—September. What were you doing in Low Wickam?" His eyes glint with curiosity. The only true shred of scientist I've seen from him so far.

As if he's getting an answer.

The elevator arrives at last, and I step in, Percy on my heels. The ride down is silent.

Everything's been ripped out from under me. My hypothesis. My internship. My future. *I'm so sorry, Maybelle.* I walk through the lobby in a haze. Percy takes my lanyard and hands it to security, then one of the officers escorts me to get my things from the staff locker room and walks me out of the building. Ejected, rejected.

The wind kicks up, whipping at my face. Snippets of Dr. Juncker's words play on repeat in my head.

I can't give your application to Carbon Junction University a favorable review.

Instinct has me reaching for my phone. A month ago, I would have called Dottie. Bo. Gone to the Ruins or the waffle house. But that's not where I go for comfort anymore.

Before I realize it, I'm pelting around the western edge of town, boots pounding up Gravel Ridge Road. Flint's been radio silent since our kiss, but I have to tell him.

Fired. I just got FIRED from my internship. What am I supposed to do now? I'll have to tell school. I'll have to stay there for all seven periods. My GPA is going to be a disaster, but it won't matter, because every biochem college in the country will throw my application right in the trash.

I run up the steps to Flint's front door. I can hardly breathe through the pressure in my chest. I'm a ticking time bomb about to explode.

The door opens, and I look up, wiping a sniffle from my nose. It's Flint's dad.

"I need to see Flint," I say.

He clears his throat. "He's not—"

"Tember?"

At the sound of that familiar voice, Mr. Larsen steps aside to give me a clear view of the room. Flint's not here—but my grandma is. And she's on a job. Flint's mom is perched on a barstool, wearing one of Gigi's garishly patterned neck capes. Folded squares of foil glint in her hair.

"September! Come on in." Mrs. Larsen beckons. I can tell she wants to get up, but she stays on the barstool. "Thank goodness for your grandma. My roots needed serious attention."

"Flint should be back any minute," his dad adds. "We just asked him to run and get some Diet Coke for your grandma."

Seeing Gigi makes me wobble a little. I go to stand beside her, and I must look bad, because alarm flashes over her face.

"What's going on?" she asks, keeping her voice low.

"Work stuff. I need to talk to Flint."

I slide a surreptitious glance over to Flint's mom. She doesn't seem very good. I wonder if she has a terminal illness, because she

210

looks gaunt and there are purple smudges under her eyes. God. I've been so wrapped up in my own problems that I haven't even asked Flint if he needs . . . support or something. He's about to lose his mom.

I chew on my thumbnail. Maybe I should go, or wait for Flint outside. I stare at the front door, willing him to come back.

Flint's mom gives me a sweet, tired smile. "It's lovely to finally meet you properly, September. We're so grateful Flint's had you through this. It's been a difficult time for him."

Gigi nods sympathetically and gives Mrs. Larsen's shoulder a squeeze. And then Mrs. Larsen's face crumples with such raw grief I have to take a step back. Should I look away? I've never seen an adult cry before, other than my own parents, and it has panic jolting through my veins.

"I'm glad he has friends to talk to," she continues, sniffling. "He didn't want to use the Institute's counseling services, even though they have that dedicated line for minors."

"Oh, honey," Gigi clucks, gathering Flint's mom in for a hug.

I frown—because one word doesn't fit here. *Minors.* What is she talking about?

Flint's dad gets a tissue box, looking uncomfortable in the face of all these tears. Flint's mom composes herself, then tells Gigi she's ready to take the foils out.

But something's very wrong here.

"Hold on," I whisper.

No one notices.

"Hold on," I say, louder. This time it makes everyone stop.

211

I home in on Mrs. Larsen. "I don't understand. Didn't you come here for *your* deathday?"

Her eyebrows quirk in puzzlement. "No, of course not. We came here for—" She stops. Alarm flashes over her face. "Maybe I shouldn't—"

"No—what were you about to say?" I demand.

It's so silent I can hear the foil in her hair crinkle as she breathes. Her eyes are brimming with pity when she speaks.

"We didn't come here for my deathday. We came here for Flint's."

For the second time today, I'm knocked sideways. I can only whisper, "What?"

"Shit, Leslie." Flint's dad pulls a hand over his jaw. "She didn't know?"

The front door opens. Collectively, the four of us turn. Flint freezes in the doorway, holding a pack of Diet Coke.

And it just takes one look.

How I didn't see it before, I'll never know. That sadness surrounding him. The thick cloud of it, the sullenness he wore like a cloak when we first met. I thought it was because he was about to lose a parent. This whole time, that's what I assumed it was.

For one beat, he's confused. Wondering why he's walked in and we're all just staring at him, not saying a single thing.

And then he gets it. He knows exactly what's happened.

The color drains out of him.

"September—"

"I'm an idiot," I whisper.

"Tember—" Gigi starts.

"Don't." I storm across the room, shoving past Flint and into the open air. I'm wheeling. Spinning. So *hurt* that I can't think, can't make a decision.

What the *fuck*.

Flint's dying.

He's post.

I trek down the hill, fueled with rage and pain and a hollow grief, skidding on slick leaves.

Footsteps crash through the underbrush behind me. "September, wait, please—"

I whirl around. I raise a finger in warning. "Don't. You. Dare."

He flinches. "I should have told you," he says, his face a wreck of regret.

"You think?!" I'm about to lose my shit. It takes everything I have not to bring my hands out and shove him.

"How many days do you have left?" I demand.

"That's not—"

"How many days, Flint?!" I shout. I'm unhinged now, wild-eyed and furious.

"Eleven," he whispers.

I press a hand to my stomach. I'm going to be sick. *Eleven?* As in, *less than two weeks?*

"Get away from me," I croak.

"September—"

"Get away! I *never*—*NEVER*—want to see you again."

I'm shouting now. The forest absorbs it and makes me want to shout louder.

"You don't understand—I was such a mess when I got here, and—"

"You don't think I understand death? Grief? That my life has been untouched by it? Fuck off, Flint."

"No—I don't think that at all—I know it hasn't." Flint holds out his hands, open-palmed. "And you haven't told me about what happened to you, and I'm fine with not knowing the details if you really don't want to tell me, but that's a secret too—"

I'm LIVID.

"My thing is *not* the same. Not AT ALL, Flint."

He's crying now too. But I don't give a damn.

"I'm sorry. You're right, and I know I can't fix this. Not in eleven days, not in eleven decades. I just—I didn't expect any of this. I didn't expect *you*. September, please."

"You know why I came running to your house today, Flint? I got fired. That awful woman from Low Wickam called the Institute. Percy sold me out, and I got fucking *fired*. But that's not the worst thing. I finished going through Araminta Kovak's file. There's nothing."

His voice wobbles. "What do you mean, there's nothing?"

"All of our trips, and whatever was happening with you and me, it's all a huge flaming dumpster fire, and none of it was worth it, because there *is no* hypothesis. I was wrong. I can't do anything about the half-life. No one can."

Shock has his face going even paler. It feels good to knock him down another peg.

"I wish I'd never met you." I strike out the words like venom.

I turn on my heel and stomp right through the rushing creek. The water drenches my boots, but I don't care. I scramble up the other side of the hill, leaving this tall, sullen, prickly boy behind me forever.

flint

11 DAYS, 12 HOURS, 3 MINUTES

I WATCH SEPTEMBER splash through the creek. I'm shivering, and I can't stop crying.

I saw this coming. I tried to protect myself from something like this for eight miserable years, and now that it's happening, it feels worse than I'd ever imagined. So much worse.

I sink to my knees. I want the ground to swallow me up, for the minutes on the clock to have pity on me and race down to zero, because I can't bear to be with myself. This is the worst thing I've ever done.

Someone's thrashing through the woods behind me. Before I know it, my dad is hauling me up to my feet, and we're staggering back to the house. He grunts with exertion—my body's still straining for September.

Once we're inside, there's a blur of conversation, but I'm so out of it. My parents meld into a perfect team, taking care of me like they did when I was a little kid, peeling off my clothes and tucking me into bed. They sit on either side of me in my dark bedroom, talking to me, soothing me, but I'm still crying, and nothing's getting through.

And then I'm alone, and I want to beg them to come back, but it was my voice that said, *Leave me alone*, my arms that shoved at them, my hands that swatted at my mom's cool palm on my forehead.

The silence is worse.

My chin starts to wobble, and I press my fists to my eyes. What was the whole point of me? Right now it looks like it was to hurt my parents and to hurt September. To cause them that deep, aching kind of pain that takes up residence in your heart forever.

september

I WRENCH OPEN the back door and stalk through Gigi's house, leaving puddles of creek water on the shaggy old carpet.

I turn in circles, fighting the urge to drop to my knees and scream. How could he not tell me? How could he kiss me like that at the Castle and not tell me?

Every muscle in my body contracts toward a sob, but I yank myself up straight. I won't cry for him. I didn't cry for Maybelle, so I'm sure as hell not going to cry for this. I'm not sad—I'm mad. I want the anger to burn, because I know once the burn is gone, I'll break.

If it had been one thing, I might have been able to handle it. The internship. My hypothesis. Flint. But all three are hitting at once, and I don't know how I'm going to stay standing. I've lost everything.

Maybelle.

The back door slides open, and Gigi brings a gust of cold air inside with her.

"Tember? Where are you?"

When she sees me standing in the dark, swaying on the spot, she drops her bags and comes right for me. She wraps me in a hug, but I can't drag up the energy to bring my arms around her.

"I'm fine," I bite out. "Just angry." My fists are clenched so tight my nails are about to break the skin. "What the hell was he think-ing?! How could he not tell me?"

Gigi whispers *shhh*s as she tucks a strand of my hair behind my ear.

"Don't. I'm not going to cry—I'm furious."

Her face contorts with pity. "Honey, I really think you need to talk to someone. You've been barely holding it together the last few weeks."

I wrench away from her hug. She thinks *I* need therapy? My parents are the ones who need it, not me.

"I thought I was doing pretty damn well, Gigi. Of course, not as good as you. It hasn't even been a year, and you're already perfectly fucking fine."

Gigi steps back. "Tember—"

"How did you put it out of your mind? Did it just not bother you that your four-year-old granddaughter died?"

"Of course it bothered me; I loved Maybelle very—"

"No. There's no way you loved her. Not if you can be like this, like you don't have a care in the world."

She just looks at me with soft pity. "I think you need to be careful about what you're saying, or you might regret some of this once you've calmed down," she says, voice soothing as ever.

"What are you going to do?" I shout. "Kick me out? I don't even need to live here anymore, because the Institute fired me."

"What? What are you talking about?"

"I don't want to get into it. I fucked up, and they fired me."

"Oh, Tember." Gigi shakes her head sadly. "I kept telling myself that you just needed time. I haven't said anything, and that was the wrong approach. That's not your fault, it's mine. But I can't sit here and watch you destroy yourself."

"I'm not destroying myself! I'm holding myself together!"

Something snaps in her. "Holding yourself together? Look at you; you're a mess!"

I bark out an offended laugh. "Wow, thanks a lot, Gigi."

"It's not healthy, how you're handling this, and we need to talk about it."

"I don't *want* to talk about it! That's the whole fucking point!"

"And you think not telling anyone here that your sister died is going to work, do you?"

I'm done with this. I whirl away and stalk to my room, slamming my door so hard a picture in the hallway falls off the wall.

I'm shaking from the toxic spill of the stress-response chemicals in my veins. The regret Gigi warned me about—*Did I really just say all of that to her?*—is already tugging at me, so I pull out my phone, desperate for a distraction. My thumb, out of habit, taps on my messages with Dottie and Bo.

There hasn't been a new text in over two days.

What would I say, anyway? *Hey, guys, what's up? The boy I'm falling for is dying, and it's fucking me up a million times more than it should because I watched someone die six months ago, and I can't do it again?*

I slam my phone down on my pillow. I lost my internship, I pushed Dottie and Bo away from me, my research is a joke. And Flint's dying.

I can't take my hand off my stomach. I'm afraid if I move even an inch, my organs will spill out. This is exactly what it felt like after Maybelle, and I hate Flint for making me feel it again.

How did I not see it? Because it was there that first time I saw him, on that day I found him at the Ruins. That tangle of sorrow and stubbornness followed him around like a little gray cloud. Like he didn't want to let himself have any fun. It's all so obvious now. This was why he was weird about food. Why he never wore a coat. Some people half-life and chase every possible high as their lives blaze out. Some people do the opposite.

I never stopped to examine his grief. That snap reaction I made, thinking it was his mom or dad about to die, just *stuck*. I was too wrapped up in the messy business of falling for him to put it together. There were so many new sensations: the way the heat coursed under my skin when we were hiding during flashlight tag, the way my stomach fluttered when I combed my fingers through his hair that night by the creek, the intoxication of those touches to my knee under the table.

When I think about the way he kissed me, I can't help but press a hand to my lips, feeling a thrum of heat at the memory. I was so happy. *He* was so happy. For a few minutes afterward, his personal storm cloud was nowhere in sight.

A single tear tracks down my cheek.

I smack my palm over it. *No.*

Who cares that my friends haven't texted. I need to get out of here and do something fun.

It only takes me ten minutes to run to Dottie's house. I rap on her window, and the curtains rustle, then fling open. When she sees it's me, her confusion shifts to alarm. She heaves up the sash window and pulls me gracelessly through. I push my hair out of my face, and oh—she's not alone.

Bo's here, on the beanbag in the corner. It stings, knowing that they're hanging out without me *again*, but it's a paper cut compared to what Flint just did to me.

Bo jolts to his feet. "What's wrong?"

I wasn't going to say anything. I was going to come over and pretend to be fine, but the words come out anyway.

"He's post," I blurt.

"Who's post?" Dottie asks. Realization wipes everything else off her face. "Oh, holy hell. Flint?"

I nod. "He's dying in eleven days."

Dottie's eyes go wide. "Jesusaurus rex."

And then there's this weird, perfectly still moment where they wait for the details. A normal person would gush, would tell them everything. But I know if I start, if I tell them how I feel about this grief, I won't be able to keep Maybelle out of it.

"Let's do something," I blurt. "Drive to Atlantic City, go bowling, I don't care. We have to do something."

The way they're looking at me, pity etched on their faces, makes me feel like crawling out of my skin. This isn't what I wanted. I want things to be how they used to be with the three of us, bright and happy and fun. I want everything to go back to the way it was before Flint came to Carbon Junction and ruined everything.

"I can't do this," I whisper.

And then I'm moving.

"Tember? Where are you going?" Bo asks.

"September, wait," Dottie says, but I'm out the window, already halfway gone.

flint

I STAY IN my room for hours, drifting between tears and fitful patches of sleep. I stare at my phone, at the numbers counting down. *Tick. Tick. Tick.*

When night falls, I sneak past my dad, who has camped out on my bedroom floor *just so someone's there when you wake up,* and then I step out into the moonlit living room.

Out the back porch window, the Crown towers over Carbon Junction, lit as white as bone. Through the trees, September's house is dark.

I've never felt so alone.

This is why I shouldn't have said yes to driving September around. Why did I have to meet her *now*? If I'd met her a year ago, maybe we could have made something of this. Maybe I could have told her up front, and she'd have been okay with it, and we could have spent a few bittersweet months together.

I press my forehead against the glass. Leaving wreckage behind was exactly what I came here to avoid, and now my last days are going to be worse than I ever could have imagined. But as much as I'm hurting, I don't deserve a shred of sympathy. September is the one who's been wronged here.

On my way back to my room, my elbow hits the kitchen counter.

A manila folder falls off, papers scattering everywhere. I kneel to pick them up.

A deposit invoice from a catering company. Another from an event space you can rent out on Main Street. A deed to a burial plot in Carbon Junction Cemetery.

These . . . are the plans for my funeral.

The papers fall from my numb hands. One skates across the floor and disappears under the couch. For one motionless minute, I sit there on the floor, barely breathing.

Then I get up and go back to bed.

I stare at my ceiling until the weak light of early morning seeps in. I slept with my window open, and there's a damp feeling to everything in the room, like when you go camping. We're slipping toward the freezing temperatures of December, and my face is numb from the cold, but I don't want to be warm.

After all the crying yesterday, I feel hollow and wrung out. I'm sure it'll hit me again once the sun's up, but for now, I'm in a zombie-like trance that feels almost identical to how I used to be before I came to Carbon Junction.

I prop myself up on my elbows and listen. The house is perfectly still, and there's a wash of gray silence over everything.

It's Thanksgiving.

We don't have any big plans, just the three of us and a turkey, so I don't need to get up and get dressed or anything. Not that I would, after yesterday.

I roll onto my stomach, then hang my head over the edge of

my bed and reach underneath for my Last Day tent.

I glance at my bedroom door. I don't want to risk Mom or Dad coming in, so I get up and turn the lock as slowly as I can, muffling the click with my other hand.

I drop the tent bundle onto my bed, then open my sock drawer and dig out the protein bars I've been hoarding. A water bottle. A high-powered flashlight. From the corner of my mostly empty closet, I grab my old black backpack and start to pack.

Thanksgiving Day plods on, and I stay in my room. Mom must not feel like cooking the turkey, because the day comes and goes without much more than cereal and sandwiches. I don't eat much of either.

I lie in bed and stare at the countdown on my phone screen and the house across the creek. When leaves blow in through my open window, I don't get up to close it.

The next day, the doorbell rings.

I pry myself up from the couch, where I've been lying listlessly for hours. I assume it must be another delivery for Mom. I open the door, but instead of a driver, it's Aerys.

"Hey," she says stiffly.

I bristle. "What, are you coming over to make sure I told September? I didn't, but she found out anyway."

Aerys shoves her hands into her hoodie pocket. "I actually came to get my Wii back."

"Oh." Embarrassed heat floods my cheeks. "Fine. I'll get it."

"I'll wait out here," she says.

I bring the Wii and transfer it to her arms. She turns to go.

"Is that seriously all you came for?" I ask.

"Uh . . . yep," she says.

"So what, I make one mistake and that's it?"

"It wasn't 'one mistake,' Flint, it was a colossal fuckup," she says.

"You think I don't know that? I'll never not hate myself for it."

Aerys shakes her head. "I still can't believe you were just going to ghost her."

"What's wrong with that? It's what you did to your friends when the first hot girl came along."

Aerys's eyes widen, and the air between us goes very still. I know instantly that I've overstepped.

"That's really interesting, Flint, coming from someone who never talked to their *best friend* after they moved away."

"It's not like you tried really hard to talk to me either," I point out, hating how my voice is rising. "Besides, we were *eight*, and I was *dying*!"

"Oh, get over yourself. You've been dying for years."

My blood surges in my veins. She knows *nothing* about what it's like to live with a deadline.

I sharpen my words to a knifepoint. "Let's stop pretending that you were hanging out with me for any other reason than to give yourself a pat on the back. You can't make it up to the friends you ignored by pitying me."

Aerys blows out a sad breath. "This was never about pity, Flint."

"No? Poor little dying kid needs a friend, needs to get out of the house. Well, news flash, I didn't want a friend. I didn't want you to show up on my doorstep, and I never should have walked by your house."

Aerys's eyes go glassy with tears. "God, you're such an asshole, Flint. Everybody gives you so much leeway, treating you with kid gloves, but half-lifing young doesn't give you an excuse to be a shit-head." She shifts the stuff under her arm. "Look. We're done, okay?"

"We shouldn't have even started," I shout as she turns her back on me and walks away.

It doesn't hit me until later, after I've stopped shaking—that was the last time I'll ever see her.

On Saturday, I go out into the woods. I walk for hours, thinking about how, if September hadn't found out I was post, we'd be on our way to another hospital right now.

Somehow I end up at the crumbling, ruined house where I met her. I sit there for a long time, propped up against the wall like I was on the day she burned into my life.

I'd be lying if I said I wasn't half watching for a flash of color between the dying leaves.

I text her. The exact same message I sent her yesterday and the day before that. One text a day. More than that would be annoying.

> I'm sorry.
> I'm sorry.
> I'm sorry.

Maybe once a day is annoying too.

I can't stop.

Am I really never going to see her again?

I go to the Ruins again the next day, but this time I bring my backpack with me. I zip it into a big waterproof bag and bury it under a pile of rocks.

I was worried that this place wasn't remote enough for my deathday, but I haven't seen a single person out here so far. It's clear that September's not coming back here either.

Each time I return, it feels more and more certain that this is where I'll die.

Later that evening, Mom cracks my bedroom door open. "Flint? Come out and watch a movie with us."

"Stop asking," I snap. "I'm just going to keep saying no."

I should have stuck to my initial plan all along: be an asshole son. So that when I go, they can feel relief instead of sadness.

When the house is dark and the moon is up, I hear Mom crying. She cries every night now. Dad comes into my room.

"Flint?"

"I'm awake."

Dad sinks into the chair in the corner. "You're making this really tough on your mom, kid."

I clench my jaw. "Do you think it's *not* tough on me?"

"We know it is. We've always known that. But this isn't how you should be spending your last week."

"It's exactly how I should be spending it. I deserve this."

He stares out the window, but he doesn't deny it.

I bury my face in my pillow. I wish they'd let me go already.

It's after midnight the next time I check my phone.

Seven days left.

SEVEN.

A sickening dread spills through me. I'm running out of time.

september

IT'S BEEN ALMOST a week since I found out about Flint.

On the outside, it looks like I'm keeping it together. I get up. I get dressed. I go to school. But on the inside . . .

When NASA sends up a rocket, everything has to be perfect. The physical stresses of launch, the g-forces, the high temperatures—if even a single bolt comes loose or a piece of cargo shifts, it throws off the center of mass. Then the rocket starts shimmying, and systems fail in a domino effect until the whole rocket's shaking, wobbling, corkscrewing—and then it blows up.

I feel like I'm at the "everything shaking" part.

I was hoping that once I stopped hanging out with Flint, I'd be able to be the old September again. That I could hitch up the mask and fool everyone. But joke's on me, because now I can't smile at all anymore. There's only one person I've ever been able to be around when I've felt like this, and he's off-limits now.

I hate that I'm hyperaware of how much time he has left. Every class I sit through, every silent dinner with Gigi, every night lying awake in the dark. It wasn't that long ago that I was counting days for another loss, and this feels sickeningly familiar. The worst kind of déjà vu.

Today he's down to six days, and my alarm clock is going off for school.

Out of habit, I check my phone before my feet even hit the floor. There's a message from Bo, saying he's bringing coffee for us. I click off my phone screen with a burst of irritation. After I left Dottie's house, they blew up my phone so hard I had to turn my notifications off. Every moment with them this past week—by the lockers before first period, excruciatingly long lunches, my new seventh-period gym class with Dottie—has been an exhausting effort to act normal. I wish that they'd leave me alone or that I had the courage to simply not talk to them, but it feels impossible to do that when our friendship is so woven into the fabric of my school day. I wonder how much they'll be able to take before they jettison me.

Gigi's in the kitchen when I come in for breakfast. I sit down across from her and pick at a piece of toast. She hasn't said anything about our fight, and she's treating me like my outburst didn't make her love me any less. Still, I've been keeping our conversations clinical and quick, just the bare minimum that we need to be living in the same house together. But this morning, Gigi wrenches me into a discussion I don't want to have.

"Tember? I talked to Mrs. Larsen yesterday," she says gently.

I stand and push my chair back from the table so hard it shrieks across the tiles. With my back to her, I dump what's left of my toast in the trash.

"Whatever's going on, he's a fucking liar, and he deserves it," I say, nearly spitting the words.

"His mom says she can barely get him to eat."

The instant she says it, I can't see anything but Flint's face. Fresh pain sears through me. Why does it hurt to know he's suffering? It's not fair that someone can do something so horrible to you and it doesn't instantly wipe away the love. It should.

Instead of heading out the front door, I go back to my bedroom. After Maybelle, I used to grab a scholarly article to read anytime I felt the pressure of grief behind my eyes. I lie stomach-down on my bed and navigate to one of my favorite peer-reviewed open-access journals. But the words don't make any sense to me today.

Six days.

Sometimes it catches me out: I think of something that I want to tell Flint, or I forget that I'm not researching my hypothesis anymore, and I start to make a mental note to add a certain chemical to my list to investigate, or I pull out my phone to message him. And then I remember that he's going to be gone soon, gone in a way that I'll never be able to tell him anything ever again.

It seems impossibly cruel, to be so close to two people who half-lifed long before they deserved to.

I remember whispering *Six days* to myself before, in my bed in my house in Colorado. I hope it wasn't one of the days where I was down a rabbit hole of genetics, still looking for a loophole that would save her. I spent too many days doing that and not enough just being with her.

For one ridiculous second, I think . . . what if I could handle it? I did it before, for Maybelle, and it can't be harder than that. What if I can pull my shit together enough to see Flint one more time before he dies?

The bright peal of my ringtone spills into my room. It's my dad. Again. He's been calling every day. Irritation has me jabbing the green button—if I talk to him once, maybe he'll leave me alone for a week.

I don't bother with hello. "What, Dad?"

On the screen, he flinches. "Uh, just calling to check on you. Mom and I are worried. Gigi told me about your friend."

"It's fine," I say stiffly.

"Are you sure? Because—"

"I'm sure, Dad. It's not a big deal. It's nothing compared to losing a sister."

Dad blinks. We've never talked about Maybelle on any of these calls.

"Um, maybe you can pass me to Gigi," he says, floundering.

"I would, but my battery's low," I lie. "You'll have to call her on the house phone. Talk to you later, Dad."

I hang up and burrow into my sheets, pulling the pillow over my head. I never want to move again. It's dark here, and warm, and if I can just force myself to sleep, maybe I can get through the rest of the day.

I frown into the pillowed darkness. Is this what my mom is doing, thousands of miles away? For the first time, my heart aches with understanding. I see now, how leaving the nest of your bed sometimes feels impossible. That you just want to hide from everything, slide into sleep so your brain shuts up, because everything hurts less in the dark.

I suddenly want to hug her. *Mom.*

I press the pillow tighter over my head until the feeling passes.

I leave for school, walking toward another torturous day of

skirting questions and avoiding sensitive topics. I'm almost there when I get the text from Flint. I know what it says, but I tap on it anyway.

I'm sorry.

He sends it once a day. It should grate on my nerves. But I can't stop feeling this tug inside my chest that always seems to come from the direction of his house, and it's utter bullshit because *Where's the science behind that?* But at the same time . . . the fact that he sends me this every day means he feels it too. The thing between us, pulling taut but not breaking.

I start to type out Stop texting me.

But I can't send it. I don't want him to stop, because when he stops, that'll mean he's gone.

After school the next day, I pace in slow, aimless circles around Gigi's living room. The house is so quiet I swear I can hear every fiber of carpet bending under my socks. My brain is snagged on something, like I'm a loading screen with the bar stuck on 17 percent.

Something about this afternoon is swelling up in me, rising like panic. Psychology is a science, and scientifically, I realize this is emotional shock, but knowing that can't magically pull me out of it. I don't have the internship anymore to distract me, so I'm trapped here thinking about Flint.

Half of me is unforgivingly upset about what he did, and the other half is caught in the memory of that coal factory kiss. Yesterday I caught myself with my nose buried in the collar of my coat in case there was anything left of him there. I was so mad at myself after I did it that I went to the laundry room and sprayed half a bottle of Febreze on it.

I'm sure it's not helping that I'm getting basically no sleep. Last night I couldn't stop thinking about how each one of my heartbeats matches a tick forward of the clock's second hand. I woke up in the dark, pulse thudding with the sheer *dread* of being on countdown again, and for a moment I thought it was Maybelle who had five days left. And then I remembered that the countdown's not for her this time.

I go to the kitchen. Maybe I just need another coffee, or some food. There's not much in the cabinets, mostly some healthy stuff that Gigi and I have left untouched the entire time I've been here. Rice cakes, walnuts, a bag of lentils—

The memory strikes like a needle. I can hear her voice as she tried a walnut for the first time. "I know why they call it a walnut, Tember," she said, spitting it out with an exaggerated grimace. "It tastes like a wall."

The urge to cry and the urge to press my hand over my heart out of sheer fondness battle in my chest.

I shut the cabinet. I can't bear being here with all of this, not a second longer. She's here, in the photo albums on the living room shelves, in the formulas written on my bedroom walls. I'm afraid to admit it, but she's always been everywhere—in a bag of walnuts, a swing set, my red hair in the mirror.

I grab my coat and plunge out into the cold. I strike out away from Gigi's, away from the creek, away from Flint's stupid cabin. I walk until the tip of my nose feels like a chip of ice, until the cold air

236

burns my lungs. I tramp through dead leaves for so long I start to wonder if I should pull out my phone to figure out where I am, but something about the trees feels vaguely familiar.

When I see the first stone, I come to an abrupt halt.

For a few long moments, I just stare stupidly at it, my mind refusing to acknowledge where I am.

The Ruins.

I almost turn back. I left to get away from the formulas written on my bedroom wall, and by some stupid mistake, I've ended up at their sister.

Instead I step over the fallen stones and warily approach what's left of the broken building. Surely the wind and the rain have scrubbed the Ruins of my presence by now. Twigs snap under my boots. I circle around until I can see the wall. Good—only the faintest gray marks are left of my formulas.

I turn to leave this behind me too and—

There he is.

A hundred yards away but walking in this direction. Head down and hands shoved into his pockets.

Everything in me wants to run to him. To give in to the mess that's been building in me since before we met, to be sad all over him because he's made of that, and he can take it.

He looks up like he's sensed me, even though I haven't moved.

His steps stutter. There's a moment of disbelief, then one of hope—and then his expression collapses into heartbreak.

I can't move.

He starts walking again, slowly, like he's afraid I'll disappear.

And then he's here. Close enough to touch if I were to take two steps forward.

For a moment we just stare. I'm fighting back a million different feelings. Before I fall apart under the weight of all of it, I break our stare and glance off into the forest.

"Damn it, Flint," I whisper.

He takes a half step forward. Stops. "I'm so sorry. September, I'm so, *so* sorry."

I can't look at him. I *know* he's sorry.

"Yell at me," he says softly.

"What?"

"Yell at me if you want to. Anything. Just don't send me away."

Tears well up in my eyes. I don't have the energy to shout at him like I did at the creek. And it's not like he doesn't understand what he's done—he's beating himself up more than I ever could.

"September, I—"

"I'm a wreck." The words are out before I can stop them, jagged in the air.

"Me too," he says. The darkness around him swells, and instead of flinching away from it, I step into it. I think about everything that's gone wrong in the last week.

My throat closes up, and my eyes prickle. *Acetylcholine*, my brain supplies, $C_7NH_{16}O_2+$, even as it's getting flooded with it. It's all sputtering up, like he's a black hole and being close to him is sucking all the darkness in me to the surface.

"It was my sister," I whisper.

Flint freezes.

"I had a sister. She half-lifed when she was two."

"Shit, September."

"My parents tried to get me to come here to Carbon Junction before the last day. Ship me off so I didn't have to see it. But I wanted to be there. I was there when she came into the world. She deserved to have me holding her as she left it."

"Oh Christ," he says, and then he listens as it all spills out.

"We didn't want to leave the house that day at all. Didn't want to risk her being hurt, spending her last hours in pain or in a hospital or in a ditch. So we made a fort in the living room. Lugged all our mattresses downstairs, piled it with pillows and blankets.

"I sang her our favorite songs, played games with her, trying to stop her from picking up on the undercurrent in the room. I saw confusion flash across her face a couple of times, like she was thinking, *Mommy and Daddy and Tember don't do this every day with me.*

"I was singing to her when she went. It was fast, a little shudder. A far-off stare. I sang until I was sure she wasn't with me anymore."

The knot in my chest is harder than ever.

"So you see? I know what it's like to live with a countdown too," I say.

Flint looks as devastated as I feel.

"What was her name?" he whispers.

"Maybelle." It's the first time I've said her name to anyone since moving here.

I named her.

I force myself to breathe. Close my eyes. In on a count of three. One, two—

"Stop doing that," he says softly.

I blink my eyes open. "Doing what?"

"Every time it starts to come up, you throttle it and bury it deeper inside you."

My eyes burn with tears.

I tug my hand out of his. "Do you think what you're doing is so much better? It's not like you're a model example of what it looks like to face your grief."

He tenses.

"What have you been doing since I last saw you, Flint? I think I can guess. Not eating. Not coming out of your room. Not *living*. Am I right?"

He just stares blankly down at the ground.

"What would you tell me if *I* was the one with five days left? Would you want me to live the way you're making yourself live?"

He crumples forward a little, but I can't stop now. Even if by the end of this we'll both be lying on the forest floor, bleeding out.

"What would you tell Maybelle? You've had *twelve more years* than my sister had, and what have you done with them?" I demand. "What would you tell her, Flint?"

flint

I CAN BARELY breathe. September's dismantling me.

We stand in the cold forest, both of us as broken as the walls around us. The air is still, but inside me, a million things are splintering.

My heart is breaking for her sister.

I can't believe September was with her when it happened. She had to *watch* it. And afterward, she had to go on, living beyond that one horrible second that turned her into an only child.

September's words play on repeat in my head.

What would you tell her?

Shreds of my seventeen years swirl around me, every single thing I believed and didn't believe. For the first time, it feels so simple to tell which ones were *really* true.

Something is coming into focus, a glowing diamond of truth hidden under the wreckage of my life.

What would you tell her?

I think about every time September could find beauty in places where I could only see ugliness. I think about the times she showed me how to savor something that felt good. The sweetness of a butterscotch candy, a sunset, a kiss, a quiet starlit night. She made me look. She tilted my face to those things when I couldn't even lift my own chin.

I think about how I've *enjoyed* more hours of my life this past month than I have in entire years. Before I came here, my life was a miserable blur, but these last few weeks have been studded with small flashes of happiness. Playing flashlight tag. Going to that flea market with Mom. Playing video games with Aerys.

Eating a pile of waffles drenched in caramel. Wandering through that creepy, beautiful factory. Every second I spent with September.

The memories crescendo in my chest.

And, with a sudden certainty, I know: I've been doing this wrong the whole time.

I thought that by denying myself happiness, leaving this world would hurt less. But all I've done is make my *life* hurt.

And it's messed up, because it's not exactly a shocking revelation. I *knew* I was hurting everyone, but I'd convinced myself that I was doing the right thing.

You've had twelve more years than my sister had, and what have you done with them?

What would you tell her, Flint?

I'd tell her to let her family have as much of her time as she can give them. Go to the zoo, and the beach, and every museum within a hundred-mile radius if that's what they want, just to be in the car with them.

I'd tell her to soak up whatever spots of joy she can. To slow down and savor that gorgeous sunset, a long hug, a warm blanket, her favorite food. To let in that old friend and all the good memories that come with them.

I regret eight whole years of my life. It feels strangely freeing to admit that. And now I can do something with the days that come next.

I take one long, quaking breath.

My fingertips are tingling, and it's not because of the cold. The wreckage has cleared, and I can see now that living means savoring the good moments. Being able to appreciate the beauty, despite all the pain.

I want to spend my last five days drinking up as much life as I can.

I want to be more than just alive. I want to *live*.

september

FLINT STARES DOWN at the packed-earth floor of this ruined house. Processing, I guess. Well, let him process.

I scoot a few feet away from him. Talking about Maybelle's last day has taken me dangerously close to the edge. I've been trying to suppress my memories of my sister for months, hoping they would fade with time, but they're still there and vivid as ever.

Flint's silent for many long minutes. I'm about to ask him if he's okay when he straightens, as abruptly as a spell breaking.

"You're right," he says softly.

I don't know what I was expecting him to say. Not that.

He turns to look directly at me. "You're right," he says again. "I don't want to keep living like I've been living.

"I'm going to do the next few days differently than I did all the others. Get a little bit of actual living in before I go. And I know I need to do it on my own; I get that. I've asked too much of you already, and I'm so, so sorry for putting you through all of this. And now I know you were there when your sister died . . . I won't ask you to go through that again."

I open my mouth to speak, but he plows on.

"There's just one thing I have to say, and then I'll leave you alone, and I'll stop texting you, and everything. September . . ."

He takes a deep breath and looks at me, so intensely earnest that I have to clamp my teeth down on the inside of my lip to keep from looking away.

"September, I will *never* not be sorry for lying to you. But I'm not sorry we met, and I'm grateful for every second I got with you."

He lifts a hand and almost touches my cheek, then pulls back at the last moment.

And then he turns and starts walking away.

I watch him go, head down and hands shoved into his pockets. The sound of his boots crushing through the leaves get a decibel quieter with every step he takes away from me. In a minute, he'll disappear into the trees.

My heart thuds.

Maybe I should let him go. Maybe we're too broken to fix.

I can see how it will all play out. I'll walk home alone through this dying forest. Tomorrow, I'll check my phone for his daily I'm sorry, but it won't come. And then I'll wake up on December 5, the day after his deathday, and know that he isn't in the world with me anymore.

There will be no going back then. No *Let's rewind,* no *I should have spent those last days with you.* Time's running out, and I know better than anybody what that feels like.

I should still be mad at him for lying to me, but the anger's burning off, losing more and more heat by the second. And he's . . . he's Flint. I *know* him now, and I want his last days to be full of love. To be full of moments where his face lights up in wonder, or happiness, or just simple contentedness. And I know I can give him that.

245

"Wait," I croak out, even though he's too far away now to hear me.

Panic slices through me. I take one lurching step forward, then I get it together and run after him.

"Flint, wait," I call.

He turns. I sprint up to him, stopping so close I have to crane my neck.

He looks down at me, so cautious and hopeful. Like I have his heart in my hands, and I can either smash it or place it gently back in his chest.

"I can't let you walk away," I say, half out of breath from running. "I can help you have a good last week. I want to be there for it. Even if it's awful at the end, even if it's the second most painful experience of my life. I want to be there."

He looks like he might cry. "Seriously?"

"Yes. Seriously."

He does get emotional then. His mouth wobbles, and he has to press a hand over it and look out into the trees.

"Are you sure this is the best idea?" he asks.

"No." In five days, he'll be gone, and I'll still be here, and nothing will ever make that not unfair. "But it's what I want to do."

He nods, considering. "I think we should have one rule, though," he says. "You can't make it all about me and pack away all of your emotions. You're allowed to be sad."

I shake my head. "No, Flint. I don't want to clutter your last days with my mess. I want it to be about you. With Maybelle, I wasn't always there. I had two years after she half-lifed, and I spent most of it at school and the rest of it buried in a textbook."

"You were there at the end," he says.

I was. Those last few weeks, I didn't touch a textbook, just spent as much time with her as I could. I can do that for Flint too.

He plows a hand through his hair, concern knitting his eyebrows. "I'm worried about you, September. Will you do the same thing when I go? Bury your feelings and spend your life trying to outrun them?"

"Probably. But, Flint, I don't want to end up like my parents—or you, no offense."

"None taken."

"I'm afraid if I let it all catch up to me, I'll just be . . . permanently sad."

"I don't know. I think it's possible to face your grief, go into it, and still come out the other side. Not totally sure how, because I clearly haven't nailed it, but I think it must be possible."

I shake my head sadly. "I don't know if there is another side, Flint. I don't think you can ever be the same after losing someone so close."

He thinks for a long moment. "No, you're right. You won't ever be the same as you were. But it has to be better than not facing it at all, right?"

I close my eyes against the fresh sting. "Maybe."

A gust of wind blows through the trees. Flint stiffens and rubs his arms for warmth.

"First thing I'm going to do is start wearing a coat," he mumbles.

I unwind my scarf. I step in closer to loop it around his neck. He stays very still as he waits for me to finish, looking down at me. He wants me to meet his eyes, but I keep mine trained on the scarf, because my heart rate just lurched up.

247

"There," I say quietly, patting the knot.

"Thank you," he says quietly back.

There's a charged moment that reminds me of piercingly honest midnight conversations, of packages wrapped in brown paper, of the slip of his Vantablack hair through my fingers.

It's all still there, somehow. The attraction, the breathlessness. I'm not sure what to do with it, but it's there.

Flint's pinkie finger brushes mine.

"Maybe we shouldn't . . ." I whisper. I don't know if we can pick up exactly where we left off.

"It's okay," he says, taking a small, respectful step back. "I'm just grateful you're still here. It's okay if it's just as friends."

Just friends. "Okay," I say.

Now that that's been decided, something between us loosens. I'm going to have to say goodbye to him, but not today.

The thought of five more days with him feels like breathing in pure oxygen.

flint

MY BRAIN IS going a mile a minute as I approach the cabin. I need to make a list. I want to cram every day full of moments, experiences, *life*.

I let myself in through the front door.

"Mom? Dad?" My voice still echoes in this skeleton of a place. I told September that I needed to fill them in and asked her if we could meet up again in a couple hours. I'm jittery now, nearly vibrating, because I have five days left, and *there's so much I want to do with them*.

Mom emerges from the hallway, moving like she's running out of batteries.

"Flint?" She frowns and looks at my bedroom door, which is still closed. "What are you doing out here?"

I go to her and wrap my arms around her.

"What's going on? Why are you hugging me?" she says, and her voice sounds so funny muffled into my shoulder I have to smile.

"Where's Dad? I need to talk to you guys."

She draws back and notices the yellow scarf still wound around my neck.

"I saw September," I explain.

"Oh, honey." Her eyes brim with sympathy.

"No, it was good. Don't worry."

The back porch door slides open, and Dad clomps in, carrying an armload of firewood. He stops midstomp and looks at us. "What's up? Everything okay?"

"I need to talk to you guys. Sit down."

They walk suspiciously to the couch. Mom slides her hand into Dad's, and they brace for whatever I'm about to say.

"Stop looking so freaked out. It's good. I promise."

I grab a blanket and wrap it around my shoulders. I'm done with being cold.

I launch into the story of how I ended up at the Ruins and how what September said slapped me into wanting to live.

"I'm sorry, guys. I know this is what you've been trying to tell me for years."

I wait for their reaction, guilt gnawing at my stomach.

Mom nods slowly. "It's okay, Flint. Sometimes you have to hear the same thing in a different way."

Relief floods me.

"So. What's on your agenda now, kid?" Dad asks.

"For now, I was thinking . . . do you want to maybe play a board game or something? I know Mom brought some from home."

Mom's face glows, the first genuine smile I've seen from her in years. "That's a wonderful idea."

We sprawl out on the living room floor and play every game in the stack. Dad keeps looking down the hall at my bedroom door, and then at me, like he can't really believe I'm out here, really *with* them, really *trying* for the first time in years.

At one point, Mom's competitive side flares up, and she's

desperately trying to win back her lead, and she and Dad are bickering but in a teasing way, and I feel something swell in my chest I haven't felt in so, so long.

It's not quite the high-octane extravaganza I pictured, but it's a start.

september

AFTER FLINT'S AFTERNOON with his parents, we settle into the bamboo-sleek, dramatically lit interior of Carbon Junction's best Japanese restaurant, and I watch as Flint tries his first ever roll of sushi. He's never had it before, and honestly, this could go either way.

"Oh my god. This is amazing." He flags down the waiter. "Excuse me? Can you bring the menu back?"

I laugh as he orders another *six* things. While we wait for them, I twist the napkin in my lap into a knot. He's fidgety too, pulsing with a barely contained energy. There's a sense of urgency now, almost tipping into panic. It manifests as a buzz in the air, neither of us fully able to relax.

"So . . . five days," I say, even though I have to push the words out around the lump in my throat. "What should we do?"

"I was hoping you'd have some ideas. I googled bucket lists, but everything is either a plane ride away or isn't on Carbon Junction's social calendar for December. There were a few things I would have loved to do. Foam party. Watch a Pride Parade. Go to a Renaissance festival in full costume. Attend a silent disco."

I smile. "Those would have been incredible." I ache for the fact that he doesn't have enough time left to do them.

He pokes at a lump of wasabi with his chopstick. "I feel like I

should be more prepared for this. I've had years to think about it."
He looks up. "What have you loved? What stands out in your mind
as can't miss Life Attractions?"

"I'm not sure." I push some rice around on my plate. "When
people make those bucket lists online, they focus on big, flashy
things, like going to the top of the Eiffel Tower or swimming with
dolphins or whatever. They're doing those for Instagram, though, or
because they think it's what they're supposed to want. I guess they
do sound impressive when you say them out loud to other people.
But everything I remember as being the best moments of my life has
been so . . . small. Like . . . running through the sprinklers with
my best friend on summer break, getting grass stuck all over my wet
feet. The first time my baby sister smiled at a silly face I made. My
first real Eureka moment in the biochem lab."

Kissing you, I think. My cheeks flush—thanks, vasodilators. I
promptly try to dislodge the thought. *Friends.*

Flint nods. "So maybe you can't plan the small, intense stuff."

"Maybe not," I say.

There's a bleak silence, but then he shakes it off, which is more
than I can do these days.

"Okay, so let's shoot for medium thrills," he decides. He pulls out
his phone. "Should we make a list? Skydiving and base jumping are
out—those are definitely high-level thrills, and I don't want to end
up in a full-body cast—but what about something like zip-lining?
And I've always wanted to go skiing." He pops an unagi roll into his
mouth. "Wow, okay, I don't know about these eel ones."

"I think the ski slope on I-99 just opened for the season," I say.

"Really? I'm sure my parents would be up for taking us. Mom wanted this whole vacation to be full of stuff like that, so I think they have some money saved. I'll ask them."

He brings his napkin up from his lap and lays it next to his empty plate. I've never seen him eat so much in one sitting before.

The moment hangs, and I can see why he's been so talkative tonight. Every time there's a silence, the countdown looms, reminding us that every second is another one gone.

He looks so *alive*. It's bizarre to be sitting across from someone so perfectly healthy and know that in a week they'll be gone. I can't wrap my head around it, even though I've been through it before.

"I guess we should head home," I say.

He shakes his head. "I don't think I'm ready to call it a night." I hear what he's really saying: *We're running out of time.* "Can we do something that involves being warm?"

I tug my phone out. "Let me see what I can find."

"Do a search: top things to do in Pennsylvania before you croak."

I ignore him and tap around on my phone. Warm. He wants warm . . .

"I think I found the perfect place."

On our walk back to the Jeep, I try to ignore the brutal white column of the Institute looming over the town. I remember the first time I saw it, when I was a little kid visiting Gigi for Christmas. The building was so alien, and I used to imagine what went on in there.

Now I know. Dr. Jackson will be roaming the top-floor lab, squeaking equations onto her whiteboard. Percy's probably sitting in my spot in the observation room this very moment, poised to take the place in the biochem program at CJU, about to live the career I wanted. The life.

Flint stops walking. "Hey. You okay?"

I shrug. He knows the answer. I can't think about my colossal career screwup right now. That—and everything else—can be postponed to next week.

We keep walking. Once, his arm brushes against mine, like it did when we were on our way to the factory party, but he doesn't let it happen again.

When we pass the general store, display windows lit up with Christmas lights and mannequins, Flint grabs my hand and says, "Hold on a sec, I have an idea," and then he pulls me into the store. He beelines for a rack with dozens of puffy winter coats.

"What color should I get?" he asks.

"Not black," I say, a smile tugging at the corner of my mouth.

He rolls his eyes. "Fine, not black." Then he grabs one, frees it from its hanger, and slides it on. "This one," he says. The tags ruffle at his wrist as he wears it to the cash register.

It's burnt orange, and it matches the color of my hair exactly.

According to the "Top Ten Things to Do on a Fall Weekend in Pennsylvania" list I found, the apple orchard and pumpkin patch in Sugar Grove stays open late for "cozy autumn evenings." They have a giant stone fire pit, surrounded by an assortment of rocking chairs, egg chairs, and gliders. They even lend you blankets.

When Flint and I sat down on one of the two-person gliders, the seats were all full and kids were running around everywhere, but now there's only one older couple left.

"Well, I'm not sure if *drink apple cider* was ever on anyone's bucket list, but it should be," Flint says. "I'm categorizing it as a medium-life-thrill item."

I take a sip from my own mug. It is pretty satisfying.

"Are you warm enough?" I ask.

He looks down at his brand-new orange coat and the thick plaid blanket laid over our laps. "Nope."

"Come on, you used to wear a T-shirt in this weather and not even flinch."

"If you recall, I did actually *pass out* because of that life choice," he says.

For the half hour that we've been sitting here, I've been achingly aware of how close we are. He's been steadily rocking our glider this entire time. It's not that late, but between the hypnotic rocking and the fire, I feel drowsy.

I pull the blanket up to my chin. "Sorry this isn't more of a medium-intensity thrill."

He looks at me, and something hovers between us. Like he's trying to convey that just being with me *is* the thrill.

I look away.

God, wouldn't this all be easier if we weren't attracted to each other?

Across from us, the last two people rise, say goodnight to us, and disappear into the darkness.

We're alone now. The fire crackles, and the orchard whispers around us. The stars above are pinprick clear, but tonight I'm having trouble finding the beauty.

Flint stops rocking us and leans forward to set his empty mug on the edge of the fire pit. He holds his hand out to take my mug, and when I give it to him, his fingers accidentally close over mine.

The touch is enough to have my brain releasing a tiny burst of those heady, dizzying neurotransmitters. *Dopamine, norepinephrine, serotonin.* $C_8H_{11}NO_2$, $C_8H_{11}NO_3$, $C_{10}H_{12}N_2O$.

"Sorry," he says quietly, like he thinks he shouldn't touch me.

What would the last five weeks have been like if he'd told me up front that he was dying? Would we have had some beautiful, bittersweet, end-of-days love story? Probably not. I would have left him alone and not gotten involved.

I press my eyes closed.

"I can't do this," I whisper.

Flint slumps. "It's okay," he mumbles. "I thought it might be too hard to stay until the end, and I totally get it. It's fine, and I'll be—"

"No. That's not what I mean." I touch his arm, but he won't look at me.

Maybe we won't have a whole love story, the kind that lasts years or decades, but we have the next handful of days.

"Flint." I reach out, fingertips at his jaw to guide him back to me. Our eyes lock, and I try to pour everything I'm feeling into this one intense stare.

"I don't think I want to be just friends. I know we don't have much time, and I know I should be mad at you forever for not telling me about your deathday, but there's something here, and it's too hard to keep flinching away from you, and I—"

I stumble. *I can't press pause on falling for you, even if you won't be there to catch me five days from now.*

"I just—I don't want to spend the next five days pretending we're only friends."

My declaration hangs in the air between us. The firelight flickers over his face. I wait for him to say something. *Anything.*

The old Flint's at war with the new Flint. I can tell he's swallowing down the worry, the *What if it hurts you more*, the *This might be a very bad idea.*

Finally, something changes in the electrical field between us.

"Good," he says softly. "Because I don't want to pretend either."

A thrill hums inside me.

"So . . . now that we're not friends," he says slowly, "does that mean you want me to . . . do things like . . . this?"

He leans forward and brushes the softest kiss to the edge of my jaw.

The chemicals flood me instantly. My skin buzzes, going tight all over. I nod, helpless in the onslaught of sensation.

"And what about . . . this?" he asks softly.

The next kiss is on my cheek, right under my eyelashes.

"That's fine too," I say.

Before he has a chance to say *Like this* again, his lower lip brushes mine infinitesimally.

It obliterates my control. I surge forward, and our lips interlock so perfectly, so exquisitely it makes me want to cry. He licks a stripe on my lower lip, and it lights something up inside me, has me tugging at him, holding on to him.

The blanket falls, and he pulls it back up, tenting it over our shoulders. Heat builds under it, searing where his hands land, where mine land.

"God, September," he says. His voice is barely a breath, shuddering and woozy.

We kiss again, and again, and it's all black cherry and firelight, and I never want it to end.

flint

THE NEXT MORNING, after an hour on the road, my parents and September and I step out of the Jeep, and our boots sink into fresh, crunchy snow.

It feels like we're in a different world. Everything is white: the sky, the incomprehensibly large mountain in front of us, the gleaming hotel to our left. There are people everywhere—the slopes are covered with skiers slaloming down the face of the mountain, some of them a thousand feet above us and small as ants, some of them life-sized and close enough to bump into as we walk through the ski resort's base camp.

Mom and Dad lead the way. September's hand brushes against mine, and even though it's the lightest touch, it still feels electric. I twine my fingers with hers and look at her to check—*Is this okay?* It feels like we're still finding our way back to each other.

"Equipment rental's over there," Dad says, pointing.

When we get to the front of the line, September grabs a snowboard and says to the guy handing out boots, "Size seven, please—Burtons, if you have them."

I do a double take.

She smiles faintly. "Colorado, remember?"

"You're about to make me look like a total noob, aren't you?"

260

She laughs. "Yes."

She shows me how to click into my skis, and a little conveyor belt takes us up to the top of a small slope—the bunny hill, she calls it.

The snow, spread out in front of me, is sparkling, reflecting a million rays of sun.

"You ready for this, kid?" Dad asks, squeezing my shoulder.

"Sure. Bucket list here we come," I say.

It's . . . not easy. Mom and Dad have skied before too, so all three of them are shouting tips at me and laughing at my mistakes.

"I think I'm getting the hang of it," I call out to them on my fifth or sixth trip down.

For ten blissful seconds, I'm flying. The wind slices through my hair, and the thrill rushes in my veins.

I'm free.

I'm also gathering speed—quite a lot of speed. I try, but I can't get my skis to do the "vee" thing—

"DO THE VEE!" September yells, but my skis are sticking together, and—I can't stop and—

I wipe out. Spectacularly.

I look up, spitting snow out of my mouth, batting at my face to get the ice-cold slivers out of my eyelashes.

September whooshes to a halt in front of me on her snowboard, spraying up a wall of snow that frankly makes her look like a badass.

Once she's sure I'm unhurt, she starts laughing.

"Guys, I hate to say it, but I'm not coordinated enough for this. I think maybe I should return the skis—maybe we can just go snow tubing?"

"Like a child?" September teases.

"Yes, like a child. You only live once, and, wouldn't you know it, snow tubing is on my bucket list."

The sun's dipping below the horizon when we step out of the alpine-themed restaurant where we had dinner.

"Tubing is where it's at," I'm saying to my dad. "All of the adrenaline rush, none of the risk of broken legs."

Mom hugs me. "I'm very glad you didn't break anything, but I do wish we'd videoed your wipeout earlier," she says.

I squeeze her back. My heart swells with fondness for all three of them.

Out of habit, I pull out my phone to check the countdown.

It hits like a punch to the chest.

A second ago, I was fine, and now it's taking everything I have not to break down and cry, to thrash around at the unfairness of it all, to pick up a piece of wood from this disgustingly picturesque lumberjack stack of firewood and hurl it through the gorgeous Christmas-lit lodge window—

September's hand slips into mine.

My heartbeat settles.

I turn away from September and my parents while I compose myself. The mountain looms in my view.

"I want to go to the top," I say suddenly.

September squints doubtfully up at the peak—it's where all the expert runs start.

"Not to ski down," I clarify. "I just want to see."

I want to stand on top of a mountain with her.

Dad starts toward the ski lift, but Mom grabs him. "We'll let you two go up."

The chairlift is almost as exhilarating as the skiing itself. Feet dangling over empty air, knowing the only thing stopping me from falling out is a clanky metal bar. There's something about toying with the edge of death that feels even more thrilling now that I've got so little time left on the clock.

At the top, we crunch through the snow to the observation point. The valley sprawls out in front of us. The twilight is ethereally gorgeous on the snow. We breathe in the ice-cold air and marvel at the scenery rolling out from our feet. And this is just one valley, in one mountain ridge, in one continent of this huge world that I've seen so little of.

It's easy to find the beauty in places like this. It's harder, what September can do—like when she found the beauty in dismally gray Merrybrook or in the slump of the old houses in Carbon Junction's Old Town. In me.

A bracing wind slashes through the air, but it doesn't budge me. I've never felt healthier, or stronger. And isn't that a fucking joke.

For a few hours, it felt like our problems weren't real, and I wonder if part of that magic is because we left Carbon Junction.

"It says there's an observation deck where we can see down into the valley on the other side," September says.

To get there, we have to walk through a narrow pass flanked by towering pine trees. For a few minutes, we're completely alone. The only two people in the world. I turn to look at her, and she's so utterly, gut-wrenchingly beautiful, I have to stop walking.

She turns, probably to ask me why I stopped, but the words die on her lips.

For a moment, we just stare at each other.

Then something snaps, and she's on me, colliding with my chest, her mouth hot on mine. The back of my jacket scrapes on the bark of the tree she pushes me up against.

My body responds to her in a thousand ways: fizzing warmth in my cheeks, lavalike heat coursing down my spine, an antsy need building in my lungs. My heartbeat is everywhere, pounding in my ears. I can't get enough of her.

Her fingers fist almost painfully in my hair, and her body arches. I haul her closer. When her fingernails skate under my big puffy jacket and under my shirt, goose bumps break out over my whole torso.

I break away to catch my breath. "Is it really messed up that I just want to spend all day doing this?"

She drops her head to my chest, breathless. "If it's messed up," she says, "then I'm messed up too, Flint. And I don't want to do *just* this," she adds in a whisper.

My whole body heats. Just the thought of *more* has my brain stuttering, so to show her how on board with that plan I'd be, I kiss her again, hard.

I'm addicted to how being with her makes the countdown fade.

I could stay here all day, but she finally takes my hand and tugs me to the observation point, which is just as stunning as the other side. We're walking back to the ski lift when she asks quietly, "Flint? Have you ever . . . before?"

"Yes. Twice. I got it in my head last year that I probably shouldn't die a virgin."

"Sensible," she murmurs.

I look down at my boots, afraid to meet her eyes. "Have you?" I ask.

"Yes. A few times, with a guy I dated over the summer."

I'm a little relieved. I think if it were any other combination—if either of us hadn't before—things might get even more complicated than they already are.

Our chairlift arrives, and it carries us down the mountain, our gloved hands twined together, our breath puffing in the air.

september

I'M ON MY way to the kitchen the next morning when thoughts of Flint and our snow-dusted kisses flash over me. I have to stop and lean against the wall, touching my fingertips to my lips, stunned all over again at the electric hum that hasn't quite faded.

Four days, my brain warns me, slicing through the hum.

I grimace against the countdown and shove off the wall.

In the kitchen, Gigi's standing over a skillet of scrambled eggs with her back to me.

Things are still tense between us. I know I owe her an apology, but I'm too preoccupied with Flint, and besides, nothing's changed. I still don't understand her nonchalance about Maybelle.

"Gigi?" I say tentatively, preparing to deliver the lie I've rehearsed. It's Thursday—but there's no way I'm going back to school today. Not after yesterday with Flint. "I'm not feeling so good. Maybe I should stay home."

She turns around. "Honey, I was already going to call you out of school again today. We'll pretend it's the flu—I figure we can buy you a week."

Grateful tears sting my eyes, and I can only nod.

• • •

I don't know which medium thrill we're doing until Flint flicks on the blinker and guides the Jeep over to an exit marked with a sign for Western Pennsylvania Wildlife Park.

"Oh, Flint. A roadside zoo? Please don't tell me that's where we're going."

"Yep. There's a thing at this one where you can ride in a cage on the back of a truck through the lion enclosure—"

"Please no." I rub my temples. "Maybe this is why people die on their deathdays—deciding to do stupid shit. Are you sure this isn't classified as a high-level thrill?"

He pats my knee. "It's perfectly safe."

I shake my head disparagingly. "Fine. It's your bucket list."

The place does look respectable, at least, and it's AZA accredited, which means that it treats the animals ethically and that it has trained veterinarians and zoological PhDs on staff.

A staff member leads us to a platform and we board the truck. As we step into the cage with three other visitors, it's momentarily ironic that the humans are the ones in the cage this time.

"Whatever you do," the guide says, "don't use the mesh above your heads to hang on. If the lions see anything poking out of the cage, they'll think it's food, and they will be over here *fast*."

Fabulous.

I grip the safety rail tight as they drive us out into the African lion enclosure. It certainly doesn't look like Africa—it's a cold, overcast Pennsylvania day—but at least the animals have tons of space.

One of the lions saunters over to us right away.

"Come look," Flint says, beckoning me closer to where the lion is prowling.

"No, I'm good, I'll stay over here." I wrap my coat tighter around myself. I wonder if bright colors like Flint's orange jacket and my red are going to make the lions angry.

The animal keepers feed the lion with special tongs that can't be tugged through the cage.

"Jesus Christ, Flint," I mutter. The cuts of raw beef the keepers are giving the lions probably taste a lot like the flesh of my arm.

In one graceful bound, the lion leaps at the cage. Distressingly, the meshed metal bars rattle, and the truck rocks on its tires. The animal's sheer size has fear curling into a tight ball inside me. He licks at the cage, three-inch-long ivory-white incisors clacking against the metal.

Flint leans forward. I hook a finger through his belt loop. I don't want to begrudge him this, but it feels like his behavior is starting to verge on self-destructive.

For one long minute, I watch as Flint and the lion have an intense stare-off.

The lion shakes his head, as if he's bored, and then he slinks away.

Flint turns to me, eyes blazing, the adrenaline hitting him hard.

"Did you see that?"

"I saw," I say faintly.

The truck engine starts up and trundles us over the uneven ground back to the main building.

The lion lies down, stretching his huge body—

And roars.

I've never heard anything like it. I'm not sure it was my ears that absorbed the noise—it was more a vibration that reverberated through every cell in my body.

Flint's arm settles around me, pulling me close. This—us—is still so new that it surprises me. He's so solid—he's real and warm and right here where I can wrap my arms around him.

I'm going to lose him.

The thought rips through me as fast and powerfully as the roar.

I look at the lion, staring straight into his amber eyes. *I understand how you feel.*

It's what I want to do too—roar at the unfairness of the world.

"Does this mean you're an adrenaline junkie now?" I ask as we navigate through the zoo's gift shop.

"I don't think so, but that was incredible."

His cheeks are flushed pink, and he's swinging our linked hands between us jauntily. I just hope skydiving isn't on tomorrow's list.

There are bins and barrels full of stuffed animals on both sides of us. We're meandering through, not really paying attention, when I spot the little gray elephant.

It's just a flash of a thought:

I should get that for Maybelle—

But it has everything in me plummeting.

"You okay?" Flint asks, grabbing my elbow to steady me.

A few weeks ago, I would have said yes and plastered on a smile.

"It's just . . . she would have loved this," I say quietly. "She was obsessed with elephants."

"You should get it," he says.

I run a finger over its floppy little ear. Its plastic bead eyes stare up at me like *Please love me.*

"Yeah."

Back in the Jeep, holding the elephant on my lap, I stare out the window and try to swallow down the lump in my throat.

"What happened back there? Memory?" Flint asks gently.

"No. I think the worst thing about losing someone is in the little moments, when your mind is on autopilot, and, just for a split second, you forget."

Flint takes one hand off the wheel and fastens it over mine. I grip his fingers tight.

"We used to share my room when we came to visit Gigi. The other night, I caught myself sneaking in there late at night, stepping quietly so I wouldn't wake Maybelle up—only to realize the room was empty."

I press my eyes closed. What will be the thing that trips me up in a week's time? What will remind me of Flint when he's gone?

He pulls the car over and turns in his seat to give me his full attention.

He doesn't say anything, just listens, and I find myself telling him more. "I had alerts set so I'd hear about any minuscule bit of progress on half-life science. Everything I read, I would apply it to her case, checking to see if it was a breakthrough big enough to make it so I wouldn't have to lose her. And then there was a day where I read an article and it didn't matter anymore. Because it was too late. She was gone."

"There was nothing you could have done," Flint says.

I shake my head. "I should have spent more time with her. I shouldn't have been so wrapped up in all that research, because it was useless and pointless and stupid anyway. Fucking Institute," I say. The words catch, ragged in my throat, and the venom behind them surprises me.

Something in me is saying, *All right, that's enough, get it together. Suppress this.* I was conditioned to pretend everything was okay. I spent so many nights lying awake in my bed in Colorado, swallowing down sobs as I listened to her singing herself to sleep on the other side of the wall.

I'm not crying, but his eyes are damp, and it makes me feel like a robot. Like I'm broken.

"I never cried, Flint," I whisper.

"I don't know that grieving always means crying."

"Yeah, well, I'm pretty sure I haven't grieved in any way. I don't talk about her because I don't want the floodgates to open. I'll just go around seeing her in everything, talking about her all the time, and crying all over everyone."

"I don't know what it's like to lose someone," he says carefully, "but I think—I hope—it gets so that you can sometimes talk about them without crying. Not all the time. But sometimes."

I nod, and the lump eases a little.

"What was one thing she did that made you laugh?" he asks.

I think for a moment. It feels weird, to try to pull up a specific memory, when I've spent so much time shoving them down.

"I guess . . . there was this one time, we were in the grocery store with my mom, and the intercom came on, just someone saying 'Good afternoon, shoppers, there's a deal on raspberries' or something, and Maybelle looked up at the ceiling and said, 'Thank you, lady in the sky!'"

I don't smile. But for the first time, I feel like maybe I could smile at this memory one day.

Flint draws me closer, wraps his arms around me, and hugs me. Just hugs me. The weighted blanket of him around me has everything in me settling.

After a few minutes, I tell him he can drive again. He kisses me on my temple and turns the key in the ignition. As he pulls back onto the highway, I check my phone and see a slew of frantic messages.

> BO: Are you not at school today?
>
> DOTTIE: Okay, you're definitely not here. Text us. We're worried.
>
> BO: Where are you? Are you okay? I mean obviously you're not okay but are you at home?

I'm about to put my phone away without answering when something makes me stop.

I look at how Flint's handled today. And maybe he's the exception to the rule; maybe he can handle all of my mess because he lives every day with worse, but maybe there are other people out there who can handle me too.

I can feel something in me loosening, opening up. For the first time ever, I . . . want to tell Dottie and Bo.

If they can't take it, I can move on, and then at least I won't have to avoid them at school or pretend to be okay over awkward lunches.

I hug the stuffed elephant. "Flint? Can you drive me to Dottie's?"

Half an hour later, I'm sitting on the beanbag in the corner of Dottie's room, a mess of nerves. How are they going to take this?

"Pumpkin, we're so sorry about Flint," Bo says.

I stare down into the mug of champurrado Dottie's Tía Leticia made for us when I came in. Here goes, I guess.

"It's not just Flint, guys. That's not the only thing that I've been falling apart over. Remember when I moved here in May? It's because my four-year-old sister had just died. She wasn't sick. It was a kill switch death."

Their faces go slack with shock. I'm sure *dead sister* was pretty low on their list of suspicions. The room is so still I can feel my blood pulsing in my cheeks. Maybe this was a bad idea.

But then Dottie reaches out and takes my hand and whispers, "Oh, September."

"I'm not sure if it was meeting Flint or working on my hypothesis, but it all started coming up, and I've been . . . just really struggling. I'm sorry that I dropped off the radar for you guys. I know I've been acting so weird."

I exhale, and most of the tension leaves my body. I'm surprised at how good it feels now that my truth is out there.

"Stand up," Dottie commands.

"What? Why?"

"You too, Bo."

Once we're all standing, Dottie wraps her arms around me in one of her signature hugs, and a second later Bo loops his around both of us.

"I'm so sorry. So, so sorry," Dottie says.

I squeeze my eyes shut and let them hug me. Dottie's magnolia body spray clusters in my throat, and the scientist in me knows that it's burning off a microscopic layer of cells, the way inhaled corrosive irritants like NH_3 do.

It's worth losing a few cells for this hug.

"We knew there must have been something," Bo says quietly, after we all sit back down.

"I did a pretty good job of hiding it until about five weeks ago."

"Mmm . . . no. We always knew," Dottie says. "It was like you'd put up this wall sometimes. Which is fine—you're allowed to have secrets."

"Why didn't you tell us when you moved here?" Bo asks.

I shrug. "I didn't want to be the girl with the dead sister from day one. I think an overwhelming majority of people don't want to deal with this kind of shit. I'm glad we had some time to get to know each other before I started losing my grip. I was my funniest with you—like, remember that day we met, when I had to come to school for the last two weeks of junior year to prove my residency for the internship? I swear I wasn't that fun in Colorado, but we just clicked, and I could return your zingers, and I felt . . . *fun*, for the first time in two years."

"You'll be that again," Bo says, patting my hand.

"I don't know . . . after next week, I might be miserable forever. So if that's a friendship deal breaker, you might want to back out now."

"It's not a deal breaker," Bo says firmly. "And you won't be miserable forever. We're going to get you through this."

"Bo and I have been *extremely* pissed off at Tall, Dark, and Sullen, by the way. If you want to go toilet paper his house or slash his tires, we are on board."

Oh. It didn't occur to me that they'd still be mad at him. So much has changed in the last few days.

I can still taste last night's kisses.

"Why are you looking all dreamy?" Bo demands. "Is there something else you need to tell us?"

I flush. "I guess you guys need to hear the whole story. You might not be quite as mad at him after."

"Good, because I was getting fond of the old grump, and I don't want to have to donate my cherry purse to Rag House on principle," Dottie says.

flint

2 DAYS, 12 HOURS, 15 MINUTES

I'M IN THE echoing, vaulted room of an art museum in Pittsburgh, staring at a painting of a black hole—not a NASA kind of black hole, literally a black circle someone's painted on a twenty-foot-tall canvas—when I start to lose it.

Dad comes up behind me. "Flint? You coming?"

Apparently ten minutes isn't a socially acceptable length of time to spend staring at a black hole.

"Leslie? Flint looks like he's about to puke," Dad says.

Mom power walks from the other end of the huge room, inspecting me for damage.

"I'm fine," I say. "It's just . . . this painting."

Maybe modern art wasn't the best idea. Nearly every painting in here amplifies my impending doom.

Mom guides us to a bench and furnishes me with a water bottle, even though I'm pretty sure we're not allowed to eat or drink in the presence of all this existential dread.

I lean forward, sandwiched between my parents, and press my eyes shut.

"It's getting really scary, Mom." I whisper the stark truth of it into the sterile museum air.

She rubs my arm. "I know. You're being so brave."

Not long now. She doesn't say the words, but I hear them.

I drink all the water and stare at the grout between the squares of marble on the floor.

"I'm so sorry, honey," Mom says. "We should have done something else today."

"No, it's cool, Mom." I know this is her idea of a day well lived.

"Welp. Let's blow this pop stand," Dad says after a while, slapping his knees and standing.

On our way to the Jeep, Mom says, "I know you want to spend as much time with September as you can, but why don't you have Aerys come over when we get home?"

"I would, but I think I kind of threw a grenade on our friendship."

"What? Oh no!"

"Yeah."

It was such a dick move to throw her ex-friend issue in her face.

"I guess there's not really time to fix it now," I say bleakly as we pile into the Jeep.

Dad puts the car into reverse and twists in his seat. But instead of backing up, he says, "Hey. Even if you can't fix stuff with Aerys, you sure that's the note you want to leave things on with her?"

"That . . . is actually a really good point."

"I know. Love ya, kid," Dad says, and then he steps on the gas and takes us back to Carbon Junction.

I'm standing outside the high school when the bell rings, scanning the people streaming out of the building. After a minute, Aerys breaks away from the crowd, slinging her backpack over her shoulder as she heads away from me. Her swaggering, confident stride eats up the sidewalk.

"Aerys!" I call, sprinting to catch up to her.

She stops and looks around. When she spots me, she stiffens, but she doesn't immediately storm off. I guess that's a good sign.

I jog over to her. "Hey," I say.

"Hi, Flint," she says, sounding tired.

"I owe you a huge apology. The biggest. Can we talk for a second? Totally fine to say no, and I'll get out of here, but I thought you should know that I'm sorry for saying that shit the other day."

She narrows her eyes. Measures me up. "You know . . . when I tried to get my friends back after Darcy . . . I groveled."

I nod eagerly. "I can grovel. I can totally grovel."

She crosses her arms. "But . . . they still didn't want to hear it. They didn't care anymore."

"And . . . do you not care anymore?"

She sighs. "We were *so* tight, Flint. You were like my brother when we were little. So yeah. I still care. And I think it's really shitty that my ex-friends didn't give me a chance to make it up to them. So I can *try* to forgive you. But it will depend on what you have to say, really."

"I have a lot to say. A lot of 'I'm an asshole. I'm the worst.'"

"That sounds like a promising start."

"Can I maybe continue the apologies while I take you on a little trip down memory lane?" I ask.

She hitches her backpack higher on her shoulder. "Sure. Where's your car?"

We pile in, and, on the way to the bowling alley where we had our joint seventh birthday party, I fill her in on everything she missed. And I mean everything.

I apologize again, in greater detail, as the machine sets up our pins for our first game.

"That's probably enough," she says, picking at the laminated edge of our table. "You're forgiven."

"We're good?" I ask. "You're not just giving in because I'm the dying kid?"

"Nope. Unconditional forgiveness, because people screw up sometimes. So . . . you're out of the house," she says. "And at a bowling alley, no less. You're really doing this, huh?"

"Yep. Flint Larsen, living it up."

She starts to get up from our table to choose a bowling ball, but I clear my throat.

"Hey, Aer? I just need to say . . . thank you for not giving up on me. After I stormed off that first day."

"It's no big deal."

"It kind of is, though. It would have been easier to not talk to me after that. And it took guts to come to my house that next day. You opened yourself up to . . . a lot. A countdown, a guaranteed good-bye. At the time I thought it was a stupid thing to do, but now I get it. I think it's so fucking brave, and I'm grateful, Aer. You're a really good friend, and those people who dumped you sound like total idiots to me."

She looks down, bashful from the praise. "Thanks, man. And yeah, I guess it did open me up to some hard stuff. But also some good stuff. There was a reason we were best friends, and I still like

279

hanging out with you. Better to have loved and lost than never to have loved at all, right?"

"I used to think that saying was schmaltzy and ridiculous," I say.

"But you don't anymore?"

I shake my head no.

"Wonder what changed your mind," she says teasingly. "And does she have red hair and skin like a makeup commercial?"

I smile. "September definitely had something to do with it. But you did too." Then I glance down at my scuffed-up rented bowling shoes. "I'm sorry that I'm going to have to peace out on you. Will you be okay?"

I need her to be okay. I need someone to be okay, after.

"I think so. I have my mom. She'll hold me up for a while if I need it."

When we climb back into the Jeep later, Aerys scrolls through her phone to queue up some music for our drive home, one of the songs we were obsessed with as kids.

"Oh, by the way," I say, "you've got plans tomorrow."

"I do?"

"Yeah. You're hanging out with September and me."

She looks momentarily surprised, then pleased. "Do I have to watch you make out?" she asks.

"Maybe, but her friends will be there too, so at least you'll have someone to suffer with."

She turns her face to the window so I don't see her smile, but I catch the reflection of it in the glass.

september

I LIE IN my bed and watch as the numbers on my alarm clock twitch from 11:59 to 12:00.

Another day gone.

Unsurprisingly my thoughts keep circling back to Flint. He came over after spending the afternoon with Aerys, and we took a walk along the creek. He seemed fine at first, but as the sun set, I could feel the tension coiling tighter in him.

I'm about to roll over for the twentieth time when something taps on my window. I know it's Flint before I even pull the curtain back. He's on the other side of the glass, eyes wild with panic.

I fumble with the window sash and haul it up. Icy air tumbles in with him, and my room feels suddenly tiny, full of cold night and this towering, distraught boy.

Flint drags his hands through his hair, then paces to my desk and back again. Alarm skitters through me—he looks like he's about to come apart at the seams.

I glance at the door. Down the hall, the Home Shopping Network blares from the TV in Gigi's bedroom. She's probably asleep, but if Flint keeps stomping around like this, she might wake up and come investigate.

"Flint, has something happened?" I whisper.

"No," he says. "It's just— I've had two Red Bulls, and I don't want to sleep, and I can't—" His voice clogs with grief. "I hate this. I *hate* this. I'm going to wreck everyone. Should I just leave Carbon Junction now?"

"Of course you shouldn't leave." I steer him to the edge of my bed and sit beside him. He leans forward and drops his head into his hands. "I'm sorry. I was going to try not to do this. I was trying to be so good and just live, just enjoy life, and you."

He finally notices the murmur of the television down the hall. "Shit. Will your grandma be mad if she finds me in here?"

"If she didn't hear you come in, then she's asleep. You're good."

I lean my head on his shoulder, heart still aching for him. He's vibrating faintly. I can't tell if it's a shiver or nerves, but his clothes are so cold it feels as if he's just pulled them out of a freezer.

"What happened to your coat?" I ask. "You need to warm up." I pull back my comforter and nudge his arm. "Lie down," I order.

He does, his teeth nearly chattering. Without thinking, I climb under the covers too, some survivalist instinct telling me to wrap him in warmth and make him feel safe and soothed.

We wriggle until we're lying on our sides, face-to-face. He grabs one of my hands and stares into my eyes like I'm a lifeboat that he's clinging to in a storm, like if he breaks our gaze for even a second he'll go under.

I start stroking his hair with my free hand. Every touch seems to unwind his frown a tiny notch, until finally, finally, his breathing calms and his gaze softens.

"Better?" I whisper.

He nods and exhales, melting deeper into my mattress.

That's when his leg brushes mine under the covers.

I'd been so focused on his face and on bringing him down from his panic that I hadn't realized.

We're in bed together.

The room contracts around us. In the stillness, the thing tugging him to me is more powerful than ever. He brings one hand up to my face. "September," he says, my name carried on a breath, and then we're both leaning in as slowly as if we're under a spell.

The first kiss is a melting slide, slow and lapping like moonlight and waves on a shore. Just like every other time we've kissed, it's like being sucked into a place where nothing hurts and everything feels good.

He kisses me, spanning his palm over my waist, moving first over my shirt, then under it. His progress falters when he gets to my rib cage.

"Oh god, you're not wearing a bra." He sounds half-broken, and I can tell it takes a monumental effort to pull his hand away. "Sorry— was that okay?"

"Very okay," I say.

Soon we won't be able to do this. At the thought, a fresh wave of desperation crashes through me. I grab his shoulders tight. *Don't leave me.*

We're clinging to each other now. And then he nudges his hips against me, and I nearly pass out. I can *feel* him through his black jeans.

My body wants things I can't even begin to articulate.

I tug at the hem of his shirt and whisper, "My turn." He shifts to pull it over his head.

"How much do you want to do?" he whispers. "Want to make sure we're on the same page."

I catch his face between my hands so I can look in his eyes when I say it.

"Everything," I whisper. "You?"

"I want everything too. It makes sense, right?"

"Perfect sense." There's so much that we can't have. Time. A future. But I want this with him.

"Oh my god." He groans, dropping his forehead to my collarbone. "I don't have any condoms here. Can you wait? I'll go get—"

"It's okay—I have one," I say. I lean over the edge of my bed to get one from the pack I bought this summer. It's a little clumsy then; a desperate rush to get back to where we were without losing our momentum. I shouldn't have worried, because a minute later I'm back in a delirious spiral of kisses.

"How will this ever be enough?" I whisper. I need a hundred nights like this with him.

"It won't be," he says, his forehead pressed to mine.

I loop my arms around his neck and find his mouth, and then millions of shimmering sensations take me under.

Afterward, I'll remember this night in flashes. Slow kisses where it feels like we're trading one breath back and forth between us and quiet moments where he matches his fingertips to mine. It's not all smooth, though, and there are times where we both wince with embarrassment. There are knocked shoulders and leg cramps and embarrassing sounds, but it's us, it's *him*, and there are also moments that stun me with their perfection.

Flint falls asleep with his head heavy on my chest, right over my heart, his arms wrapped around my waist like he's trying to make sure I don't go anywhere before the sun comes up. As if I'm the one in danger of leaving.

I play with a lock of his Vantablack hair. I stare at him and think, *How did the grumpy boy from the Ruins turn into* this?

In that moment, I know, without a doubt, that this is love. Has always been love. The all-in, consuming, want-every-good-thing-to-happen-for-the-other-person kind of love.

A thought spikes into me, sharp and painful.

There has to be something I can do to save him.

On my walls, the formulas, black Sharpie on white paint, seem to dance in the half dark. I'm a scientist. I had one hypothesis that didn't pan out, but maybe I can have another, and I can—

But then I think about Maybelle.

About how I didn't give her the sister she deserved because I was stuck with my nose in a book trying to save her.

A thick sadness gathers in my chest, and I curve my hand over Flint's bare shoulder, holding him as close to me as I can while he sleeps.

I have to just love him, then let him go.

flint

TIME STARTS MOVING faster, blurring with noise and color and speed. On Saturday night, Dottie hauls us all to a grungy bar to watch one of her favorite local bands.

I'm standing at the edge of the crowd with Aerys, getting my eardrums pummeled with metal music. The musicians on the stage all have unkempt hair and Rip Van Winkle beards, and they've been furiously head banging for the last twenty minutes. It's kind of a miracle that they can actually play with their heads slamming all over the place like that.

I'm a little buzzed from whatever Dottie's got in the bottle stashed in her purse. She screeched when I told her I'd never been drunk, saying, *"You can't kick the bucket and never have even gotten a good buzz on."*

I may be standing in a dingy bar, but in my mind, I'm in September's bedroom, in September's bed, running my hands through her hair. I was in bad shape yesterday at the museum, about to rattle apart at the seams, but after last night with her, I'm euphoric. I never want to forget a single detail of the things I saw, the things I heard, the things I felt.

A screeching whine of feedback brings me back into the moment. Beside me, Aerys is watching Dottie and Bo, who dove into the fray as soon as we got here and are jumping up and down with reckless abandon.

Aerys chews on her lip.

"Hey," I say, elbowing her. "You okay?"

"Yeah. I'm just scared I'll screw it up with them."

"Aer—you're not a bad friend for one bad choice you made. Plus, I have a feeling these two are the kind of friends you keep, no matter who you're dating." I take her by the shoulders and peel her off the wall. "Go."

She takes a deep breath, nods, and plunges into the mosh pit.

September slides up beside me, and it feels so natural to wind my arm around her and draw her close. Like we've been doing this for years. Her fingernails rake lightly over the inside of my arm, and it feels so fucking *good* I almost tell our friends they can finish the night without us.

When the next song starts, she presses one ear to my chest and brings a hand up to cover the other.

"You don't like the noise?" I shout.

"Not the biggest fan, no."

I wrap my arms around her so I'm blocking out more of the sound. Her arms loop around my waist, and we stand there for the whole next song, a statue frozen in time.

The next time the band breaks between sets, Bo and Aerys and Dottie come bounding over. Dottie's made a list of possibilities for where we can go next—the finest things Carbon Junction has to offer to round out my medium-thrills week.

"Wait. Have you ever raced shopping carts at midnight in Walmart?" Dottie asks.

"I can't say I've had that distinct pleasure," I say.

"Get your coat on."

Ten minutes later, I'm looping my fingers in the metal mesh of the cart as Aerys pelts me down the Barbie aisle. We race until a sour-faced guy with a comb-over and a walkie-talkie makes his way toward us.

We leap out of the carts and run out the front doors into the cold night, laughing and hollering and breathing in life like we have an unlimited supply of it.

But there's only so much anticipation I can take, and I've wanted to be alone with September since I snuck out of her house this morning.

We say goodnight to our friends, and this time it's September who crosses the creek and taps on my window.

After we chase the Pop Rocks fizz of the feelings, I gather September into my arms. And then we're drifting.

I don't want to sleep. I fight it for as long as I can, and she does too, tracing patterns on my bare shoulder while I just look and look and look to permanently impose the image of her face in my mind.

When everything in the room is still, and it feels like nothing in the world is moving, I say, simply, "I love you, September."

It echoes in the room, feeling a hundred times bigger and more true than any other words I've ever spoken or will speak again.

"I love you, Flint Larsen," she says, and it's not a whisper either; it's a declaration to meet mine.

And then her chest goes concave under my palm, the sort of breath you exhale just before you start to cry.

I kiss her so she won't have to cry. I try to pour a million apologies into it, a million days of *September and Flint* that we'll never get.

"Flint? What if I never have this again?" she asks quietly, later.

"You will," I say, even though it hurts to think about. "And hopefully whoever they are, they'll be much less miserable than me."

"I wish we had more time," she whispers.

"Me too."

When I close my eyes, the blackness is as soft and dark as a charred candlewick.

flint

THE DAY BEFORE my deathday is perfect.

The five of us—me, September, Aerys, Dottie, and Bo—pile into the Jeep and drive to an amusement park that opens for a few select days in December, bedecked with Christmas garlands and twinkling lights.

Swaddled in coats and gloves and hats, we ride roller coasters until Bo turns green and poke puffs of cotton candy into one another's mouths and take turns making faces for the cameras at the tops of the big drops. September and I barely let go of each other's hands. I pretend that I have a million days left. I smile, because this is how I want them to remember me.

Maybe it's not some rapturous, drunken whirl through every extreme thrill life has to offer, but it's more life than I ever thought I'd get.

It's funny, how the things most people put on their bucket lists don't guarantee joy. They're not the memories that stand out in your mind when you look back on it all. Sometimes the smallest things are the things you remember the most. I didn't climb Kilimanjaro or see the Northern Lights or ride a camel, but my knee brushed September's on November 15. I carved a really amazing jack-o'-lantern with Dad when I was six. Mom and I put together a two-thousand-piece puzzle on our dining table. Grandpa and I shared a funnel cake as he pointed up at the airplanes whizzing above our heads. Aerys and I stayed up until we were giddy to beat the final boss. In the dark last night, September told me she loved me.

There's a moment, when we're taking a break on a patch of grass, and my friends are laughing at something I didn't catch, and September smiles at me and leans her head on my shoulder, and I feel so full I think, *I could go now.*

It's been eight years since I half-lifed, and I've never felt that before today. It's clean, like taking my first deep breath in my entire life.

The ride home from the park is bittersweet. The mood in the car tips toward melancholy as the sun sinks down. I'm glad I'm driving, because it keeps my mind off the pressure building in all of us.

In eight hours, the countdown timer on my phone that's been ticking off my days will hit 0:00:00, and it'll officially be my death-day. I don't know how many hours of December 4 I'll get. I don't know if I'll die at a minute past midnight or sometime tomorrow afternoon—or if I'll get lucky and see one more sunset, one more twilight, one more moonrise.

Dottie leans through the gap in the seats and finds a more upbeat tune, then offers me another piece of cotton candy. September lays her hand on my knee, stilling me, calming me. Keeping me here.

Aerys is showing Bo the photos she took. She was so animated today, and if there's one entirely good, untarnished thing that's come from all of this, it's that she found a place to belong.

Then it's time to drop Dottie and Bo off.

We all pile out, shivering on the sidewalk. Dottie hugs me tight, and when she steps back, her eyes are damp.

"I'm not going to say the G-word, okay, mister? I refuse."

"I refuse too, then."

But even though we're not saying it, we all feel it: This is the first of my real goodbyes.

Bo squeezes September's hand. "We'll pick you up at nine tomorrow." He's orchestrated a road trip out to Atlantic City for the four of them, so they'll all be together when I go. My dad's in charge of sending them a text with the news.

I hug Bo hard. I'm so grateful that he and Dottie will be there to take care of September and Aerys when I won't be here to do it anymore.

Then there are three of us. We drive in silence, and for all the lightness of the day, the dread of tomorrow is getting hard to ignore.

I walk Aerys to her door.

"So this is it, then, huh?" she says.

I swallow. "Yeah."

"But you can call us tomorrow, if it doesn't happen right away, or whatever. If you want to."

I don't know if it'd be better to leave her with a clean break or the hope that she might speak to me again, so I nod noncommittally. Which I guess is choosing hope.

We hug forever.

I'm halfway down the sidewalk when she calls out, "Hey, Flint?"

I turn around and take in the image, her and her house and the changing leaves and the spiked crown of the Institute rising over it all.

"I'm glad you came back," she says.

"Me too."

And when I fold back into the Jeep, I have to just sit for a while, my forehead on the steering wheel. Part of me wants to run back up to the door, soak up every last second I have with everyone, or gather them all in my living room and let them hold me in one big group huddle, but I don't know that my parents would appreciate that. We decided—well, I decided—I needed to be with Mom and Dad for the actual event. Like September and her parents did for her sister.

"Well, that was rough," I croak, finally raising my head.

I put the car in gear, and we drive away from my best friend's house for the last time.

"Me next, then, I guess," September says, sounding as devastated as I feel.

I reach over and take her hand. "Actually, I have something planned for us. You up for it?"

She perks up, nodding like I've given her an extension of years, not just a few hours.

Funny how, near the end, some hours feel like a blip and some an eternity.

Dusk is falling when the road suddenly dumps us out of the thick forest and into a flat, grassy field. I slow when I see the hulking building up ahead and the sign on the road that reads *Clearfield-Victoria Regional Airport*.

I pull the Jeep in behind an outbuilding. From where we are, we can just about see the main office, where a single square of light shines yellow in the dark. We get out of the Jeep and skulk around the back of the enormous hangar. It's as big as a football field and the same height as a four-story building.

There are several fire exits on the building's back wall, but I lead us around to the yawning mouth of the open hangar door. They must be expecting a late-night landing if they haven't closed up yet.

I hold a finger up to my lips, then peer around the edge of the opening.

"I think we're clear," I whisper.

We slip into the hangar and hide behind a row of rolling tool cabinets to wait. After a few minutes, we hear the sound of a puttering tow tractor, guiding a Cirrus SR22 into its place for the night. The airport mechanic—a rangy, tanned-to-a-crisp white guy wearing a dusty baseball hat—whistles a tune as he shuts the giant hangar doors and locks up. He leaves through a side door, and then we're alone.

We step out of hiding. The smell of the hangar takes me back. Jet fuel, black coffee, baked tarmac.

I let out a disbelieving laugh. "I didn't actually think that would work."

September spins in the space, eyes lit with wonder, her coat flaring out around her. "Tell me what kinds of planes these are, then."

I start with the one in the far corner. "Okay. This is a Cessna Skyhawk—my grandpa used to fly one like this. And this is a Piper Saratoga—super reliable."

I name all of the planes for her as we walk through the hangar. Our hushed voices bounce off the roof high above our heads.

She stops next to the sleekest, most expensive plane. "This one's very fancy."

"Gulfstream IV," I say. "Probably some billionaire jetting from his mountain mansion over to Philadelphia or New York City."

September steps onto the portable stairway that's still pushed up against the jet. "Will it be stupidly swanky inside, do you think?" she asks.

I'm about to say you can't go in there, because a respect for pilots and their property was drilled into me from a young age, but then I think, what the hell. I'm dying tomorrow.

She cracks open the door. "Wow, okay. It really is stupidly swanky."

I can smell the price tag. Buttery leather, lacquered wood, new carpet. September runs a hand over an armrest. On the left side of the plane, there's a row of three seats that blend into a sort of bench, for anyone who wants to lie down at cruising altitude. There's a dining area and a gleaming flight attendant workstation, but it's the cockpit that I want to see.

I stand in the gap between the two pilot seats, scanning the expanse of switches, gauges, buttons. The memories flood in, and in all of them, child-me is wearing a huge, heavy headset. Grandpa was fearless—he let me flick switches and hold the yoke, and he even let me talk to ground control to request permission to land.

I slide into the seat, settling into the nubby sheepskin covering that's standard for cockpits.

When I take hold of the yoke, I feel a simple, uncomplicated happiness roll through me. I'm in an airplane again.

I run my hands over the controls, and, for a moment, I pretend I'm forty thousand feet in the air, with atmospheric pressure tugging at my eardrums. I imagine what it would feel like to pilot the plane through inversions and stall turns and rolls. What it would feel like to bring the plane back to earth, that moment when the landing gear connects with the ground.

I open my eyes and ease up out of the seat. Enough of airplanes. I want September.

She's right there, in the cockpit doorway, and we're so close that the oversized buttons on her coat click against my coat's zipper.

She looks up at me, this exquisite, determined, brilliant girl. We've spent so much time together this week, but there's still a tug inside me that's nearly painful, a *want*, like I might die early if we don't start kissing in the next two seconds.

She rises on tiptoe, and I dip to meet her.

With her kiss, all my dread evaporates, every bad feeling suddenly a distant, fuzzy memory. Time falls away. It's almost a miracle, that there's this little escape, this peace, right at the end.

In some corner of my mind, I know I should be keeping track of time so I can get home before midnight, but she catches my bottom lip again, and my thoughts scatter. I kiss her, on this perfect last day in this perfect airplane, and I wish this moment could be infinite.

september

I KISS FLINT like somehow it will keep him with me. He tastes so *alive*, like black cherries and goodbyes, and I can't get it through my head that this really is the last time. It doesn't feel real.

One last kiss. Another.

And through it all, a terrified, dreadful pressure is gathering in my chest.

I kiss him, because when I'm kissing him, he doesn't look quite so scared.

Sometime later, my phone vibrates. I tug it out so I can turn Do Not Disturb on.

That's when I see the time.

A hot strike of pain runs down the center of me.

"It's past midnight," I whisper.

It's Flint's last day. I could lose him any minute now.

My hearing goes dull, like we really are on an airplane and the pressure's changing.

I think back to another night, when I set my alarm for five minutes before midnight and met my parents in the dark upstairs hallway, and we went into Maybelle's room to wake her up together on her last day.

And suddenly, everything I thought I could handle about this moment, I just . . . *can't*.

I can't bear to go through this again. I can't lose Flint like I lost Maybelle. The universe can't throw that much at one person. Inside me, a thousand blaring sirens start screaming.

I surge to my feet. Start pacing up and down the aisle.

Flint's saying my name, trying to get me to sit down. My mind is scrambling for an out. Something to make this not happen. Was he 100 percent sure he half-lifed? Did he get the date right?

"September." He catches me, makes me look at him. "Stop. Please."

"I have to do something."

His face is all pity. "There's nothing we can do. You know that."

I shake my head, thoughts churning. There has to be something. I'm a half-life scientist.

My hypothesis still *feels* right. I still think there's a little instruction card embedded in our DNA that says *When chemical X drops to 10 microliters, trigger the half-life. When it drops to 5 microliters, shut everything down.*

But I couldn't find it. There were some good candidates. L-tyrosine, acetylcholine, enkephalin. I was sure it was one of them. I thought the anomalies would all have just a little extra "chemical X" in their systems.

I have to try *something*. If I let this go, he'll be dead for sure, so what do I have to lose? If I can get him to the Institute, there's a chance.

I whirl.

Flint takes a step back. "Why does it look like you just got an idea that I'm not going to like?"

"I'm taking you to the Institute."

flint

I LEAN AWAY from September.

"That's a terrible idea," I say.

"Why?" she asks, a desperate light in her eyes. "Don't you *want* to live?"

Pain crumples in my chest. "Of course I want to live. But I was never going to. You even said—your hypothesis didn't pan out in the end."

"All those formulas on my walls? There are only a handful of chemicals it could be. So what if I give you *all* of them? I can give you an injection. If I'm right, and the instructions in your DNA are telling your body to switch off when the level of one of those chemicals drops below a certain threshold, we'll just top it up. And keep topping it up. It has to be one of those ones I was looking at."

I wince. "You're just going to stick me with a bunch of needles and pump a bunch of medicines into me?"

"Isn't it worth a shot?" The determined heat in her eyes knocks me back.

"September, it won't work."

"Don't you want to *try*?"

She's asking too much. What the hell am I supposed to do here? The last thing I wanted was for my final hours to become a race against time.

"Please don't say no," she says. "Please. I can't lose you too."

"September, this is—"

With a jolt, I remember my parents. I can't believe I lost track of time so spectacularly. I'm supposed to be with them. There are things I want to say to them, and I had it all lined up for midnight. What if I die before I get a chance to talk to them?

I fumble for my phone. There are three missed calls from my mom and a slew of texts. They're freaking out.

"My parents—September, I can't. I need to be with my parents." I feel terror about my dying all the time, a low-level poison in my blood and a dull ache in my bones, but now it's flaring out of control. *I'm dying. Today.*

"We can get them to the Institute too," she says. "I need to work out how, but we have a little bit of time. Statistically, only three percent of kill switch deaths occur in the first hour."

God. I can't believe we're having this conversation. Three percent?

She looks at me, wild and gorgeous and desperate. "Please, Flint. Let me at least try to save you."

It's a bad idea. The worst idea.

But if I don't let her try this, will she be messed up forever, thinking she might have been able to save me?

I got my perfect last day. She changed everything for me, made this month more than I ever thought it could be. I can do this for her.

On the count of three, we bust out of the emergency exit at the back of the hangar and dash for the Jeep. I fire up the engine like a getaway driver and peel out. Alarms blare. Some unlucky person on the airport staff will get rousted out of bed to come deal with this, but they won't get to the airport in time to catch us.

Of all the things I thought I'd be doing on my last day, this wasn't it.

September won't let go of my hand. We're holding on for dear life—literally—on the center console. A thought flickers through my mind: I probably shouldn't be driving. But September's eyes are bright, her mind whirring like a computer now. "I need to make some calls. The Institute should be quiet, but still . . ."

I glance over to catch her chewing rabidly on her thumbnail, phone pressed to her ear.

"Hey, Dottie—no, he's okay. I'm with him. Listen. I need to fig-ure out where Percy lives."

september

"PERCY'S NEVER GOING to go for this," Dottie says, wrenching the steering wheel to the left. "He's such a little twerp."

She's driving Flint's Jeep, because that's one of the cardinal rules of the half-life: Never drive on your deathday.

"Turn left here," Aerys says. She's riding shotgun, navigating. I was surprised to see her at Bo's—apparently they'd all felt so down after saying goodbye earlier they decided to have a sleepover.

We rattle over a pothole, and Flint's head knocks on the roof.

"Just keep your eyes on the road, Dottie—and for Dolly Parton's sake, slow down," Bo says from the seat next to me.

Flint's on my other side, holding my hand, and I'd be lying if I said I wasn't counting his pulse rate under my fingertips. It could happen any minute now. Any second.

Not yet. Please.

Flint looks wiped, and I know he's not the happiest with me that we're doing this. Well, he can forgive me tomorrow. When he wakes up the day after his deathday.

Bo twists in his seat to look at me. "Do you really think Percy will agree to this?" he asks.

"I'm going to kick his ass if he doesn't," Dottie vows. "He got September fired, so he owes her big-time."

Finally, we see Percy's house, looming in the dark. Dottie rides the brakes hard, and we all lurch forward, seat belts jerking against our chests.

There's no turning back now. We need Percy—it's the only way I can get Flint into the Institute.

We climb out of the Jeep and head to the front door, our breath puffing in the cold. All the lights are off. The sweet, melodic ring of the doorbell sounds so out of place in the pitch-black, one-in-the-morning silence.

We wait.

And wait.

I push the doorbell again, jabbing so it *ding-dong*s a dozen times.

Percy himself finally answers, rubbing sleep from his eyes like a little boy. And . . . he's dressed in a green T-shirt and dinosaur-print pajama pants.

Bo coughs to cover a laugh.

Percy juts his chin out defiantly, trying to look down his nose at all of us. "What are you doing at my house at"—he checks his wristwatch—"one a.m.?"

"I need you to come with us. To the Institute."

"But it's not time for our shift," he says stupidly.

"No shit, Sherlock," Dottie snaps, but I signal her back with a hand.

"I need to get in. This is Flint, and it's his deathday today."

"What does that have to do with me? Just book him into Intake, or call the hotline. You should have registered months ago, so I gather you're using whatever connections you think you have to jump the line—"

"Listen here, Percival," Dottie says, drilling a finger into his bony shoulder. "You're going to get us all into that building, whether you like it or not. Get in the car."

Percy visibly gulps. "Okay, jeez," he mumbles.

Dottie marches him to the Jeep.

"Uh, Dottie? I think you're getting a little *too* into your role," Bo says.

On the way back to Carbon Junction, Percy rains questions on us.

"I don't know why you think *I* can help you. Why didn't you just go to reception to see which doctor is on rotation tonight? You know them as well as I do."

"I'm not taking him to Intake, Percy. That's not the plan."

"And do I get to know what that plan is?"

I'm about to snap at him, but then it hits me—all the technical details, the science and the formulas behind my hypothesis—Percy actually will understand.

So I run him through it.

And as the minutes tick by, as Dottie swerves us around corners, Percy starts to sit up straighter in his seat. He gets the shine in his eye that all scientists get—he's hooked. And he's blasting questions at me, trying to poke holes in my work, but not in a mean way—that's just what we do. Make sure the work is strong. Watertight. Which I know it's not, and he'll figure that out sooner or later.

"Do you have a piece of paper?" Percy asks.

"Not sure. Flint?"

"There might be a pen in the glove compartment," he mutters. "Napkins or something." He never takes his eyes off the darkness outside the window.

I feel another stab of guilt. I should be paying all of my attention to him, the way I did with Maybelle on her last day. He shouldn't be stuffed into a car with all of us.

Bo finds an old road atlas that has some white space and passes it back to Percy. He starts scrawling things on it. The same things I have at home, tattooed on my walls. I take the pen and show him what I figured out.

"This is . . . You really did all of this?" he asks.

"Of course I did. What do you think I am, an idiot?"

"No," he says softly. "I never thought you were an idiot. I knew you could do stuff like this. Heard about it, but never saw it."

"Yeah, well, fat lot of good it did in the end. Look," I say, grabbing the pen, adding a few numbers, symbols, showing him where the flaw is. The link I was waiting for that never came. "Of all the possible chemical candidates, the anomalies I studied didn't share any."

"But you're going to give him something anyway."

"I have to try," I say, setting my jaw against the fear that's growing inside me.

Percy presses his lips together, like there's more he wants to say, but he knows it won't be met with calm reason. I know. I *know* this isn't good science, that this isn't rational, but I can't see why I shouldn't just *try*.

I press Flint's hand between mine, memorizing the feel of it. Is this a waste of time?

In the parking lot behind the Crown, we spill out of the car and into the cold.

"Let's go over it one last time. Tell me what you're going to do," Dottie prompts Percy.

"I'm going to go in, tell the security guard that I—"

"*Casually* tell the guard," Dottie corrects him.

"Casually." Percy nods.

"That means don't act like a total dickweed, Percival. But don't be friendly either; he'll suspect something right away."

"O-okay. I'll tell him that I forgot some notes that I really need for my AP Calc BC test, and that I have to pull an all-nighter tonight if I have any hope of passing it. I'll take the elevator up to the Intake floor but then take the emergency stairwell back down to the loading dock, where I'll open the door the smokers use. But—what if an alarm goes off or something? And there are cameras and stuff." His nerves are getting to him.

"If the alarm goes off, we'll run," I say. "We'll be upstairs and hiding in a room before security can find us."

I hope.

"This is such a bad idea," Percy says, looking hideously ill. "I like the science, and I want to try it—but this is—man, my parents are going to kill me."

"Percy?" Dottie lays her hands on his shoulders and looks him in the eye. "Shut up, and go get 'em, tiger."

He takes a deep breath, nods, and heads for the Institute's front door.

The five of us skulk around the back of the building and crouch behind a row of bushes. We wait, staring at the loading dock.

"It's taking too long," Aerys whispers. "What if he squealed?"

"He didn't squeal," Dottie says firmly, her mouth a hard line and her eyes laser focused on the door.

The seconds tick by. Beside me, Flint shivers.

"Are you okay?" I whisper.

"Well, I'm still here," he says.

And then the night moves. The door cracks open, and a panicked hand—Percy's hand—reaches out and flails wildly at us in a *Come on* gesture.

We sprint to the door. We don't dare stop once we're inside, just pelt up the stairs. I take them two at a time, never letting go of Flint's hand.

Four flights of stairs. That's where we need to be: fourth floor, Diagnostics and Pathology.

When we get there, Percy stands next to the retina scanner.

It beeps red, and my stomach plummets.

"It always does that," he hisses. He repositions his face and tries again.

Green.

He cracks open the door to the silent hallway.

Crap, I think, fear squeezing me again. I really didn't think any of this through. How will I know if the mini-labs are empty? They should be, but you never know when some workaholic will come in to run tests or catch up on paperwork.

Indecision and panic burn under my skin, but everyone's depending on me to make a choice. *This one.*

It's empty. Relief.

We all pile in, and I shut the door behind me. Percy slides down the wall, trembling. He looks like he's going to puke. Bo paces in the corner. Flint leans quietly on the edge of the examination table, crosses his arms, and looks down at his shoes.

What was I thinking? Have I done the wrong thing? God, I'm about to fall apart.

Bo grabs my shoulders and turns me to face him. "Tell us what you need. Like IVs and monitors and whatever." He's got his producer, no-nonsense, *Pull your shit together* look on his face, and it revives me. We're too far in this to back out now.

"Okay." I press my hands together to stop them from shaking. I survey the room, scanning the labels on the cabinets and drawers. And then I start doling out instructions. I have Aerys and Bo collect the easy supplies. Percy gets involved quickly, because this is what he knows. He's even arguing with me over some of the equipment.

I freeze, midway through digging through a drawer, suddenly feeling terrifyingly out of my depth. I've seen Dr. Juncker insert IVs dozens of times, but I've never done it. What if I miss? What if Flint has some sort of reaction to the chemicals I'm planning on giving him? I don't know how to man a crash cart. What the hell am I thinking? I'm just an intern with a knack for remembering scientific formulas and—

"September." Percy taps me on the shoulder. "Who's going up to the vault?"

The vault is the refrigerated chemical storage room attached to the top-floor lab.

I glance at Flint. I don't want to leave him, but it has to be me. If anyone else gets caught, stealing bags of saline is one thing; stealing raw chemicals and experimental drugs is another.

"Me," I say. "I'll need your badge. I'll grab some L-tyrosine, acetylcholine . . . everything on that list. I'll be back in five minutes, ten minutes, tops."

I reach for the handle, but before I can turn it, the door flies open.

Standing on the other side, wearing a cold, chiseled expression, is Dr. Juncker.

"What," she says in the coldest, sternest voice I've ever heard from her, "is going on here?"

Silence.

Her eyes shift to my right. "Mr. Bassingthwaighte?"

Percy makes a strangled noise, and I think, *Shit, this is it.*

Panic slides through my body, an icy chill followed by nauseating heat. If I wasn't completely blackballed in the scientific community before, I will be now. This is bad. She has every right to call security. And the police.

But then, Percival Bassingthwaighte, bane of my existence, steps forward.

He smooths down his ruffled hair, attempting to look dignified in his dinosaur-print pajamas. "Dr. Juncker," he starts, his voice as cool and collected as if it were any other workday. "Ms. Harrington has been researching and proving a hypothesis that, in my opinion, holds merit. This is her patient, Flint Larsen, aged seventeen years two months. Today is his deathday, and we brought him here to administer an experimental cocktail of L-tyrosine, acetylcholine, and other psychopharmaceuticals in an attempt to elongate his life."

Dr. Juncker's frown grows deeper with every word that comes out of Percy's mouth.

When he finishes, she crosses her arms. "So. You are meaning to tell me you brought this boy here to inject previously untested levels of proteinogenic amino acids into his system in the hope he will live past his deathday?"

I swallow. "Yeah, that's kind of it."

I'm so screwed.

"You have to see her research, Dr. Juncker," Percy pipes up again, and I'm swamped with such a fondness for him that I take back all the angry thoughts I've ever had. He takes the road atlas page out of his pocket and carefully smooths out the folds. "It's brilliant," he says.

Dr. Juncker raises one skeptical eyebrow, but she takes the paper. She fishes a pair of glasses out of her lab coat pocket and scans, lips pressed together in an unwaveringly harsh line. Finally, she pulls the rolling lab stool out from under the counter and sits. She takes off her glasses and presses her fingertips to her eyes.

"The hypothesis is incredibly interesting. I think we should take it to Dr. Jackson, and the board, to pursue the idea in earnest, as a company. But if we were to give Mr. Larsen the drugs you're suggesting, it'd be a guessing game, shots in the dark. It's too late for . . . well, it's just too late."

The room goes still.

"I'm truly sorry, September," she says. "The work you've done toward this *is* brilliant. I've always thought you were a talented scientist."

I should feel something at that, because it's the closest I'll ever get to a compliment from my boss—ex-boss—but I feel nothing.

"Are you going to call the police?" Dottie whispers.

Dr. Juncker sighs. "No. But I am going to call your parents."

I slump backward. Flint's close behind me, and he steadies me, but that only breaks my heart more.

Everything in me starts to shut down.

flint

IT'S STARTING TO get real.

I was so smug, thinking I knew all there was to know about living on a countdown. But nothing compares to it being my actual deathday.

I could die at *any minute*.

With every second that pounds by, more pressure builds up in my chest. My stomach is a knot that will probably never unknot. Not in my lifetime.

But as terrified as I am, I can't let September see it. She's just . . . staring. Glazed over and looking blankly ahead, like she's completely stopped working.

The terrifying German woman leads us down the hallway and into the elevator, where she presses the button for the fifteenth floor. The plaque next to it reads *Psychology and Support*. Great.

We file out into a curved white hallway that looks exactly like the one we just came from. I have this horrifying fear that if I whip my head around too fast, something in there will just snap, and everything will end. Dr. Juncker leads us to a spacious sitting room and tells us our parents will be here soon. I've been texting Mom, so she knows what's going on, but I want her and Dad here. The sooner the better—we're almost three full hours into my last day. The things I want to say to them are swelling inside me, desperate to get out before it's too late.

I try to get September to look at me, but she keeps staring off into space. I can't tell if she's going into full-on-emotional-shut-down-avoidance mode, like she did after her sister died, or if she's about to have an awful, messy breakdown.

Dottie, Bo, and Aerys leave first. Our goodbyes—our real last goodbyes this time—are unceremonious and awkward, watched over by September's weird boss and a roomful of frowning parents. And then it's just me, September, and Percy, waiting to be collected.

I hear my parents before I see them, calling my name as they search for the right room.

Mom comes in first, moving so fast I barely have time to stand up before she gets to me.

"Oh, Flint, you're still here," she says. *You're still here.*

Her face crumples, and her hands flutter to check that I'm still in one piece. Dad's right behind her. When he gets scared, he talks less, and I know it's really bad now, because he doesn't say a word when he sees me. Just grabs my hand and presses it tight between his.

I never should have put them through this. I should have been home at midnight, like Cinderella. If I'd died sometime in the last three hours, they would have gotten a *phone call* about it.

A month ago I was hell-bent on not letting them witness my death. Now I think they'd be more broken if they weren't there for it.

"I'm so sorry," I whisper. "Please don't be mad at September. It was my choice—I had to let her try this. So she'd know she tried everything she could."

313

Mom squeezes me to her.

"Thank you for letting me spend time with her this week," I say. "I know this whole trip hasn't been what you wanted and that you're probably kind of mad at her—"

"Honey, we're not mad," Mom says. "We've actually been sort of thrilled for you, because there were times . . . well, there were a few times where you looked happier than you had since you were little."

Dad nods in agreement.

"I'm glad you got to fall in love, Flint," Mom says softly. "I always wanted that for you. Everyone should get to feel it, at least once."

They both squeeze me, and I feel like a little boy again. I want to be here, tucked between my parents, until the end.

"I'm sorry I've been such a little shit for the past eight years," I mumble into my mom's shoulder. "You guys have put up with so much."

"Shh. We can talk when we get home."

But we can't. Because I don't know if I'll make it back to the cabin alive. I have to say this now.

"I'm so sorry for ruining your lives." A sob catches in my throat.

Mom brushes my cheek with her thumb. "You never ruined anything. We love you. We've loved every minute of you."

My dad clears his throat, pushing through the wad of his own emotion. "Even when you were being a little jerk."

"Don't let me hold you guys back, okay?" I say. "Have another kid or something if you want. Don't, like, forget me, obviously, but don't let it hurt you for a long time, okay?"

Mom's eyes fill with tears, but she nods and hugs me again. "Being your mother has been a privilege," she whispers fiercely in my ear.

Dad's crying now, and seeing the tears spill silently down his face sets me off.

It takes us a while to pull ourselves together, to notice that everyone in the room is studiously pretending not to listen to us.

I'm swamped with the overwhelming urge to just go *home*. Not to the cabin. Not to Dad's apartment in Philadelphia.

Home is eight years ago.

Or maybe, for a few fleeting minutes, in that airplane hangar. On the ski lift. In September's bed.

I rub my eyes.

"Mom? Can we go?" My voice comes out small and pitiful.

"Of course." As she goes to talk to Dr. Juncker, I look over at September. While I was talking to my parents, her grandma bustled in, and she's taken September's limp hand in hers and is madly texting someone with the other—September's parents, I'm guessing. September is still zoned out, sitting ramrod straight on the couch.

Going back to the cabin means saying goodbye to her. Right now.

I glance at Dad. He squeezes my hand and nods in solidarity and lets me go to her.

september

THE COUCH CUSHION sinks as Flint sits down next to me. I look down at where Gigi's hand is holding mine, avoiding his eyes.

"September? I have to go," he says softly.

Gigi sets my hand down and pats it. "I'll give you two a minute," she says.

I'm afraid to move. I'm not sure what's going on with me. It's like I'm having a million thoughts at once, but they're all behind sound-proof glass.

I wish I'd stayed in that airplane with him. Instead we're here, in the one place he didn't want to die, and it's all my fault.

This dread—it's exactly the same thing I felt that last day with Maybelle, even though the setting's diametrically different.

Something twinges in my scientist's mind.

Different.

The thought floats away.

"September? Please—talk to me," Flint says. "We can't end like this."

I shake my head. "I'm so sorry for bringing you here. You should have been with your parents."

"Look—it's all a little different than what I pictured. But this whole—"

I know I should be paying more attention, but there's that word again.

Different.

It's like trying to think through molasses. I force my brain to think the way it does when I'm in the observation room in the top-floor lab.

The anomaly files—Mitsuki's, Marvin's, Araminta's—cascade through my mind. The pathology reports, the medicines, the autopsies. I close my eyes, recalling the formulas scrawled on the stones out at the Ruins, on the wall of my bedroom.

Different.

"It's not over," I whisper.

Flint grabs my hand. "It is, though. Please, September—let me say goodbye to you before I lose my chance."

"No. It's not over, and I'm not giving up yet." I try to tug my hand out of his. "I need to talk to Dr. Juncker."

His face is etched with the same pity I saw when I made him leave the airport. That *Stop trying* look. *Don't do this. Let me go.*

Damned if I will.

I yank my hand loose and cross the room to Dr. Juncker.

"What if everyone is different?" I ask.

She frowns. "What are you talking about?"

I snatch the atlas page from Percy and hand it to her. "What if each person's body is monitoring a different chemical? Like your half-life is watching the level of a different chemical than mine? That could be why I couldn't find a correlation."

I talk faster, desperate to get this out before it's too late. The kill switch could come for Flint at any second. "I think these chemicals are the most likely candidates," I say, pointing to my list. "With more scientists working on it, and more anomaly files, we can confirm it. We know how to get some of these chemicals across the blood-brain barrier already, so we can give Flint a combination of all of them."

Dr. Juncker rubs her temples, scanning my formulas again.

"Please," I say. "We have to try." I hate that I'm begging, that I'm the furthest thing from a scientist in this moment, that I've probably made a thousand mistakes in my formulas because I'm a ball of emotion and not a cold computer.

She looks conflicted. "It's not good science, Ms. Harrington. We can't just go around pumping chemicals into people on a hunch."

"But we *know* he's going to die," I burst out. "We can't keep waiting; someone's got to *do* something. We can't hurt him, so why can't we try?"

Dr. Juncker shakes her head, even though she's still raking over the formulas. "We have to wait for the research to bear it out."

There's something wooden in the way she says it, like she's delivering lines. Hope sparks in my stomach. I think I know how to get through to her.

"What about Magnus?"

Dr. Juncker goes still.

"What would you have done if this was him?" I ask.

She closes her eyes. Inhales, slowly.

The rest of us wait, silent. I'm starting to shake. I've gone too far, and I'm going to lose him—

Her eyes snap open.

And she turns to Flint.

She levels a serious look at him. "There's no guarantee that we can prolong your life; in fact, the odds are close to zero, and—"

"I want to do it." Flint's voice is firm. "I know it's a long shot. But I want to do it."

"And *I* want to be very clear," Dr. Juncker says. "This would be an intensive experiment, and performing it is a courtesy to Ms. Harrington for her field-advancing research—and to you for assisting her."

A favor. This is a favor.

"Even if we get the right chemical," she adds, "we don't know how much to administer or how to administer it most efficiently."

"I understand," Flint says.

Dr. Juncker turns to Flint's parents.

"Mrs. Larsen, Mr. Larsen—do you consent to admitting your son in an emergency research capacity to the Half-Life Institute?"

Flint's parents, bewildered, nod, then choke out yeses.

"In that case, we're going to the top-floor lab. Percy, I need the emergency numbers for HR and legal. Mrs. and Mr. Larsen, we'll have consent documents drawn up for you to sign as soon as possible.

"In the meantime, I'll call Dr. Jackson. We're getting everyone in."

Within half an hour, the main lab is teeming with scientists. It's lit up blazing white, as if it's a normal day at work and not two in the morning.

They're all orbiting around my beautiful, lanky boy. He's sitting upright in a hospital bed, and his black clothes have been replaced by a hospital gown and a spiderweb of electrodes, but his hair is still the darkest thing in the room.

Whenever I can, I stand next to him, our hands clasped tightly. Dr. Juncker set up two chairs by the head of the bed for Flint's parents, but I keep having to step out of the way for the dozens of preparations the med team has to do.

Dr. Juncker and Dr. Jackson siphoned my formulas out of my brain and onto the big whiteboard. At first, I try to stay involved. I'm not wearing my lab coat, but the research scientists, seniors and principals and associates alike, all listen to me like I'm worth listening to.

I float between stations: the bank of people tasked with calling hospitals for more anomaly files, the long table where others comb through stacks of pathology reports, still others at the whiteboard working out which chemicals they're going to give Flint and in what doses. Every now and then they nod at a stream of formulas and approach Flint with a loaded syringe.

The Cs and Hs and Os and Ns all start to run together. I'm exhausted, and this is too close to me now. I tell my bosses they can take over, relegating myself to the outskirts of the operation. Percy goes home to get some sleep, and a tiny part of me is jealous, but then I look at Flint and know there's no way I can leave him now.

The scientist in me keeps shouting *There's not enough time; there's not enough time.* I feel like everyone here knows it too. There's an excitement in the air, and they're eager to do this because it's important work, but it's not fever-pitch like it would be if we'd already found the exact right answer. Everything we're trying is a *guess*.

Each time Flint's eyes meet mine, it feels like he's trying to say something to me. But it's not like I can blow a whistle and tell the scientists to stop so we can kiss and cry for a minute.

So I hold his hand, feeling worse and worse about this whole plan by the second.

At around seven in the morning, there's finally a lull. Dr. Jackson and Dr. Juncker have narrowed it down to seven possible chemicals, all neurotransmitters. Three more than were on my list. They've given Flint injections of each. Tiny doses—because messing with someone's brain chemistry is no joke.

Now we just have to wait. Check the work. Keep observing and recording his vitals. We're making more progress on the half-life tonight than we would be able to make in months.

Someone brings a rolling privacy panel and angles it in a crescent around Flint's bed. It's not much, but it's better than nothing.

He's holding up well. A little bit of nausea, a headache, some drowsiness—but all of that could be from being awake for almost twenty-four hours straight.

I perch on the edge of his bed, careful not to bump his IV or the wires sprouting out of the monitoring machines. His parents turn away to give us some privacy but stay close enough to reach him in a split second if . . . it happens.

"Your bosses said I can have a break," Flint says, his voice rough and low. "Want to rest with me?" He scoots over to make room.

We lie on our sides, face-to-face. It shouldn't feel intimate, in this airy, open lab, but he draws the sheet over us, right to our chins, and we might as well be in a world of our own.

"Hi," he whispers.

My knees bump against his. He runs a hand over my hair, twists a strand around his finger.

"How are you feeling?" I ask.

"Starting to get pretty tired."

I smooth Flint's hair away from his eyes. "I know this isn't where you wanted to be today." I swallow. "I'm sorry, Flint."

"Hey—no regrets." He smiles sadly. "You taught me how to live. I can do this for you."

I draw back an inch, frowning. "You don't think this will work."

He doesn't answer.

I open my mouth to tell him that he'll make it through today, but I can't get the words out. Dr. Juncker's right. It's not good science.

So instead, I press my forehead to his collarbone. Between us, his hands find mine. He squeezes tight.

"I'm so tired," I whisper. "But I'm afraid to close my eyes, in case—"

I break off. *In case I'm wrong. In case none of this works. In case you go.*

He's quiet for a long moment.

"September—it's okay if you miss it."

I shake my head, still burrowed into him. "It's really not."

"It's going to be quick—you know that. Kill switch deaths always are. If you're asleep, or if you're on the other side of the lab getting some water, you can't regret it for the rest of your life."

It occurs to me then: Even though I spent Maybelle's last day by her side—from midnight until 11:16 a.m. exactly, I didn't say *goodbye* to her. I couldn't, because she had no idea what was happening.

"I never said goodbye to her," I whisper.

Flint drops his voice to a soothing hum. "It doesn't matter if you don't say the G-word. So many people torture themselves about last words. What they said, what they didn't say. You have to trust that the sum of all your moments with them outweighs the last words you said to them. Hardly anyone gets a perfect goodbye."

I close my eyes against the sting of new tears.

"Hey. Kiss me," he says, bumping the tip of my nose with his.

He still smells like black cherry, even though that should be impossible.

His lips touch mine. For the first few seconds, I'm only half here, lost in my own fear. My heartbeat thuds in warning: *Last time, last time, last time.*

It's not. It can't be.

But then there's a spark, and kissing him pulls me into the present, like always.

He draws back first—his parents and twenty scientists are in the room, after all.

"Thank you," he says.

"Anytime."

"Not for the kiss. For everything." He stares at me like he's about to convey something important. "September, this last week has been the best week of my life."

My throat gets unbearably tight.

"I need you to promise me something." He cups my chin and looks right into my eyes. "You can't outrun it forever. You know that." I'm not sure if he's talking about losing my sister or him. "When it catches up to you, promise me that you'll let yourself feel it."

I look down.

"Please, September. Promise me. It's bad form to deny a deathbed wish."

I want to scream, *Stop saying that; stop acting like it's over*, but he's got a point. He's here, with tubes sprouting out of him, this boy who hates the Institute. And he's doing all of this for *me*.

"I promise," I say. "I'll let myself feel it."

He relaxes, then draws me in closer.

"Okay, wait—I might have another request," he says sheepishly.

"Don't get greedy," I say, dragging up a small smile.

"Just one more?"

"Mm. I'll allow it."

"Please don't forget how to be alive. I'm so in awe of how you can still see the magic in the world, even after what happened to you. It floored me, that first time you did it. I think it's the most courageous and amazing thing a person can do, to find the beauty despite all the pain. If you lost that . . ." He trails off, looking guilty and broken. "Promise me you won't lose that, September."

I tell him I'll try. I tell him *I promise*.

"But none of this matters," I add firmly. "Because you'll be fine."

"Right," he says. He rubs his eyes. "God. If I don't sleep, I think I might start hallucinating."

"Sleep," I say. "I'll be right here."

324

He's out in minutes, but I try to hang on a little longer.

I stare at him. Burn the lines of his face into my mind. The wave patterns of his inky hair. The exact placement of that mole over his lip. The fan of his eyelashes on his pale cheeks.

Maybe he's right. Maybe that's all any of us can do—find the beauty and soak it up. And enjoy it while we can.

flint

0 DAYS, 0 HOURS, 0 MINUTES

THEY WAKE ME up after two measly hours of sleep to inject more things I can't pronounce into my IV, and then they run some other tests.

As the hours pass, the mood in the lab relaxes a little, but the panic inside me is building. An hour from now, I might not be here.

I look around. It's not where I expected to spend my last day, but people I care about are clustered around me, and my body is giving the Institute reams of data for September's hypothesis. But still, the dread gets louder. At one point, I have to clench tight to the rail on my bed so I don't yank out my IV and run out of the lab, because the only words going through my head are *No, no, this can't be real, not today.*

I don't want to leave.

When the clock hits 9:00 p.m., September comes and curls up next to me in the hospital bed. I love her so much in that moment that I have to glance at the graphs to see if it's registering on the equipment.

"Finish line's in sight," she whispers. "We should try to stay awake."

I nod. Just a few hours to go, and we'll know if it worked.

It's eleven. September fell asleep a minute ago, her head going heavy on my shoulder. I watch as the frown she's been wearing all day slides away. I trace my thumb over her cheek. Press a kiss to her forehead.

I blink, and my eyelids go heavy. I try to drag them open, but they refuse.

I drift away.

I dream of September. Of all the things we'll do, starting tomorrow. For the first time, I let myself imagine what it would be like, to be the first person to live without knowing when I'll die. Every day I'll wake up and venture out into a world where a hundred things might kill me. I won't hide, though—I'll apply to a flight school to become a pilot. We'll walk out to the Ruins and scratch our names on the stones, *Flint + September*, and I'll listen as she talks animatedly about spectrometers and chromatographs and other things I'll never understand. I'll watch the autumn sunset braid into her hair. When I get my pilot's license, I'll take her flying.

When I wake up, the lab is humming and quiet. Someone's turned off the blazing white lights again, so it's dim and blue. The scientists are milling around noiselessly, and everything's so peaceful it feels like I'm still dreaming. Is it past midnight?

September's still tucked up at my side, her cheek warm where it's resting on my shoulder, and I think, *Maybe I've made it.*

And then I feel the sharp pain behind my left eye, bright and hot.

And I know that I haven't.

Terror blooms in my stomach. Every muscle in my body cramps at the same time, making my hand contract sharply around Mom's. She jolts forward, instantly alert. When she realizes what's happening, she grabs for Dad's arm.

They only have a moment, but they pour love into me, Mom whispering, "It's okay, I love you, it'll all be okay."

I'm looking into their eyes when my sight goes.

And somehow, impossibly, in the black, there's one image, flaring as brightly as reality: a forest, and a flame of a girl in a dark red coat, staring at the rain-washed remains of the marks she made on the day we met.

I didn't climb Kilimanjaro or see the Northern Lights or ride a camel, but I met September forty-one days before the end, and it was everything.

september

I WAKE UP with someone's hand on my cheek, tugging me up so I'm sitting instead of lying down.

For a second, I'm groggy and disoriented, then I remember where I am—the lab, the treatments, Flint. Instinctively I try to turn to check on him.

Dr. Juncker's hand stays firmly on my face. To stop me from *seeing*.

And that's when I know.

He's not here anymore.

Dr. Jackson calls it quietly. "Flint Larsen, time of death, one forty-eight a.m."

A spontaneous aneurysm. Too much damage to come back from, even with all the backup life support the Institute can provide.

He made it longer than any other anomaly. We *turned him into* an anomaly.

It's a big deal, scientifically.

But I can't bring myself to care.

Flint. I put my hand over Dr. Juncker's and gently set it aside.

He looks like he's sleeping, only his eyelids aren't quite all the way closed, and there are three tiny bubbles at the corner of his mouth. There's this feeling of *wrongness* in the room, tight around my ribs, and no one's talking, hardly anyone's moving, and it *gathers, gathers, gathers.*

I can't breathe.

I kissed him an hour ago.

I blink and see Flint's parents. His mom, her forehead pressed to Flint's unmoving shoulder, still stroking his hair as if he can feel it. His dad, sitting in the chair he's been in all day, leaning forward and pinching the bridge of his nose.

I blink and see someone turning off the machines that tried to keep him alive, that have never kept any of the patients in this building alive.

I blink and see the inside of a pink princess tent lit with Christmas lights. See a small pinkie finger linked with mine. Copper-red hair tangled with my own, the color so exactly the same I couldn't tell which strands were mine and which were my sister's.

I blink and look up at the empty observation room where I used to watch Dr. Jackson on my lunch breaks.

I blink.

Gigi's there. She tugs me gently from the bed, but there's one last thing I need to do.

I lean down by Flint's ear. His Vantablack hair is cool on my cheek.

"I miss you already," I whisper.

I squeeze his hand, but his skin already feels like clay, like something inanimate.

Gigi tugs me away then, guiding me to a corner and gathering me into a tight hug.

"I'm cold," I whisper. I'm shaking the way some people do after they get epidural anesthesia. Every fiber of me is fighting to shut this down like I did with Maybelle, to compartmentalize the ache.

Don't. Let yourself feel it.

"I'm so sorry," Gigi murmurs.

They start to wheel the machines away from the hospital bed.

Promise me.

And because I'm tired of fighting the darkness, and because I promised him, I leave my defenses on the polished tiles of the top-floor lab, and I let myself feel it.

Gigi and I walk home in the 3:00 a.m. dark. They didn't need me in the lab anymore. I couldn't bear to be there anyway. My eyes are open and staring at the quiet streets, but I keep stumbling. We pass house after house of sleeping people who have no idea what happened an hour ago on the thirtieth floor of the Institute.

I can't believe he's really gone.

Gigi steers me to my room, but I balk and reroute to hers. Her walls are bare, unlike mine. And I was never with him in here.

"Do you want me to stay?" she asks.

I nod. She perches on the side of the bed and starts stroking my hair. I close my eyes, and it presses tears out in a watery spill. It's different from losing Maybelle, because no one needs anything from me this time.

I try to recall how it felt when I was in the passenger seat of the

Jeep on that first drive to Merrybrook, being next to that pulsing, black sadness of his. How, when I let myself slip into it, it felt like relief.

I slip into it now.

It's quieter than I thought it would be, falling apart.

I thought I'd howl and scream and thrash.

Sometimes I cry silent, leaking tears. Sometimes it's a million sharp, fast gasps that I can't stop—like the Intake floor patient last year who started hyperventilating.

But most of the time I'm not really even here.

Dottie and Bo come over after school the next day. They drag a bucket of old paint out of the garage and paint over the formulas on my walls so I can move back into my room.

It still hurts to sleep in the bed where he slept. Where *we* slept.

Percy collects my homework from school and brings it by in the evening. Not that I have any plans to do it.

All I want to do is sleep. I think about Mom, in her dark room on the other side of the country. I breathe in deeply, sending my forgiveness out over the miles. *I understand now, Mama.* Nothing hurts when you're asleep.

And when I'm only half asleep, that's okay too—because I can convince myself that the pillow under my cheek is Flint's shoulder, that the one pressed against my back is his arm around me.

I pretend that we're on the top floor of the Institute again, on his deathday, before it all went wrong. My last words to him were *We should try to stay awake*, but all I can do is sleep.

I wake sharply to find myself in darkness. My heart is thudding. It's the first time I've felt alert, and *real*, since it happened. *Adrenaline dump*, I think, diagnosing the panicked drumbeat of my heart in my chest. $C_9H_{13}NO_3$.

I fumble for my phone. In a lapse of memory, my brain thinks it'd be a good idea to check my texts from him.

There's nothing new, of course, and that hits me right in the lungs. We were nearly inseparable last week, so the last texts I have from him are from when I found out about his half-life. The week where we didn't speak.

I'm sorry.

I'm sorry.

I'm sorry.

I stare at the words until they're burned into my vision.

And then the screen goes dead.

The panic behind my ribs swells. Those texts are all I have left of him. Suddenly it's of utmost importance to my scientist's mind to find other proof that he was here, that he was real. I toss my room. Pull all the covers off my bed—did he leave a sock under the sheets on the night he spent here? Did he leave his wallet on my bedside table? There must be something. *Please*. But even as I search, I know I won't find anything. He was so self-contained. Just his black clothes and his piratical boots and the keys to his Jeep.

I bury my face in the pillow he used, but there's no trace of the black cherry smell of him. I rifle through my closet, bunching every dress and shirt up to my nose, trying to remember what I wore each day last week, praying that something missed the wash cycle.

I freeze when the screech of the hangers across the bar reveals something I'd tucked in the back of the closet a long time ago.

A box. Plain cardboard. Sealed with packing tape.

I stare at it for a long moment.

Maybelle.

I can't. I'm afraid if I let myself feel both of these losses at once, I won't be able to function.

I shut the closet door and pace my room. There's nothing left of Flint in here. Where is he? Where is the proof that he loved me? In wild desperation, I rush through the living room and out into the cold. There's ice on the edges of the creek, and the frozen night air bites at my skin. I'm halfway up the other side of the creek when I notice—

The cabin is dark and lifeless. It's just because it's the middle of the night, I tell myself; that's why the lights are off. I pound on the back window. *I need proof.* Vaguely, I'm aware that what I'm doing is socially unacceptable, but I don't care. I pound until the glass warbles, then I slap with my stinging cold palm, over and over, but no one comes.

I cup my hands and peer into the dark room. There are no dishes by the sink, no papers on the bar.

His parents are gone.

Just like him.

Panicking, I pull out my phone, and even though it's god-knows-what-time in the morning, Dottie answers right away.

"I don't even have a picture of him, Dottie," I whisper, and then I start to cry.

"Shh, shh, babe. You do have one. I took one. That day at the amusement park. I'm sending it to you now."

My phone chimes, and there he is.

Flint.

Neither of us is looking at the camera. We're looking at each other, and *oh*, there it all is, hovering in the air between us. I zoom in on him and press my fingertips to the screen.

There you are.

september

ONE WEEK AFTER Flint's death, Gigi wakes me at dawn and we get dressed together.

We're burying him today.

Dottie and Bo pick us up. The car is cold, and the ride is rickety, nothing like being in the passenger seat of the Jeep.

When we arrive, Flint's extended family stares. Not because I'm his, what? girlfriend?—but because I'm wearing a rust-orange dress that flares out around my calves and my wine-red coat.

We stand, huddled in the December cold, next to a group of people who must be distantly related to Flint. They're all in black wool coats, and I wonder if they had to buy them especially for this.

Sometimes I forget that Flint was born here, that he lived his first eight years here. He said once that Philadelphia never felt real to him. I'm glad his parents decided to bury him in Carbon Junction.

The sound of a motor hums from behind us, and a hearse—*his hearse*—pulls to a stop on the narrow cemetery road. A man in a suit and a stupid top hat that I instantly want to swat off his head gets out and opens the back doors.

I stand, stock-still, just staring. He's in there. Flint is right *there*.

His parents pull up in the Jeep, and my heart nearly stops. But it's not Flint who climbs out of the driver's side, it's his dad, his face pale and serious.

Dottie nudges my arm, and I turn back to see the pallbearers placing Flint's coffin—seventeen years old and he has a *coffin*—on the straps that will lower him into the ground.

The tension in my chest ratchets up.

His coffin looks too long, like a stretched-out cartoon version of a coffin, and it's gloss black. It shines like his hair did on the night he walked into Le Belgique.

I wonder if he's wearing his boots or if they've given him polished dress shoes and a badly tailored funeral suit.

My phone buzzes in my coat, and for one weightless moment, I imagine reaching in and finding a new I'm sorry text waiting for me. But it's probably just my dad calling again, so I dig my hand into my pocket and click to stop its buzzing.

I stand there in the cold, and, instead of wiping away the tears when they come, I leave them on my cheeks for the wind to take.

When it's done, I join the line of people hugging his parents. His mom's smiles and *thank-you*s are fragile, but they're still smiles. I wonder what the difference is between his mother and mine, how she can do this when my mother could only crawl into bed.

When it's our turn, I hug Mrs. Larsen.

"We're glad he knew you, September," she says into my hair.

My chin wobbles. I took Flint's last day from them, subjecting him to treatments that didn't work in the end, and they're *thanking me*.

"I came by the cabin," I say, my voice rough with disuse.

"Oh, honey." His mom glances uneasily at his dad. "We moved to a hotel right after. We couldn't bear to be there, and we're going back to Philadelphia tomorrow. I'm so sorry, September. What did you need?"

The question hangs in the air.

Him.

"Nothing," I whisper.

Nothing.

A few hours after the funeral, Gigi calls me over to the window by the front door. We peek out the blinds and see a few reporters on the sidewalk, shivering in the cold, clutching fuzzy microphones.

"Well, shit," Gigi says.

"What are they doing here?" I ask, frowning.

"You kept Flint alive past his deathday—*with medicine*," she says gently. "It's big news."

I reach up and spin the rod on the blinds so they're as tightly closed as they can be. I guess it was inevitable that word would get out— there were at least twenty people in the lab that night, and news spreads quickly in a small town. Especially when it includes the words *half-life* and *cure*.

We stay in all day and eat toast and canned soup. Well, Gigi eats. I pick at the edges of one slice of toast.

Later, I check my phone and find sixty-four unread emails and a dozen voice mails. I listen to messages from the Institute's managing director, a few board members whose careers I looked up to, and the head of HR.

They all say that Dr. Jackson and Dr. Juncker refuse to continue the research without my involvement—or at least my permission.

I tap out a short email to Dr. Juncker, giving them permission to keep working on it without me.

They can have my research.

It didn't save him, so I don't want it.

I can't stop thinking about the box in my closet. I can feel its presence, swelling in the house.

Flint's absence is a constant ache in my ribs, in my head, in my stomach . . . but I'm surviving it. I'm still here. And I'm not pretending he never happened.

Maybe I can deal with both losses. Get a two-for-one deal on grieving, I think morbidly.

I go to my closet and slide all of my clothes to one side. The box is there, waiting.

When I moved in with Gigi, I came with two suitcases, a carry-on, and this cardboard box. My memories of packing it are hazy, but it must have been after I got the acceptance letter for the internship at the Institute. I remember easing open the door to Maybelle's room. The blinds were closed, and the air was still, like not even the oxygen and nitrogen particles dared move, and it still smelled like her.

I took three things, and then I sealed the box up and never told my parents I'd even gone in her room.

Now I take the box out and rip the tape with my fingers.

When I look inside, it's not the devastation I thought it'd be.

Maybe it's because knowing Flint eased me into being comfortable with grief, the way you wade slowly into cold water.

The first thing I see is the small stuffed cocker spaniel puppy I won for her at a fair. It was her second-favorite toy—we buried her striped sock monkey, aptly named Sock, with her.

Underneath the puppy is a gray hoodie with elephant ears that she wore all the time. Under that, the rainbow heart dress that flared out when she spun circles in the living room. She'd cry every time it was in the laundry, so Mom would let her wear it for days on end, just twirling through the house.

One stuffed animal. One tiny hoodie. One dress. I lie down on the bed, curling myself around them.

"I miss you," I whisper into the bundle of her old things.

Maybelle.

I'm already in the dark. It doesn't take much to slip in deeper.

"I miss you, and I wish you were still here. I'm sorry for all the times I didn't look up when you asked, for all the nights I had my nose buried in a textbook instead of being with you. I was doing it to save you, but I was too late. I wish I was still a sister."

It's a relief to stop running, to stop stifling every thought of her.

I finally let myself picture the years we should have had together.

When she's five, I'll walk her to the bus stop and wave her off to kindergarten. When she comes home, I'll be there waiting.

When she's six, we'll have a sleepover and watch the movies I loved as a kid.

When she's eight, she'll steal my nail polishes and forget to close

340

them, and I'll find them clumpy and dried out. I'll snap at her, then find her later crying out of guilt.

When she's sixteen, she'll hate the boyfriend who dumped me, and she'll egg his car.

When she's twenty-one, we'll go to Hawaii for a week and drink piña coladas the whole time, and she'll tell me everything about her first serious relationship.

When she's fifty-four, she'll sit with me as we say goodbye to our parents.

When she's sixty, we'll meet for coffee every week and share pictures of our grandchildren and flirt with the barista.

The half-life took all those years from us in a split second. An entire sisterhood.

I cradle Maybelle's puppy to my chest. I navigate to the photos I have of her on my phone, the ones I'd hidden from myself in an album within an album within an album. They've been with me this whole time, in my pocket, in my memory, but I'm only just now ready to see them. I go through the pictures, slowly, lingering on the ones where we're together.

Eight months after her death, I finally start to grieve for what I've lost. This time, it's not quiet. It's ugly, and gasping, and it feels like it will never end.

september

GIGI FINDS ME there, swiping through the photos on my phone. She sets a tray of food down on the nightstand, then sits on the edge of my bed and lays her hand on my arm.

"Gigi?" I whisper. "How were you okay after Maybelle?"

She shifts. "You were only little when your grandpa died, so you probably don't remember much about him. But he was so gentle. Such a sweet man. It hit me hard when I lost him." She stops to tuck my hair behind my ear. "Grief can last a long time for some people, like a constant ache, and other people manage to get through whole days or weeks before a memory knocks them down. Before a moment comes when they turn to say something but find the air beside them empty."

I nod—I've done that so many times this week.

"I was a real mess in the beginning. Talking to my clients helped. I joined a group of widows who quilted. I hate quilting, by the way—but the talking was nice."

"I'm sorry," I say. I feel guilty—I never thought about it. I knew I had a grandpa, obviously, but Gigi's always seemed so bright to me. Losing a husband, after so many years together, must have been horrible. And for my parents . . . losing a child is the most awful thing.

"So I guess to answer your question," Gigi says, rubbing her hands on her floral trousers, "losing Maybelle did hurt me. But when you're older, death still hurts, but you can weather it a little better. You know what to expect, maybe." She pushes my hair behind my ear again, and I lean into her touch. "And then you turned up on my doorstep, and I needed to take care of you."

I bury my face in the side of her leg. She smells powdery and old, and one day I'll lose her too.

"I'm sorry," I say, for Grandpa Dan and for keeping her at arm's length since I arrived in Carbon Junction and the way I blew up at her the day I found out about Flint's half-life.

"You're forgiven. And I'm sorry too. I understand why you were upset. I should have talked to you, instead of just bandying her name around like that." She picks up the elephant hoodie. "But it looks like you might be ready to talk about her now. You want to?"

"Yes, please," I reply.

That night, I thumb my phone to life and scroll through my missed calls.

In the entire time that I've lived here, I've never been the one to call my parents.

I tap on *Mom and Dad*. Just audio this time. My nerves jitter as I wait for it to connect.

Dad answers. "September," he says, his voice bleary. "Honey, we've been trying to get ahold of you. Gigi's been keeping us up to date."

"Hi, Daddy."

343

"How are you, uh . . ." He stops, clears his throat. "How you holding up?" he asks, in the same careful tone that people used on him after he lost his four-year-old daughter.

I swallow. I could say that I'm fine, but I didn't call so we could repeat the lines from every other call.

"Honestly . . . I'm not great," I say quietly.

The line crackles with silence.

"I miss her, Daddy. I miss Maybelle," I whisper.

I hear a rustle, like he's sitting down.

"I miss her too," he says, and his voice breaks halfway through the sentence.

More silence.

I feel an overwhelming urge to say more. It seems impossible to hold the words in, like the iron plate I'd kept over everything just doesn't exist anymore.

"I've been trying so hard to hold it together," I blurt. "I felt like I wasn't allowed to fall apart because you and Mom were a mess." My voice cracks, but I'm gathering steam. "I felt like you forgot me, Dad. Like I wasn't important enough to you to even try to hold it together. For two years, you'd kept it together for Maybelle, and then as soon as she was gone, you both just . . . stopped. I had to cook and get myself to school and everything."

"Tember," he says, when I finally taper off. "I'm so sorry. That's never what we meant to make you feel. You seemed so capable, and we—well, I think your mom and I tried to hold it together for so long *before* the deathday that when it was over, we just collapsed."

"I know. I understand." I think of how hard it was to get out of

344

bed after Flint died, how I still just want to slip into the blackness and rest sometimes. "I'm not mad anymore."

I hear a rough sniffling noise as Dad shifts around.

"I know I don't say it enough. But we really are so proud of you, September. For how hard you worked to get that internship and everything. Gigi's filling us in on all the half-life progress. I can't really wrap my head around what you've done, but I know it's incredible. It's going to change the world."

"I guess," I say, looking down and picking at a thread on my comforter. "I just wish I'd been able to do it three years ago."

"Me too." He sounds so broken. I wish we could all rewind, be the people we were before, when we were a family of four. He clears his throat. "I wasn't sure if I should tell you last time we talked, but, um, Mom's actually started seeing a therapist."

Just hearing that makes me start crying all over again. "That's great, Dad," I say. "Tell her I love her, okay?"

"I will."

After we hang up, I lie in bed and stare at my painted-over walls for a long time. The heaviness in me feels a little more bearable, like the very air's a little more oxygenated than it was before.

Aerys rings the doorbell the next day, holding a huge shopping bag.

"Hey," I say, wrapping my arms around myself against the cold. "Come in."

"Dottie said you were looking for something of his." She reaches into the bag. "He made this when he was a kid. He made them all the time back then."

It's a model airplane. The craftsmanship is neat, and the delicate propeller spins gently. I study the meticulously applied decals and try to imagine where his hands held the pieces together as the glue dried.

"Oh, and," Aerys says, reaching into the bag again, "I asked his parents for these. They said you can have whatever else you want, just text them. I'll give you their number."

Out of the bag come the worn black pirate boots, zipped up as if they're still on his feet. My heart stutters in my chest.

I thank Aerys and hug her tightly for a long time.

"Are you sure you don't want the airplane?" I ask when I pull back, my nose a little runny, fresh tears starring on my lashes.

"I'm good; I have a few more at home," she says.

I hug Flint's boots to my chest. There's an awkward silence as she fishes a tissue out of her hoodie and wipes at her own nose.

"This sucks," she says. "I really miss him, the grumpy old bastard."

"Me too."

For the first time, I think about what it must be like to be in her shoes, to have lost her childhood best friend right after finding him again. Flint told me she's been having a hard time with friendships for about a year, and now that I'm looking for it, I can see the loneliness clinging to her. I wondered why she was so cautious around Dottie and Bo—like she was afraid she'd do something wrong and we'd all turn our backs on her.

"Hey," I say, an idea forming. "Maybe once a month, you and me should hang out and play video games and wear all black, in honor of him."

She looks up, gratitude flooding her face. "You're on."

"And you can tell me what he was like when he was a little kid," I say.

"For sure," she says, and then we're hugging again, and, for a moment, it feels like he's here with us.

After she leaves, I take Flint's boots to my room. I sit on the edge of my bed and stare at them for a long time, and then I slip my feet in. They're huge. My feet slide around inside, seeking a warmth that's no longer there.

I set them on top of my bookshelf next to Maybelle's puppy, and I hang his airplane above my bed.

Six days after Flint's funeral, I go back to school.

I hesitate outside the front door, feeling like I want to throw up, but if I miss any more time, my GPA is going to be nonexistent.

After I check in with reception, I walk down the main hallway toward my locker. People literally veer to the side when they see me, giving me an extra foot of room as they pass me. Like they think if they get too close, or if they speak to me, someone they love will drop dead. It feels so much like Colorado, and the lump in my throat tightens. But then Dottie appears, linking her arm with mine, and I make it through first period, and then second.

At lunch, a guy in the next cafeteria line over asks for an extra milk, and his low voice sounds so much like Flint's that my stomach drops like I've missed the bottom stair on a flight of steps.

"You can go in front of me," I say to the girl behind me as I tuck myself against the wall.

"You sure? Are you okay?" she asks.

"Yeah. I just need a minute to be human."

I let the wall hold me up and let the grief shake through me. Having the occasional moment where I sit with it is better than trying to outrun it, living in fear that it'll swallow me whole.

For the rest of the day, every time I get shaky, I know it'll only be a few minutes before I can meet Bo at my locker or before Aerys finds me during a passing period and falls into step with me.

When I climb into Dottie's car at the end of the day, I feel like it might be a tiny, tiny bit easier to do it all again tomorrow. Or harder. Who knows. I wonder if this hollow pain will ever leave me or if I'm going to have to carry it around like a backpack full of textbooks.

When I get home, Gigi has the TV on. A CGI-rendered DNA strand flashes on the screen, next to a title that reads *Breaking Half-Life News*. On the screen, people mill around in a lab—a familiar lab.

The next shot shows Dr. Jackson at a podium. The white column of the Institute towers behind her like a sentinel. Reporters cluster around her, arms outstretched so their microphones can pick up her speech.

"Scientists at the Half-Life Institute are hard at work," a faceless narrator reports. "There have been recent scientific breakthroughs that could very well change humanity's relationship with death."

I watch for a minute, but it seems so far removed, like I had nothing to do with it. I should be grieving this loss too, because science was a whole part of my identity, the biggest part, but it's like my brain has reached the limit of what I can process right now, and it just blends with all the other loss.

Life goes on. And I go on. Without Flint, without Maybelle, and without the future I thought I'd have as a scientist.

september

THREE WEEKS LATER, after the quietest Christmas of my life comes and goes, Gigi knocks softly on my door. "Tember? There's someone here to see you."

I shuffle down the hallway—and stop abruptly when I see Dr. Juncker sitting at my kitchen table.

"Ms. Harrington," she says, her accent hitting the *g* like a *k*.

I slide into my chair as Gigi sets a steaming mug of black coffee in front of her.

"I don't know how much you've heard, but we're hard at work, figuring out how to type people so we can determine which of the chemicals is triggering their half-life. We think there are nine in total."

Something sparks, deep inside me. I want to ask more—what typing methods they're testing, how they administer treatments, what the dosage patterns are.

But it only lasts a fleeting second. There's not enough in me for the spark to catch and burn.

She slides an envelope over.

"What's this?" I ask.

"Open it."

I tear the seal and pull out a single sheet of creamy, expensive paper.

Dear Ms. Harrington,

It is my pleasure to inform you of your acceptance to the Biochemistry and Genetics Program at Carbon Junction University.

I look up. "I don't understand," I say hollowly.

"You applied for early decision, remember?"

"I . . ."

And then I do remember. I applied in October. *Before* I met Flint. It seems like a decade ago. I put my application in as soon as the window opened.

"But . . . why would they accept me? You fired me," I say, frowning. "Asking for the Low Wickam files was unethical."

"That transgression pales in comparison to what you've contributed to the history of the Half-Life Institute, September. The university board agrees."

I sit, stunned, staring at the acceptance letter.

"We'd also like to have you back at the Institute," Dr. Juncker adds. "To finish your internship."

"Why?" I whisper.

"I don't know if you've checked your emails recently, but we've been getting calls from institutions and universities all over the world trying to poach you. Labs in the UK, France, and New Zealand all want you to come work for them. The decision is yours, of course. But Dr. Jackson and I would love to have you back on our team. This," she says, tapping the offer letter, "is the start of a career. One as great as any scientist could hope for."

I look at the letter, and I wish I could feel the euphoria I would have felt if I'd received it two months ago.

I shake my head. "I'm not a good scientist. I'm not clinical and perfect. I never was."

Dr. Juncker looks down, twisting the plain gold band on her ring finger. "You and I, we know the pain. We can make a difference now."

I swallow hard. "I have to think about it."

"I understand. Reach out when you feel ready." She pushes her chair back and stands. "And, September? Being cold and dispassionate isn't what led to the single biggest breakthrough in the history of the half-life."

Her words echo in the air long after she's gone.

February passes. And March.

Every now and then, I pull the CJU acceptance letter out from my desk drawer and stare at it. Each time, I put it back in the drawer.

And then, on a day that feels like all the rest, I turn on the TV to see some news anchor trying to explain the more complicated science behind my research.

They show a convoluted graphic, complicated science boiled down into layman's terms.

"Well, that's not right," I mutter.

And then I'm wondering what the real formulas are, what Dr. Jackson is writing on the whiteboard this very moment, what dosages Dr. Juncker is experimenting with, what the side effects are in the clinical trials I know they've started.

Caught in the frenzied thrill of scientific curiosity, I rush to my room. I stare at the walls, as if I can x-ray vision through the paint to see my formulas.

It's starting to sink in now. My hypothesis was right. It just needed more work and a team of skilled scientists dedicated to hammering out the details.

We did that. Flint and me, and the scientists at the Institute.

How far have they taken my work? How are they typing people? Have any trial subjects lived past their deathday? What happens to them after?

The pull of curiosity is too strong. Science, the thing that's always driven me, that's been so quiet inside me these last few months, wakes with a rush.

I grab my phone and find a number I never thought I'd dial again.

"Dr. Juncker? I'd like to take you up on the offer to come back to my internship, if it's still on the table."

september

I STOOP TO touch the small yellow bud of a daffodil pushing up through the soil.

"Pumpkin, come on, you're going to be late!" Bo calls.

Dottie, Bo, and Aerys skipped their afternoon classes to walk me to the Institute for my first day back at my internship.

It's been a week since I told Dr. Juncker I wanted to come back, and it's a gorgeous afternoon, the sky a cloudless pastel blue. We hike up the flight of marble steps leading to the Institute. When we get to the top, I tug my lab coat on over a spectacular dress that Dottie pulled out of the donation pile at Rag House, with an outrageous '70s print and a ruffled hem.

I hear Flint's voice in my head: *You know that your clothes won't make you less of a good scientist, right?*

I can be more than one thing: I can be grieving and laughing and awestruck, sometimes all in one breath. I can be meticulous scientist September and bright fun September and grieving sister September.

I decide to leave my lab coat unbuttoned to show off the dress.

"Have a good day at work, babe," Dottie says. "You got this."

I hug them, then turn to face the building's revolving door.

I'm early, so I go to the observation room, to have my first glance at the place where I lost him on my own. The lab is brightly lit and empty, and it's been rearranged, which I appreciate.

A light rap on the door has me looking up.

"September," Percy says, linking his hands behind his back and drawing himself up straight in the way that used to annoy me. There's a sparkle in his eye.

"Percy!"

"It's good to have you back. But god knows you can't be trusted to remain professional in the environment," he says, eyeballing the explosion of my outfit.

I smile and realize that Percival Bassingthwaighte and I are something I never thought we'd be: friends.

"And . . . it looks like you'll have to put up with me for a few more years—I got into CJU too."

"That's great news, Percy!" He deserves it. "But how? They can't have two people from America in the program, can they?"

"Apparently they created a special spot for you, Ms. Save the World, on top of the six places they usually have. But enough about that. I think our presence is required downstairs."

"Oh, right. The press conference."

When we get back down to the lobby, the door to the lecture hall opens and noise spills out. Through the opening, I can see that almost every seat in the auditorium is filled. Pops of light flash.

Percy and I slip inside and stand against the wall.

At the front of the lecture hall, sitting at a long table, are Dr. Juncker, Dr. Jackson, a man I think might be on the Institute's board of directors, and a girl around my age with dramatic eye-liner and a thick black fishtail braid. She's wearing a smart suit jacket that doesn't quite seem to fit with the rest of her style, and the nameplate in front of her reads *Ms. Nandika Dhillon—Clinical Trial Subject*.

"I want to be clear," Dr. Jackson says, smiling. "We have not cured *death*."

A ripple of laughter goes through the room.

"We have not found a way to get rid of the half-life altogether. People will still get the seizure that indicates they're halfway through their life, but in many cases that will serve as a useful notification, and they can start treatment, either here at the Institute or, in the near future, at their local hospital. Ms. Dhillon is one of one hundred and fifty clinical trial subjects who have heroically agreed to help us develop treatments to prolong life beyond the deathdays.

"Ms. Dhillon's deathday was February eighteenth. A full five weeks ago."

The crowd erupts with applause.

A reporter in the crowd raises their hand. "Ms. Dhillon—without a deathday, and assuming the treatments you're receiving continue to work, you could live for another year, or seventy. How does it feel not to know when you're going to die?"

"Honestly? It's really weird," the girl says, followed by a smoky laugh. The room laughs with her. "If I ever get seriously ill, or if I get in an accident, I'll have no idea if that'll be the end of me or if I'll pull through."

"Dr. Jackson," another reporter asks, "is it true that people who are terminally ill in the weeks leading up to their deathday won't be saved by this treatment?"

"That's correct," Dr. Jackson says. "Our treatments can only bypass the Blumenthal effect, colloquially known as the kill switch. People will still die if they have advanced-stage heart disease, degenerative illnesses, and anything else that's not yet medically curable."

The reporters turn their attention back to Nandika, peppering her with more questions.

"Sure, it's a little scary knowing that anything could kill me," she says. "Driving a car. Crossing a road. Pneumonia or a mugging or a drive-by shooting. But it's the kind of terrifying that makes me feel like every day is a gift."

The crowd likes that, and more flashes of light pop from dozens of cameras.

"Will you live more cautiously as a result?" someone asks.

"No. I don't want to live in a bubble. The Larsen therapy has given me more life than I ever thought I'd get—I'm going to live it."

I have to lean against the wall and press my hand to my ribs. *The Larsen therapy.*

I can't help but think that's exactly how he'd have answered that question if he'd been the one who lived, and I smile at Nandika Dhillon.

"That's all we have time for today," Dr. Jackson says. "Thank you all for coming."

The reporters clamor, desperate to ask more questions. The

Institute security guards hold them back to let Nandika and my bosses file out through the side door.

Percy and I slip out into the lobby right before them.

Dr. Juncker sees me and guides the group over to me and Percy.

"September, I'd like for you to meet Nandika Dhillon. Although she's not the only person to benefit from our new treatments, she's our press-facing patient spokesperson. Nandika, this is September Harrington."

Nandika steps closer. "Oh—wow—it's an honor to meet you," she says, and I can tell she really means it.

Her presence fills up the lobby just like it filled up the lecture hall. Her mom comes up beside her, smiling proudly.

And then a ten- or eleven-year-old girl pops out from behind the mom and slides her hand into Nandika's.

Nandika smiles and pulls the girl close.

Dr. Juncker nudges my arm. I'm standing there, frozen, and they're all waiting for me to say something.

"Nice to meet you," I say, shaking their hands.

Nandika's eyes lock on mine. "Thank you," she says, giving the words as much weight as she can.

It feels like she's thanking me for a thousand things, a thousand memories she'll get to make, a thousand days she'll get to live.

You're welcome seems inadequate, so I stare back. *Go be a sister,* I say to her in my mind. *Take her for ice cream dates, just the two of you. Bicker over what your parents let one of you do that the other can't. Sit with her after a fight with a friend or a rough day at school. Hold hands in the waiting room when one of your parents is in surgery. Savor the moments where you get lost in*

358

something together—a project, a game, making pancakes, a road trip.

Go be a sister.

When I step out of the Institute that evening, I step right into a sunset that rivals the one Flint and I saw on the day we met. The sun is a burning golden coin, and it sinks through a perfectly smooth ombré sky: buttery yellow down into coral, coral into soft purple.

The light it throws over Carbon Junction is very nearly magical. Wisplike clouds hang still in the air like streaks from a paintbrush. I stand with my face upturned so I can absorb every color.

I've been doing this thing where I pause whenever I see something gorgeous or joyful so I can give that moment to Maybelle and Flint.

I think it's the most courageous and amazing thing a person can do, to find the beauty despite all the pain.

In the dreamlike light, I pull out my phone and look at the texts he sent me.

> I'm sorry.
>
> I'm sorry.
>
> I'm sorry.

I tap out a reply, one last time, to the boy who changed everything.

> There's nothing to be sorry for. I loved you,
>
> I still love you. Thank you.

As I stand there on the Half-Life Institute's steps, I think about the other half-life—how long it takes for a chemical element to decrease to half of its original amount. Sometimes it takes less than a microsecond, sometimes it takes trillions of years, but eventually that last atom decays.

But with people?

No matter how much time passes, there's always something left of that person in you.

ACKNOWLEDGMENTS

I am so grateful to all the people who have had a hand in getting this story out of my mind and into the world.

First of all, thank you to everyone who read *You & Me at the End of the World* and reached out to tell me how much you loved it. You are my FAVORITE, and your encouragement meant so much as I was stitching this story together. (Extra-special thanks to the reader who named her cat after Leo!) I hope you all loved Flint and September's journey just as much.

Enormous thanks to everyone at Madeleine Milburn Agency in London, especially to my phenomenal agent, Chloe Seager, for being the perfect blend of calm, encouraging, and fiercely brilliant. Thank you to Georgia McVeigh for the invaluable editorial feedback, Hannah Ladds for her tireless film rights work, and Liane-Louise Smith and Valentina Paulmichl for making sure my words reach readers all over the globe.

No one has spent more time with those words than my absolutely stellar editor, Jody Corbett. Thank you so much for pushing me to (and sometimes beyond!) my creative limits. I'm so grateful for your guidance and skill.

Huge thanks to everyone at Scholastic, including Janell Harris and Katie Wurtzel for turning a pile of words into an actual, physical book. Thank you to Maeve Norton for the stunning cover design—you've blown us all away again! Thank you to David

Levithan, Ellie Berger, Erin Berger, Seale Ballenger, Daniela Escobar, Rachel Feld, and the fantastic sales team.

Stepping into the world of being a published author was equal parts exhilarating and terrifying, and I wouldn't have made it through last year without being a part of an incredible debut group. Thank you to the 150+ writers in the community, with special thanks to Nicole Lesperance, Anuradha D. Rajurkar, Brooke Lauren Davis, Jennie Wexler, and Holly Green. Your books are phenomenal, and I'm honored to call you my friends.

Endless thanks to Stephanie Perkins, Kelly McWilliams, and Jennifer Lynn Barnes for joining me on pandemic launch events—getting to chat books with you was a dream come true. Massive thanks also to Emily Henry, Marisa Reichardt, and Abigail Johnson for being so welcoming.

Thank you to Liz Flanagan and the women of Storymill for your friendship and support. Liz, you've been there every step of the way, and I'm so thankful for your generosity, wisdom, and our video chats! Thank you everyone else who makes up my own little writing community, including Taylor Lauren Wou Ross, Clare Golding, Rosie Talbot, and Brandon Arthur. Taylor—thank you so much for your incredible insights. You're a lifesaver. Rosie—thank you for helping me out during title decision crunch time! To all the other lovely writers I've met for coffee or traded emails with: You make this writing world so rich and alive. I admire your talent, resilience, and kindness.

Thank you to my real-life Dottie and Bo, Christina Rojas and Jared C. Neff. Christina, thank you for taking my book to a bar and buying it a drink to celebrate launch day. You are sunshine personified. Jared—if I can give you a minute more of life within the pages of this book, it will have been worth it. The world was way more fun when you were with us.

Thank you to my non-writer friends for making life so much brighter, including but not limited to Tonya, Lily, Jac, Liz, Burcu, and Lauren. Lily, thank you for reading so many versions of this story, and for always being on the other end of the phone to talk things through. I feel so incredibly fortunate that we're so close, in location and in heart.

To the Yorkshire Bournes: Thank you always for your encouragement and love. Best family-in-law ever. To my own family—there is not enough gratitude in the world. I love you all so much. Nani, I couldn't ask for a better "assistant" for my stateside bookish business. You're the best!

Lila—you are beyond incredible, and I'm in total awe of you. I can't wait to see what corners of the world you're going to light with your shine.

Mina—thank you, my sweetheart, for being such a joy. You are happiness and resilience and love and I feel so lucky that I get to be your mom.

And Henry—thank you for your unwavering support in this dream and all things. There's so much more to say, but I get to say it in person every day, and I'm endlessly grateful for that.

And, always, thank *you*. You picked up this book and let Flint and September come to life once more through the lens of your own imagination. I'll see you for the next story. ♥

ABOUT THE AUTHOR

BRIANNA BOURNE is the author of *You & Me at the End of the World*. When she's not writing, she works as a stage manager for ballet companies around the world. Originally from Texas, she grew up in Indonesia and Egypt and now lives in England with her husband and their two daughters. You can find out more about her at briannabournebooks.com.